GRANDMA'S LITTLE SECRET

GRANDMA'S LITTLE SECRET

BECCA C. SMITH

INIMITABLE
BOOKS
UNFORGETTABLE STORIES

Published by Inimitable Books, LLC
www.inimitablebooks.com

Library of Congress Cataloguing-in-Publication Data is available.

First edition, 2026
Cover design by Christian Storm

ISBN 978-1-958607-45-9 (hardcover)
10 9 8 7 6 5 4 3 2 1

To Rolf.

I hope you know how much you were loved.

I wish I could have saved you...

TRIGGER WARNING

Body horror/gore, violence, childhood physical abuse (off page, described), death, dismemberment, gaslighting, gun violence, suicide (off page, but Virginia's father is depicted with a noose around his neck at all times), implied childhood sexual assault (off page, but to be clear: there is no sexual assault implied or otherwise of the main character Emma), nonconsensual drugging, reference to spousal abuse/domestic violence

If there are any updates or changes to the list, you can check out beccacsmith.com for the most up to date version.

VIRGINIA

FEBRUARY 1985

Aiming the rickety old rowboat toward a rough patch of water under the looming shadow of Bentmer Island, Virginia smiled. It would be the perfect place to dump the body that currently lay sprawled on top of the wooden bench across from her.

The woman was still alive, but she wouldn't be for long.

Examining her in the coming darkness, Virginia shrugged.

She was pretty, at least by society's standards. Long straight black hair, thin, sculpted jaw. Honestly, she could have been a model if she hadn't wasted her life trying to be a hero.

Roy probably would have made a pass at her if Virginia had let him get a peek.

Heart dropping at the thought, she averted her eyes from the unconscious body.

Her only regret was the damned woman couldn't be added to her garden. But she'd mentioned an FBI friend and claimed to be psychic, so she hadn't wanted to take any chances.

Snorting out loud, Virginia kicked the woman's arm to make sure she was still out cold.

No movement.

If the lady had been a *real* psychic, she would have seen the shovel smashing her in the back of the head and wouldn't have come to confront her in the first place.

One of the oars slipped in her hand, but she caught it before it fell into the inky darkness of the ocean. As the sun crested the horizon, the Puget Sound was empty of ships. There was still some light left, but mostly everything turned to shadows. Smaller islands in the distance were black silhouettes with a red glowing sky behind them. Only Bentmer stood out in front of her.

At seventy-five years of age, rowing an old boat in the dead of winter wasn't exactly high on her bucket list.

But it needed to be done.

To protect her garden.

To protect herself.

A sharp sting on her finger jolted her hand, and she almost dropped the oar again.

Damn sliver.

Made from wood that had never been varnished, the gray poles had become tiny minefields ready to jab every inch of skin they could find.

Slowing down, she pulled in the oars, carefully balancing them on the two benches that served as the middle structure of the rowboat. Shifting her weight so as not to tip the boat, Virginia hefted the body into her arms, then tossed her into the choppy black water.

As she hit the Sound's surface, the woman's eyes flew open. In a panic, she inhaled the salty liquid and started choking uncontrollably, flailing her arms, trying to grab something for help.

Using an oar, Virginia pushed the woman's hand away from the boat. She shook her head, speaking over the woman's panicked coughs. "I would have loved to add you to my garden, but you got me worried about your FBI friend, and I can't have anyone finding it."

"Please..." She choked. "I won't...tell..."

"Lies don't work on me." Virginia lifted the oar and slammed it into the lady's skull.

The light snapped out of the woman's eyes as she drifted slowly under the water, seaweed tangling with her legs, pulling her down into the current.

She'd surface in the next couple of days, and it would be deemed an accidental death. Virginia would be free of suspicion.

In the meantime, she needed to focus on more important things.

Like planning Roy's death.

Virginia's chest tightened. She'd have to wait for the family reunion this summer. She wished it could be sooner, but the opportunity to make it look like self-defense was perfect. If they heard a fight, then a gunshot, there'd be no other explanation.

She didn't want to traumatize Emma, her eleven-year-old granddaughter, but a cute little thing like her would make a great witness.

Roy wouldn't be able to join the others in her garden either, but Virginia didn't care.

Because he'd be dead.

EMMA

AUGUST 1985

"Suicide hill. Stand on seat. No hands," Greg sneered triumphantly.

Emma groaned internally, but kept her face defiant, not willing to let him sense any fear. Because Suicide Hill was about the steepest one in existence. At least on their block, anyway. It was almost vertical. And riding down it on her bike while standing on the seat with no hands was...well, it was pretty much suicide.

Like a spaghetti western, Emma and her two best friends, Abby and Dana, stood in front of her house across from Abby's brother and his two lackeys. All six of them held their respective bikes—their steeds—by the handlebars. At eleven-years-old, it was their currency in this world. Even the style of bicycle separated the girls from the boys. Emma, Dana, and Abby all had banana seat, long-handled bikes, whereas the boys had their BMXs with cross-braced handlebars and padded short saddles.

"You're insane," Emma laughed. "No one's ever done that." The words spilled from her mouth. She hoped no one could see the fear twisting her gut. Her hands tightened on the blue plastic grip handles at the end of each metal antler. She loved her bike. Loved it so much, she couldn't imagine living without it. Was it a generic brand Toys "R" Us bike her dad got on sale? Yes. But it was her chariot. Her freedom. Her beautiful blue girl. The seat had blue and white stripes, and the cobalt paint was chipped and worn from the amount of damage she'd done to it already.

Greg's lips curled up on either side like a demented Cheshire cat.

Oh crap.

He smelled her fear.

"Scared?" he laughed.

Emma turned to her friends for help.

Abby shook her head. "Don't look at me. My brother's an idiot."

Though Greg was a good five feet away, he fake-lunged at Abby because of her remark, then lifted his fist, pulling it back as if he would somehow jump the distance and punch her.

His sister flinched anyway.

Because Greg didn't always *mimic* punching Abby. He usually gave her a bruised arm or leg. And it wasn't like her parents ever did anything about it. As far as they were concerned, Greg walked on water. Untouchable.

The boys all laughed at Abby's reaction.

Emma wished she could kick them where it counted. "If it's so easy, *you* do it."

Greg tilted his head, eyes calculating. "I dared you first."

Emma reeled back.

He said it.

The word she could never resist.

Dare.

"You never said 'dare,'" she squeaked.

Abby and Dana grimaced. They knew it was a done deal now.

Greg stared at Emma with a condescending smirk. He knew exactly what he was doing. "In fact, I double dare you."

The lackeys chimed in with a couple of *oooh*s and *aaah*s.

Justin threw out, for extra measure, "I triple dare you."

Okay, those were fighting words. The metaphorical slap hurt worse than if it had been physical.

Dana steered her bike to block the boys so she could have a private moment with Emma and Abby. "You don't have to do this. You know Greg. He's just trying to mess with you."

"Dana, he *double*-dared me. And Justin *triple*-dared me." Emma argued as if this settled the matter entirely. And for her, it had. There were codes she lived by, and refusing a dare would go against everything she believed in, especially if it came from *boys*.

Abby rolled her eyes, her brown curls blowing against her cheek from the cool evening breeze. "So? He's only doing it because he knows you can't resist."

"It's kind of your thing," Dana added as she pulled up jeans slightly too big for her.

Kind of? *Kind of?* Did her friends not know her? It was a *hundred* percent her thing. Was Greg goading her? Um, duh. But could she say no? Absolutely not.

Like any dare involving a stunt, the fear was quickly being replaced by determination. "Which is why I have to do it." At that, Emma pushed her bike past the little standoff in her front yard and headed for Suicide Hill, not failing to notice the boys all giving each other high fives. She wanted to spit on their stupid hair as she passed. What were they, the mullet triplets?

Why did it feel like she was walking toward her doom?

They zoomed past her on their bikes.

Oh yeah. Why was she walking? Was she stalling? Maybe. But it still didn't change the fact she was going to be the neighborhood champion if she accomplished the stunt. Or at least, the only one who could ride down Suicide Hill standing on her seat with no hands.

When Abby and Dana rode next to her, she hopped on her bike and joined them. They passed house after house. Living in the suburbs of Seattle, each house was either classic American Craftsman of wooden slats and contrasting trim or, like her own house, Northwest Contemporary with multiple levels, roofs of various sizes and configurations, cedar shingles, but always stained wood siding.

They passed by Dana's house first, a Craftsman with light brown siding and dark brown trim.

Then two more: One light pink, the other blue.

Almost there.

Next was Abby and Greg's, a Northwest Contemporary with one slanted roof and stained wood, windows surrounding the entire house.

One more to go. Another home with three roofs of all different sizes, looking like they were stacked on top of each other.

The squeal of brakes filled the air as they reached their destination. *Suicide Hill.*

They all got off their bikes and started walking them up.

The top appeared miles away, but it was only roughly the length of two football fields. Plenty of time to perform the stunt, she convinced herself. But also...she was already getting winded from lugging her bike up the hill.

I can do it.

I can do it.

I can do it.

This hill wouldn't get the best of her.

As if in response, a woman's laugh reverberated across the black asphalt.

It was difficult for Emma to distinguish reality from fantasy. It was possible she'd imagined the sound because of her growing fear of what she was about to do, but it didn't seem to matter. Images and people she imagined were as real as the handlebars gripped in her hands.

Sometimes though, she knew for certain it wasn't her imagination. Sometimes the things were real. Like two years ago, when her neighbor Mr. Waller died from a heart attack. The next day, Emma found him wandering around the block aimlessly.

Abby was the most freaked out, and, to this day, always asked if he was around.

But once Emma spoke to him, she found out he wanted to make sure his pet cat, Larry, was okay. Emma told him his daughter had taken Larry to live with her, and as soon as he heard, he disappeared.

But the woman's laugh? She honestly didn't know for sure.

At this moment, however, it was real. *Too* real.

Abby and Dana caught up to her, one on each side, but Emma needed to concentrate, so she stared straight ahead...or straight *up*.

Angrily shoving back a tuft of her stick-straight light brown hair as it blew across her face, Dana acted as if the strand itself was her enemy. She was the shortest of their trio, but also the toughest. Pushing her bike slightly ahead to force Emma to make eye contact with her, Dana said, "You know, there's a reason they call this 'Suicide Hill'?"

Oh boy, Dana loved her urban legends.

"Dana," Emma replied, "No one has ever died here. It's just a name."

Abby's eyes widened. "I heard Justin's cousin died sledding down it last winter."

Sighing heavily, Emma didn't miss a beat. "Justin," she called, "did your cousin die sledding down this hill?"

From the momentary pause on his face, the answer was obviously a resounding no, but he quickly switched gears and smiled wickedly. "Maybe?"

"See? Lies." Emma's calves tightened with each step. *Almost there.*

The woman laughed again, mocking her bravery.

Emma knew who the woman was, but she didn't want to face her. Not now, not ever. Who would want to battle with the most powerful sorceress in all of Winterbrook?

Not Emma.

Pushing ahead to block her out, Emma arrived at the top, followed by the others.

Three girls and three boys stood on a flat street, staring down the steep monstrosity of a hill.

"What are you waiting for?" Greg's puffed-out chest and the evil twinkle in his eyes screamed he thought Emma would chicken out.

She needed to wipe the smirk off his face. And the only way to do it was to perform the stunt.

Any moment now.

Just needed to jump on the pedals and go.

Now would be good.

Obviously trying to appeal to Emma's common sense, Dana said, "You don't have to do this."

But common sense wasn't something Emma had access to at the moment. "Yes. I do."

Not dwelling on it another second, Emma jumped on her bike, determined as ever.

Her stomach dropped at the sudden plunge down the hill.

Wind blew against her cheeks, her long blonde hair flying wildly behind her.

The woman's laugh was back and louder than ever.

Emma couldn't avoid the inevitable.

Queen Madelis from her favorite book, *The Gateway to Winterbrook*, hovered in the sky above her wearing all black, from her flowing gown to her long untamed hair. She mocked Emma with her gleeful laugh.

Emma had never had to face Queen Madelis before. She had thought the only way possible would be if she'd found the door to Winterbrook. She'd certainly been trying for years on end. But it turned out, in a life-or-death situation, the queen crossed borders into their world to take her out.

Emma supposed she should be honored. But honestly, she only wanted to get down this hill alive.

That, and complete the stunt so she could throw it in Greg's face for all eternity.

Queen Madelis raised her arms, hands glowing red.

Uh oh.

A stream of red magic smashed onto the road in front of Emma. Veering her bike to the right, she managed to avoid the blast.

"Come to life and swallow her whole!" Queen Madelis screamed.

The asphalt transformed into giant mouths, growing in size with each passing second. Their sharpened tar teeth snapped at the bike.

Queen Madelis laughed louder, which only made Emma determined to ignore her.

An asphalt jaw reached up and crunched down hard, but Emma dodged, then pulled her legs up onto the banana seat.

The bike wobbled, but she righted it instantly.

She could do this.

Halfway down.

Emma didn't have much time. She took her left hand off the handlebar.

"Destroy her!" Queen Madelis yelled.

Black tar dripped from the asphalt mouth's teeth, chomping down hard only inches from Emma's front wheel.

One more hand.

Hill almost gone.

The mouths, desperate now, snapped wildly around her.

The bike wobbled again as she evaded their toothy grip.

She had to let go of her right hand to complete the stunt.

As her fingers loosened on the handle, her legs still on the banana seat, the front tire jolted to the right.

She had a choice. Finish the stunt and crash with the bike or jump to safety and fail.

Crap.

Emma jumped.

"Coward!" Queen Madelis laughed triumphantly.

The bike flew fast to the right, and one of the asphalt mouths bit down hard on her bike like it was dessert.

Emma hit the ground at full impact, rolling away from the crash.

No more Queen Madelis, and no more of her chomper minions.

Brushing the dirt off her jeans and rising to her feet, she noted her demolished bike a couple of yards away, the body completely smashed. One wheel rolled a few yards, then fell to its death on the road. Her trusty blue girl, gone for good.

Dismounting and parking their bikes, her friends ran toward Emma.

Abby got there first. "Are you okay?"

Emma's arm stung from a fresh scrape, but otherwise she was unhurt. "Yeah, I'm good."

The boys screeched their bikes to a halt at Emma's side. They dismounted their bikes, obviously finding the entire situation hysterical.

Greg laughed. "What an idiot!"

"You looked so stupid," Justin cackled.

Blood boiling, Emma wanted to throw her broken bike in their faces. Instead, she pushed Greg as hard as she could.

Apparently, she was a lot stronger than she thought because he fell hard on his rear, his bike landing on top of him. "You're too chicken to even try!" Emma accused.

Dana and Abby recovered from the initial shock of Emma pushing down the "big bad bully" and laughed.

Angry now, Greg jumped to his feet, lifting his bike with him. "This isn't over!"

Emma examined her arm. No blood, only the top skin broken. "No. It isn't. Not until I go down that hill, standing on my seat no-handed. Something *your* sorry ass will never do."

Walking over to her bike, she lifted it up and dragged it over to the bent, destroyed wheel in the middle of the road.

Right behind her were her friends, with Dana picking up the wheel.

Greg, Kyle, and Justin watched them, back to being entertained at Emma's loss.

"Yeah, good luck with that," Greg laughed.

And he sounded as triumphant as Queen Madelis had been.

Emma's insides churned. She wanted to push Greg to the ground once more. Maybe the asphalt monsters would come back to life and gobble him up.

One could dream.

Focusing on her mangled bike, her entire being ached with dread.

If she had any chance of *not* getting grounded, she needed to come up with a good story.

EMMA

Were they mad or frustrated? Emma couldn't tell. It was always impossible to know for sure what her parents' moods were, but they obviously didn't believe her.

She tried one more time. "I'm serious. The road grew a mouth and ate my bike!"

How much clearer could she make it? This *might* be a moment where her imagination was misleading her, but on the other hand, she knew what had happened. And her bike had been chomped on by Queen Madelis's magic asphalt munchers.

Abby and Dana exchanged looks, suggesting she needed to take it down a few notches.

They were probably right.

Emma's mother stared up at the ceiling as if the answers were somehow written on its surface. "*Emma.*"

When her mother said her name like that, she was in trouble.

"What did we say about lying?" Her father's gaze pierced her soul.

Lying.

They always thought she was lying.

Yes, in this case it was possible it was imaginary, but her parents never believed her when she saw dead people, either. And she had seen Queen Madelis as clearly as she had seen dead Mr. Waller searching for his cat.

It crushed her on some level—never being believed. It wasn't her fault she experienced things others couldn't. Emma didn't know why she could see ghosts, or dream of horrible things people had done. Maybe that was why her imagination was so vivid.

She supposed her parents were blameless for not being able to tell what was real and what wasn't. Maybe thinking she was making *everything* up was easier for them.

Her mother shook her head. "Emma, we talked about this. You're eleven now. Old enough to babysit, for god's sake. You have to stop using your imagination to lie. Use it for your stories and playtime, but never to lie to me and your father."

A brilliant idea hit Emma.

Turning to her friends, who looked at her as if she'd lost her mind, Emma mouthed, "I got this."

She tried to ignore Dana mouthing, "But do you?"

Yes.

She knew exactly what to do.

Waving her hand in front of her parents' faces, she mimicked what she'd seen Obi-Wan Kenobi do in *Star Wars.* She was going to use the Force. "You will not ask any more questions. You will tell us everything is fine and to go back to my room."

Her parents stared at her, arms crossed.

"Are you trying to use the Force on us?" her mother asked incredulously.

Um.

Maybe they weren't as weak minded as she thought they were.

"This is what I'm talking about," her mother sighed heavily.

Her father tried not to laugh though, which only made her heart sink further. Her trying to use the Force was a joke to them. Another thing they didn't believe in.

"Don't encourage her," her mom reprimanded him.

As if laughing at her attempt to use her Jedi powers would *encourage* her.

Dana stepped forward. "Her wheel hit a patch of gravel none of us saw, and a rock jammed in the spokes. She's lucky she didn't get hurt."

Wasn't that what she said? Emma waved at Dana as if her friend backed up her story entirely. "Like I said, the road ate my bike."

"*Emma*," her mom sighed again, obviously still exasperated.

Dad stepped in, though, and motioned to the hallway leading to her bedroom. "Thank you, Dana, for the clarity. It's time for bed. We all leave bright and early tomorrow for Grandma and Grandpa's. We'll worry about that heap of metal when we get back."

Emma nodded and quickly led her friends to her room.

Opening the door, she took in her room. Her bed and dresser made up the right corner, and three rolled sleeping bags had been laid out on the floor next to the bed.

Each wall greeted them with posters of *Star Wars*, *Goonies*, *E.T.*, and *Indiana Jones*, but in the front left corner were two bookshelves filled with fantasy books. Most prominently, on the top shelf in its own display was a set of *The Chronicles of Winterbrook*.

Abby let out a breath. "What was that all about? The road ate your bike?"

Emma explained, "If I had told them the truth, that Queen Madelis brought the road to life, they would have been even angrier."

Abby's eyes rounded. "Queen Madelis was there?"

"That's what I saw," Emma confirmed. *They* believed her. Why couldn't her parents?

Abby sighed. "I wanna see those things."

"You will, when we find the door to Winterbrook."

It was a world full of spells, trees and animals that talked, granted wishes, and dragons that only let the special ones ride their backs. And all three of them were special. It was their *destiny* to find the door. She just *knew* Daltorine would let any of them ride her. Emma imagined the wind hitting her face as Daltorine's sparkling red wings flapped in the bluest of skies. Once they defeated Queen Madelis, Winterbrook would be paradise.

But back here on Earth, she appreciated her friend's aid. Turning to Dana, she said, "Thanks for covering, by the way."

Dana unrolled her sleeping bag. "Duh." Then she laughed. "I can't believe you tried using the Force on your parents."

And as serious as Emma had been about accomplishing the Jedi feat, she suddenly found it as funny as Abby and Dana did. They all laughed. "It was worth a shot."

Dana asked, "What are you going to do without a bike?"

Emma rolled out her own sleeping bag. "I'm going to miss my blue girl for sure, but there are probably a million bikes in Winterbrook if we could find the door. I could take one and bring it back, then tell them I found it."

Abby's eyes lit up. She was the last to unroll her bag. "You think so?"

Crawling into her sleeping bag, Dana beamed. "You really think we could find the door? We've searched the last three summers for it."

Confidence swelled in Emma's chest. "I know we can. Maybe we'll find it at my grandparents' tomorrow." There wasn't a shred of doubt in Emma. They would find the door.

Pulling over a small twelve-inch color TV from her bedside table, Emma placed it on the floor in front of them. "Let's watch some TV before we go to bed." Without waiting for an answer, she flipped it on, and an episode of *Murder in the Margins* was starting.

She loved how the main character, Jennifer Thatcher, used her talent to write murder mysteries and applied it to real-life cases.

Although Emma often thought that, even for an old lady, Jennifer Thatcher knew a *lot* of people who were murdered. But Jennifer's grandmotherly kindness combined with her astute observations made the show one of Emma's favorites.

On the TV, Jennifer stood next to her old-fashioned maroon bike with a tan wicker basket bolted to the front.

Sheriff Forbes stood next to her, shaking his grey-haired head. "We're going to need your help, Mrs. Thatcher."

Jennifer shrugged, then said, "Oh, I don't know what I can do. I'm just a writer."

Sheriff Forbes placed his hands on his hips. "Well, seeing as the victim was found with a note in her hand with your name on it, you may know more than you think."

Alarmed, Jennifer's left eyebrow lifted clear up her forehead. "Oh, dear."

Emma laughed with her friends as the show went to commercial.

A flash of pink filled the screen, and her heart stopped.

The camera panned out to the most beautiful bicycle Emma had ever laid her eyes on. She gasped at its perfection. A singular light beamed down on its magnificent frame as it rotated on display. The Schwinn Fair Lady. White vinyl banana saddle with an array of cartoon flowers sprinkled along its surface, a pink metal body, and tall silver chrome handlebars with white rubber handles.

It was a vehicle of the gods.

Her friends' jaws dropped. Maybe some drool, too.

Dana whistled low. "Whoa."

"Yeah," was all Emma could muster.

"You think there's a possibility your parents will get you *that* now that your bike is kaput?" Abby asked.

"Ha! Not a chance. You know my dad. He only buys generic. He'll want to fix my old bike." Emma didn't want it to be true, but she knew she was right.

Dana reached for the screen, as if touching it would make the bike materialize. "It's so perfect."

A tiny inkling of a plan eked its way into Emma's brain. "Maybe if I asked for my birthday and Christmas combined? For the next three years?"

"You think they'd go for it?" Abby raised an eyebrow.

Emma wanted to believe. "Maybe?"

Her mom's voice thundered through the walls. "Emma! Do you girls have the TV on?"

Slapping off the device, Emma, Abby, and Dana snuggled deeper into their sleeping bags until their heads were covered.

"Night," Emma said, thoroughly nestled inside.

Under the down-stuffed surface, she squeezed her eyes closed and prayed she'd dream of riding the Schwinn Fair Lady.

EMMA

Opening her eyes, Emma stood on a paved sidewalk in Anchor Point, the little town where Jennifer Thatcher lived on the show *Murder in the Margins.* Two rows of Cape Cod-style homes lined each side of the cobblestoned street, where Jennifer's famous house sat. The white picket fence, a guardian to the beautiful garden full of wildflowers and fruit trees.

A moment later, the woman herself stood in front of Emma on the sidewalk. In place of Jennifer's signature maroon bike with wicker basket, she held in her hands the pink Schwinn Fair Lady itself. Rolling it over, she said, "You earned it. No one can stand up to Greg like you do."

Emma was speechless. She was so honored and excited. The *actual* Jennifer Thatcher was standing in front of her and giving her the bike of her dreams. When she finally built up the courage to squeak a "thank you," a loud noise grabbed both their attention.

Rushing water.

A faucet? A hose? Emma wasn't sure.

"What is that?" she asked, turning toward the sound. A small voice inside told her she had to follow it.

Jennifer gathered herself, then gently touched Emma's shoulder. "Nothing you should worry yourself about, dear. Go on and forget you heard it and take this bike."

The roar grew louder until it was impossible to ignore, despite how tempting the Fair Lady was.

Walking toward the noise, the quaint street of Anchor Point dissolved around her. Dark, inky black clouds framed what was left of the town until only Jennifer and the bike remained, bright and colorful against the darkness.

The road in front of her was now dry, cracked dirt. Dead trees and bushes grew scattered across the landscape, with a wooden dilapidated house in the distance. If Emma wasn't already sure the sound was coming from the house, the water pouring down the front porch stairs was the confirmation she needed.

It being a dream didn't help matters. Anything could happen in a dream, especially one like this where Emma was entirely aware and conscious. Luckily, nothing usually happened, just silly things, like the one time she found herself in Mrs. Gorster's kitchen, and had to watch her eat an entire double-layer chocolate cake. But every once in a while, she'd dream of things she'd rather not think too much about. A few times, people got killed, and then later their deaths would be in her dad's newspaper. She hoped this wasn't one of those, but the creepy house didn't bode well.

Jennifer spoke from a distance behind her. "Come on now. Come and get your prize."

Emma ignored her. She knew Jennifer was only trying to help, but the compulsion to move forward was stronger.

Approaching the house, the sound grew louder. Her feet made tiny splashes as she climbed up the three rickety porch stairs to reach the front door. It was in worse shape than the porch, with the wood rotting in some places, remnants of paint peeling off its surface, along with scrapes and empty knot holes.

Carefully, Emma opened the door and swung it wide so she could peer inside. But instead of a living room like she expected, she found herself in a bathroom.

Relief washed through her when her grandmother stood in front of her. With her heavyset frame, short, curly gray hair, bright brown eyes, and permanent laugh lines, her grandmother always had a smile for her granddaughter. She wore the green pantsuit Emma had only seen her wear on special occasions.

Emma wondered what the occasion was, especially since Grandma Virginia held a hose in her hands and sprayed water inside a white claw-foot tub, but now, the water spilling over the edges turned a deep red color.

Was it blood?

Emma took a step back. Why would she assume it was blood? It seemed like a big leap when thinking of her grandma.

No. Maybe it was paint. Grandma must be trying to clean her tub after painting her walls red or something.

Emma was about to speak when a man stepped up next to her grandmother. He had a noose around his neck like the ones in the word game hangman, but the tail of the rope seemed to have a life of its own, twisting like a vine around her grandmother's arm.

Examining him closer, Emma startled when she realized it was her great-grandpa. She recognized him from an old, black-and-white photo hung in Grandma Virginia's sunroom.

He was the age as he was in the photo and wearing the same clothes, a plaid button-up shirt under a pair of overalls from the 1920s, when he was still alive. She had always been haunted by the photo since her grandma was in it, and she looked exactly like Emma.

Exactly.

Supposedly, her great-grandpa died when Grandma Virginia was about Emma's age, but Emma never knew the *how* of it. Now, seeing the noose, she wondered if that was the answer. Maybe he was a ghost watching over his daughter.

He stared at the tub, eyes alight, and wore a crooked smile.

It sent chills through Emma's body.

Another figure appeared next to Grandma Virginia.

Emma froze, not sure what to make of it. It was the other half of the photo. Aside from the '20s style dress, with short sleeves, rounded collar, hip waistband and pleated skirt attached, she might as well be in front of a mirror. The two of them could be twins.

More of the red liquid poured out of the tub, racing toward Emma, covering her feet, then out the front door. She reached down and touched the red substance. From the harsh metal smell to its sticky texture, her stunts over the years had exposed her to enough cuts and wounds to recognize what it was.

She'd been right the first time.

Blood.

Rooted to the floor with indecision, Emma stared at her grandma.

A woman materialized in the corner of the bathroom, arms hanging at her side, slack and unmoving. Seaweed covered the woman's body, crawling and creeping around her limbs. She watched Grandma Virginia and the two other beings.

Emma found her voice. "What's going on?"

Virginia's eyes snapped to hers, furious.

Emma had never witnessed her grandmother's anger before. And though she was in a dream, goosebumps formed on her arms and legs.

"I told you never to come here!"

"I've never been here before," she defended herself, still surprised by her grandma's rage.

The older woman reared her head back. "Emma? Is that you?"

Emma nodded, too scared to respond now.

Angry once more, Grandma Virginia yelled, "You don't belong here!"

The rope from Great-Grandpa's noose untangled from his daughter's body.

It raced toward Emma and wrapped around her neck.

EMMA WOKE UP CLUTCHING HER THROAT.

It was enough to jolt Abby and Dana awake as well.

Abby grabbed her chest from the scare. "What is it? You didn't see Mr. Waller again, did you? Is he here?" Her head swiveled around the room. "Oh, god. Is he here? Now?"

Emma took a couple of deep breaths. "No. I told you, Mr. Waller disappeared when I told him about his cat."

Abby plopped down on her pillow. "Oh, thank goodness." She sat up again. "You sure?"

Dana groaned. "She said it wasn't him. Relax."

"Don't tell me to relax," Abby huffed.

"Guys," Emma stopped them before their arguing could escalate.

Before she moved into the neighborhood, it had only been Dana and Abby, and they did not get along.

Dana had a scar from when they fought over the left-handed scissors and her hand jerked back, nicking her under her eye. But as soon as they met Emma, it was as if their issues with each other disappeared. Or, at least, shrunk to the point where they could be friends. Occasionally, though, they'd slip into their old ways. Emma somehow always managed to rein in their anger at each other.

"Sorry," Dana said, then asked carefully, "Was it one of your dreams?"

"I think so." She'd told her friends all about her dreams, especially the weird ones, but more importantly, the scary ones. "But it was even stranger because it was almost like my grandma was the bad guy."

Dana leaned in closer. "Like one of the killers you've dreamt about?"

"Yeah."

Abby hugged her pillow. "You mean the grandma we're seeing tomorrow?" She gulped. "On an island only accessible by ferry or plane?"

"Yeah," Emma repeated.

"Maybe we shouldn't go. Your dreams usually...no, strike that... *always* end up happening." Abby pointed out, veins practically popping out of her neck from worry.

But Dana was calm. "You think your grandma is dangerous?"

Emma took a moment to contemplate her accusations.

Grandma Virginia.

The woman who bought her entire third-grade class ice cream because she wanted the other kids to like Emma. The woman who made a deal with her mom that Emma could buy as many books as she wanted from the Scholastic order sheet every month at school. The woman who snuck her Hershey's miniatures under the table when her mother's attempt at meatloaf had turned into a brick of dried ketchup.

What had Emma been thinking?

This was *Grandma Virginia.* Of course, she was good.

"No, you know what? It has to be just a bad dream. You guys know my grandma. She's the best."

Abby and Dana both slumped their shoulders in relief, their faces relaxing.

Abby laughed. "Yeah, that's true. Remember when Greg got the sandbox when we were six and wouldn't let us play in it?"

Emma and Dana laughed with her.

When Grandma Virginia found out he wouldn't let them play in his sandbox, she called her friend who worked in construction and had him bring over a dump truck full of the most perfect sand and dropped it in Emma's backyard. They had made epic sandcastles and played Dune for months. It was glorious.

Abby huffed triumphantly. "I've never seen Greg so jealous."

One of the best days of their lives.

VIRGINIA

Startling awake, Virginia ran her hand through her sweaty hair.

Her granddaughter had *seen* her. Seen her in her sacred spot. The part of her brain where she re-lived her favorite kills and imagined future ones.

She had no idea how the whole psychic thing worked. Virginia hated that word, but what other option was there? She saw things most people couldn't, in real-life, in her dreams. No rules, no explanations, no guidance. Just thrown into the world with every sense magnified to the point of madness.

And Emma had it, too. Maybe worse than her.

A deep coldness settled in Virginia's insides.

What did it mean? What would her granddaughter do? Who would she tell?

Interrupting her spiral of panic, the sound of Roy's breathing next to her almost deafened her. How could one person breathe that loudly? Was he trying to steal all the air from the room in one shot?

Grabbing her pillow, she pulled it up, ready to smash it against his face and suffocate him.

Father materialized, tightly wrapping the tail end of his hanging rope around her arm. “Not yet. You couldn’t explain this one.”

Lowering the cushion, Virginia placed it back on her side of the bed, Father’s rope recoiling to let her.

Her younger self appeared next to Father, hands on hips. “Emma will only think it’s a dream,” she said, accusing.

Virginia wanted to believe it with all her heart. What was left of it, anyway.

Glancing over at Father, Virginia shrugged.

He wasn’t a ghost. She knew that for sure. She didn’t really know what he was. Some kind of manifestation of hers, like the young version of herself that was currently giving her the stink eye like she was a demon. Virginia knew she didn’t have what the news called multiple personalities either. It wasn’t as if they took over her mind or body or anything. She figured she’d just created them somehow with her gift, like imaginary friends come to life. Except they were annoying, and she wanted them to shut up most days. Her very own devil and angel.

A small smile cracked her lips, and she couldn’t help but swell with a little pride at how powerful Emma was becoming. Virginia had known the girl had the gift like her when Emma was seven years old and she’d seen the ghost of her sister Rachel.

Her granddaughter had run up to Virginia and gushed about how she’d spent the entire day with Great Aunt Rachel playing tag in the yard, dancing in the fields, and fighting monsters in an imaginary land.

It had taken all of Virginia’s willpower not to break down into a million pieces. But she’d simply smiled, laughed, and told Emma a few stories of her own about her sister.

“She could become a problem,” Father hissed.

“I don’t believe that,” Virginia hissed back.

And she didn’t.

Not Emma.

Not family.

Virginia only killed to protect herself and her family. Did she enjoy it as well? Of course. There was nothing like feeling hot blood spilling onto her hand from taking the life of someone who wronged her, or wronged anyone she loved.

Roy's breathing escalated into a chainsaw snore.

"Are you sure I can't kill him now?" Virginia groaned.

Father crossed his arms, his rope whipping around him. "Stick to the plan."

Virginia had *two*. She hoped the first one would work, but she was prepared. Always had a back-up plan.

She lay in bed, comforted with the fact that the man next to her would no longer be alive in twenty-four hours. Tomorrow night, she'd sleep soundly in the quiet.

No more breathing. No more snoring.

Just peace.

Closing her eyes, she tried to tune out his incessant sounds so she could get an hour or more of sleep, but after a few minutes, she deemed it impossible.

Glancing at the digital alarm clock by her bedside, she saw it was already 6 a.m. She might as well start the day. Plus, it was early enough to visit her garden without Roy ever being the wiser.

Carefully climbing out of bed, Virginia grabbed her favorite green jumpsuit. She'd worn it in the dream, so it felt fitting she'd wear it today. It was her special occasion outfit, and what better occasion was there than spending time with her wretches?

Slipping on the jumpsuit, she made her way out of the house and toward the backyard.

The sun hadn't made it past the long line of pines, but it still lit up the sky enough for her to see her surroundings. In an hour or so, it would be full daylight, but Virginia loved the shadowed dawn with crisp salt air.

It wasn't a long walk from the house. Her garden was partially visible from every angle on the property, which gave her comfort whenever she needed it.

And she needed it now.

Each time Virginia visited here, she took a different route, never wanting to create a worn path in the woods where anyone might stumble upon it. Not that they'd know seven of her wretches lay buried beneath, but stranger things had happened to her. She wasn't taking any chances.

She and Roy had been living on Bentmer for ten years. And before that, a little farm outside Greenwood, Indiana, for forty years. It was where they had raised their three girls.

Virginia's heart squeezed at remembering her garden there. She missed it terribly. Over twenty bodies there.

"They deserved what they got," Father said, appearing next to her.

"Of course they did," Virginia answered, ducking under a low-hanging pine tree branch. "I just wish I could visit them more often." Whenever she'd stay with Gertrude and Doris, she would return to the burial ground. She'd worried when Mary moved out to Seattle that her sisters would come with her, leaving Virginia without an excuse to visit Indiana. But Gertrude and Doris were small-town girls and would never leave. Only her Mary was brave enough to move to a real city to be closer to her mother.

"She came to be closer to Roy, her *father*, too," her younger self chimed in, sticking out her tongue.

Virginia didn't answer. She trudged ahead through the shadowed trees, admiring the few streaks of sunlight beaming through the branches.

At last, she stood at the edge of her garden. She'd marked the area between two towering pines by carving five, ten-inch lines into each of their bark beds. Anyone looking would write them off as claw marks from the wildlife. It wasn't out of the question. Black bears had roamed in their backyard a few times over the years.

The lush green grass and moss sparkled with morning dew, and for a moment, it was as if Virginia was surrounded by tiny diamonds. Even the moss on the trees shone an extra bright green today.

"They're quiet this morning," Father observed.

Sometimes, if Virginia listened very carefully, the wretches screamed. Though they were long dead, bodies chopped into pieces small enough to fit in a wheelbarrow, they'd still scream for her.

She wished they would this morning.

But Father was right. Only silence greeted her.

Virginia breathed in deep, chest sinking.

Coming there hadn't brought her the joy she'd hoped. With a snarl, Virginia turned abruptly and started back home.

Maybe they'd scream when Roy took his last breaths.

She could only dream.

EMMA

The deep blue water of the Puget Sound glimmered in the rare summer sunlight. Emma needed to appreciate these moments as most days growing up in Seattle were overcast and gray.

Plopping down on one of the long outside bench rows of the ferry boat pushing its way toward Bentmer Island, Emma motioned for Abby and Dana to sit next to her. The fresh breeze had a chill to it, and the salty smell of ocean water refreshed her. She was ready for whatever adventure awaited them at her grandparents' house.

Emma shifted in her seat. She loved taking the ferry and seeing her grandparents. It had been a while, too. Over eight months. They usually didn't wait that long to spend time together, but her dad's new job with the city constantly pulled him away.

Her parents stood a little way in front of them, resting on the railing and watching the water. Her dad had a sweatshirt with a drawing of a cartoon man in a yellow raincoat looking up at the sun and a thought bubble saying, "What's that strange yellow orb?" The image summed up living in Seattle perfectly.

Pulling out a crumpled copy of *Pride and Prejudice*, Abby started reading.

Dana rolled her eyes, and Emma laughed.

Abby's mom was from London, so she was obsessed with all things British. She dreamed of leaving her parents and brother, hoping there was some distant cousin she could move in with in England.

Emma couldn't blame her. No one in her friend's family treated her with any type of kindness, and her father on more than one occasion would utter under his breath what a disappointment she was.

Abby's one escape, when she didn't have Emma and Dana to play with, was her books and her West End Musical soundtracks. Lately, *Les Misérables* had been on repeat anytime Emma went to visit.

Amused, Emma asked, "Haven't you read that book a million times already?"

Abby lifted her chin. "Listen, you guys read fantasy. I read Regency romance. If there were a door to Mr. Darcy's, I'd be there in a heartbeat." Her face lit up. "He lives in a mansion!"

Dana responded, "Yeah, but if you were reading *Gateway to Winterbrook*, you might help us find a clue about how we'll find the door." Sitting in the middle, her head swung to Emma. "You're positive you think we'll find it at your grandparents'?"

Abby put away her book, staring at Emma for the answer.

The weight of her friends' desire pushed down on her chest. Though she had every confidence they'd find the door, it had already been a three-year search, and she worried Abby and Dana would give up. "If anyone knows where it is, it's my grandpa. He's the one who first read me the books."

"Good, because I can't wait to find Daltorine." Dana rubbed her hands together. "Maybe we can all fit on her back and fly with her at once?"

Emma was about to join in the planning of what they'd do first when they got to Winterbrook, when the ghost with the seaweed from her dream materialized about twenty feet away from them. She was sure the woman was a spirit now, though she wondered why she'd shown up in her dream last night.

And once a ghost recognized that Emma could see them, she automatically became a shining beacon to them. It always seemed to work that way with dead people. Too excited to be seen by the living, she guessed. Seaweed continued to crawl around the woman's legs and arms. Emma wondered how she'd died. Shrugging, she decided to hear the lady out.

"Incoming," she whispered.

Her friends followed her line of sight.

Abby swallowed hard. "Oh, god. Is it Mr. Waller?"

"No, it's a...fish lady ghost?" Emma answered.

"A fish lady ghost?" Dana's face crinkled in confusion. "What does that mean? Like a mermaid?"

Emma said, "I dunno. She has seaweed all over her. She was in my dream last night."

Abby gulped again. "And she's here...*now*?" Abby squeaked. "Are you *sure* it's not Mr. Waller?"

Dana groaned. "What is up with you and Mr. Waller? She just said it's a *woman* with seaweed all over her."

"Sorry if our friend seeing ghosts freaks me out a little. And Mr. Waller was creepy when he was alive," Abby argued.

Dana nudged Abby, appalled. "He was not."

"Was too," Abby said stubbornly.

"She's here," Emma informed them to stop their bickering.

The woman now stood before her, and she was far less scary than she had been in her dream. For one, she was beautiful, with shiny black hair down to her waist, deep brown eyes, and a sculpted face. Along with the constantly moving bright green seaweed, she wore a denim one-piece jumper.

"Can I sit with you?" she asked politely, her voice gentle and soft-spoken.

Emma turned to her friends. "She wants to sit with us."

They shifted in their seats awkwardly, but Dana answered, "Tell her it's okay."

The woman sat down on the bench row across from them.

Turning her full attention to the woman, Emma said, "You were in my dream last night."

"Don't you think she already knows that?" Dana asked under her breath.

The woman clarified, "I'm Freya, by the way, not 'fish lady ghost.'"

"Sorry," Emma muttered, then to her friends she said, "Her name is Freya." Sitting forward in her seat, she asked, "*Why* were you in my dream?"

Freya's lips pursed, her body tensed, then began to flicker, the seaweed crawling more rapidly than before. "It was only a partial dream. You were in your grandmother's head, and she saw you, which is why I'm here."

Emma thought for a moment, not sure what to make of the words. What did she mean she had been in Grandma Virginia's *head*? And why would that compel this ghost to come meet her? But part of her suspected the answer. "To protect me?" she asked. It didn't seem likely she'd need protection from her *grandmother*, but, for some reason, her words felt right.

Freya nodded. "Yes."

"What's she saying? Protect you from what?" Dana sat forward, her hand on Emma's arm.

Abby swallowed hard yet again. "We don't need protection where we're going, do we?"

But Emma wasn't so sure. It was strange to doubt whether her grandparents' house would be safe, but the dream planted a seed in her that her subconscious continued to sprout.

Freya raised both her eyebrows, as if reading her mind. "You're in the game now, kid. Just make sure you keep your eyes open. And let your friends watch your back." The woman's body flickered one more time, then disappeared.

"She's gone," Emma informed them.

Dana leaned back on the bench. "What in the heck *was* that?"

She worried her lip with her teeth. "You guys know I have no control over that stuff."

Sometimes, Emma wished she was normal. Or at least have a choice of who she could see. Like maybe her grandpa on her dad's side. He almost rivaled in kindness the grandpa she was visiting now. *Almost.*

Abby's head pivoted toward the looming island in front of them. "Do you think we should go home? This was supposed to be fun, not scary."

Emma hated her friends worrying, so she mustered up as much confidence as she could. "It will be. I promise. Besides, if she's really a ghost, maybe she can find the door to Winterbrook for us?" She shoulder-bumped both of them. "Then we can fly with Daltorine."

Returning the bump, Abby and Dana's whole demeanors shifted, excitement sparkling in their eyes.

Emma's dad interrupted them before they could respond. "You girls want to come and see the orca?"

Forgetting all ominous ghost visits, they leapt to their feet and to the railing, joining Emma's parents.

A single orca crested the water, then dove into the Puget Sound.

Turning to her friends, she beamed, "See? Fun."

Abby bounced on her toes, while Dana pointed to another orca farther off with her mouth open wide, but Emma sensed an underlying hesitation from them.

Setting her jaw, she decided she wouldn't let herself be deterred. She'd make sure her friends had a vacation they'd never forget.

EMMA

The ferry neared the dock as Emma's parents ushered the girls into the green station wagon with the faux wood vinyl siding. Sliding into the back seat, Dana, being the smallest, rode in the middle with Emma and Abby at the windows. The loud clunks of the ferry dock, and the yelling of men shouting orders as they grabbed the large ropes and tied the giant boat off, echoed in the car.

It didn't take long before they were on the road and driving up to her grandparents' house. They lived on the top of the island, right on the edge of a cliff face. It was so picturesque with the great pines nestled behind it and lining the winding road up to the house, Emma would have thought it was Winterbrook itself.

Holding her stomach from the car sickness rearing its ugly head from all the twists and turns of the road, Emma gazed out the window at the horizon to try to steady herself. Unfortunately, she was on the driver's side, which was all forest, so she didn't have a clear view of the Sound.

Maybe the trees would quiet her stomach.

"You feeling okay, kiddo? You look a little green." Her father's eyes met hers through the rearview mirror.

"Just a little carsick."

"We're almost there," he said. "I'll take these turns a little slower. Maybe that'll help."

"Oooh! I see another killer whale!" Abby had her face plastered to the window facing the Sound.

Dana squinted from the middle seat.

Emma attempted to crane her neck, but was immediately hit with a wave of dizziness. Letting her friends enjoy the scenery, she focused back on the trees.

A flash of darkness in the distance caught her eye. With the bright green pines surrounding it, the black patch stood out as if a fire had burnt down that exact square of land in the middle of the forest.

"What is that up there? Was there a fire or something?" Emma pointed ahead to the spot.

Everyone turned their heads, even her father, who immediately swerved slightly.

"Eyes on the road," her mom scolded.

"I don't see anything. Where are you looking?" Dana asked.

"I don't see it either, sweetie," her mom said from the front seat, head craned toward the forest.

"It's right there. We're just about to pass it." Emma rolled down the window, shoving her arm out for a more accurate pointing. "It's all dark."

As the car drew near, her queasiness intensified. Now that she had a better view, it wasn't like a fire at all. The pines, the foliage, the moss on the ground and trees, in the exact square of space was fully intact, needles, leaves, and all. They were simply black, as if someone had taken a can of spray-paint and covered every inch of the space.

"You guys don't see it?"

But all four shook their heads.

Her mother asked, "Is this like the time you tried to convince us all you saw the Smurf village on our road trip to Oregon?"

The question didn't make sense.

"I *did* see the Smurf village, so yes?"

"I saw it, too," Dana backed her up.

"But you don't see this?" Emma turned to Dana.

Her friend shook her head.

She sat back, confused. As they passed the area, the blackened ground was clearly moving, almost as if something was crawling beneath the surface. Turning away, she breathed in deeply to steady her nausea.

Abby whispered, "Are you sure it's not one of your *thingie*-things?"

Dana added, "Yeah, because we really can't see it."

Emma caught herself.

Oh. This was one of *those* moments, wasn't it?

Her mom eyed her through the rearview mirror, lips drawn into a line and one eyebrow raised.

She thought her daughter was lying again.

Making up a story.

"Maybe we're looking in the wrong place. Where exactly is it?" Her mother gave her a pointed expression.

Emma was very familiar with that particular look. It said, *Think before you speak.*

With a glance at her friends' wrinkled eyebrows, then back to her mother almost daring her to continue with what she thought was a lie, she said, "It's gone now. Maybe it was a shadow or something."

Her mother let out a breath. "Let's just focus on having a good time."

Her dad happily joined in, "We can do some clam digging, if you're up for it."

Emma smiled at her parents in the mirror, but she kept glancing back at the black chunk of forest only she could see.

EMMA

As the car turned the last curve of pines, Emma peered over her parents' shoulders. Her grandparents' house sprawled out in front of them, trees towering behind the structure like tall, skinny guardians. Whereas Emma's house had three stories, this was ranch-style, all on one level. It almost blended into the trees itself with the dark brown stained wood siding, and forest-green painted door.

The circular driveway welcomed them like two arms reaching in to hold them close. Maneuvering next to the three other cars already parked, Emma's dad stopped the engine, and everyone piled out of the station wagon.

"Looks like everyone's here already," her dad observed.

Before they could walk toward the front door, Grandpa Roy charged out of the house with a giant grin. He squeezed her mom in a bear hug, then hugged her dad a little more gently. His eyes lit up as he picked up Emma next, twirling her in his arms.

She laughed with her whole body.

Her grandpa was her favorite person in the entire universe. There was something so magical about him. As if he had left Winterbrook to live here on Earth. She wouldn't be surprised if he *were* a wizard. He certainly looked like one, with white hair and sparkling eyes. All that was missing was a long white beard, but he could be shaving so no one would recognize who he truly was.

He placed her back down on the ground and scuffed her head, right as her grandmother walked out of the house.

"Where's some of that love for your grandma? You girls, too," Grandma Virginia laughed and was nothing like Emma's dream, though she was wearing the same green pantsuit. Smiling to herself, Emma concluded *family* was the special occasion, and it filled her with warm fuzzies.

Emma, Abby, and Dana rushed over to her grandma and hugged her fiercely. As they were pulling away, she slipped each girl a brand new twenty-dollar bill.

"Yes!" Dana exclaimed.

"Greg is going to be so jealous." Abby laughed.

"Thanks, Grandma," Emma gushed, heart racing with adrenaline. She was twenty dollars closer to the Schwinn Fair Lady.

Dana and Abby echoed, "Thank you, Grandma Virginia."

Her grandma laughed and winked at Emma. "You know where to go for the good stuff."

Grandpa Roy placed his arm around his wife, but her grandmother quickly freed herself and waved for them to go inside.

As they headed toward the house though, Grandpa Roy joined Emma and the girls. "Dana and Abby, I'm so glad you two could come. We haven't seen you for a while. In fact, you know what? Along with the twenty Virginia just slipped you, Santa completely forgot to give you three something last Christmas, and he swung by our house last night to drop it off for you three."

A rush of excitement. "Grandpa, we're eleven. We know about Santa not being real."

Roy reeled back. "Not real? Well, then who was the man in the red suit that landed on my roof last night?"

"A burglar?" Emma laughed.

Dana nudged her friend with her elbow. "Speak for yourself. I believe in Santa."

"See? Dana gets it," Grandpa Roy laughed. Then he placed his hand on his chin as if thinking it over. "Well, whether it was Santa or a burglar, it doesn't change the fact he left something for each of you. Come on, I'll get them for you."

Emma didn't need to be told twice. She led Dana and Abby through the doorway and into the house. The same browns and greens from the outside spilled into the inside, from the wood paneling on every wall, to the shag green carpet under their feet, to the white popcorn ceiling.

The living room greeted them first with Emma's family sprawled about. Her aunt Doris and uncle Harold, with their kid and Emma's cousin, Lisa, stood near the fireplace.

Emma wasn't a fan of her cousin. She was spoiled and mean. But because they were the same age, everyone in the family always thought they should be best friends.

Her aunt Gertrude and uncle Doyle were talking near the half wall leading to the dining table. And behind her came Grandpa Roy, Grandma Virginia, and her parents.

"Holy mother of god," Dana mumbled under her breath.

"What?" Emma and Abby turned to their friend.

Dana pointed, jaw slack, eyes wide.

The far wall of the house was floor to ceiling windows and a sliding glass door leading to the backyard. But standing in front of the sliding glass door was something Emma never thought she'd see in person, despite her hopes and dreams.

The Schwinn Fair Lady in cherry-pink.

As if the Universe had heard the song of her soul, a beam of light shone directly on it from the skylight above, making the chrome sparkle like the diamond it was.

Emma stood in paralyzed shock, as did her friends.

Dana was the first to break when she whistled low in appreciation. "He got you the Fair Lady."

Abby sighed wistfully. "This place *is* magic."

How had her grandpa known? Did her parents tell him her bike was destroyed? But how did they guess she wanted the Fair Lady? Maybe he really *was* a wizard from Winterbrook! So many questions, but none of them mattered. Every cell in Emma's body vibrated with elation. She was the luckiest girl in the world.

As she was about to lead the charge to admire her new bike, her grandfather came up from behind and placed a small brown teddy bear in her arms, a stuffed owl in Abby's, and a stuffed elephant in Dana's. "Merry late Christmas," he said with twinkling eyes.

Oh.

Not the bike.

Don't show your disappointment.

Don't hurt his feelings.

I love this teddy bear.

It's the cutest teddy bear I've ever seen.

I love it with all my heart.

"Thank you!" Emma shouted and, with an elbow to the gut for Abby and Dana, they both joined in at the last minute.

Emma could tell Abby genuinely meant it. She was obsessed with owls and had a collection of tiny porcelain ones she kept on her shelf.

To give her credit, Dana put on a good show, but Emma knew in the depths of her heart, Dana had believed the bike was Emma's as much as she had.

Lisa sauntered over to the bike with her brown curls bouncing, her baggy overalls drooping, and turned to Emma with a smile that never reached her eyes. To her mother, she asked, "Can I go for a ride, Mom? I wanna see how fast it goes."

Aunt Doris folded her arms. "Wipe the smirk off your face. You can ride it in a bit. Say hi to your cousin and her friends first."

Lisa raised an eyebrow as if she couldn't be bothered, and Emma wanted a better view of the bike, anyway, so she took the higher road and walked over to her cousin, with Abby and Dana right next to her.

"Hey," Lisa said as if it was the most difficult word she could utter.

"Hey," Emma responded in turn.

The fact that this beautiful, perfect piece of machinery was her brat cousin's? How was it fair?

Dana and Abby didn't bother responding. They simply stared at the bike.

Lisa projected her voice with an air of bluster. "You guys like my bike?"

They nodded in unison, under the spell of the bike itself.

"I bet you wanna ride it?" Lisa taunted.

Queen Madelis might as well have cast the spell, it was so powerful, because they all nodded again like suckers.

"Too bad." Lisa delivered the final blow. "No one, and I mean *no one*, is riding it but me."

Well, that broke them out of it.

Dana's impulsive mouth didn't hold back as she whispered to Emma and Abby, "What a bitch."

"Welcome to my family," Emma groaned.

It cut deep, though. Being in the presence of her dream bike only to be told it belonged to *Lisa*? It left her with an aching hole of jealousy inside her.

Dana had had enough. "Let's go explore."

Tearing herself away from the most glorious bike ever created, Emma led her friends into the sunroom off the living room. It was roughly the size of Emma's bedroom, and windows wrapped around the walls on three sides.

A giant collage of family photos hung on almost every inch of the one wall that wasn't glass. Two armchairs and a small couch rested in the middle, facing the windows and the backyard beyond.

The photographs drew Dana and Abby's attention, and the two girls examined every picture in fascination.

Emma had seen them all a million times, so it wasn't as interesting for her, but when the alternative was Lisa lording over the Fair Lady, suddenly the pictures held more appeal. Some appeared ancient, and some were new from the last time she had visited, but somehow, they all fit together in an accurate representation of her chaotic family.

"You think Grandpa Roy would ever let us visit one of his ships?" Dana said as she examined a photograph of the man standing next to a giant freighter stacked with shipping containers.

Emma's grandfather had been piloting freighters since well before she was born. Before her *mother* was born, even. His job took him away from home for months at a time, so Emma had been thrilled to visit the ship he called home for half the year.

She'd only been there once, but it was something she'd never forget. She had imagined she'd been captured by Jabba the Hutt and was imprisoned on his sail barge. With the tall metal containers, the rough-strewn steel deck, and plenty of clunky metal places to hide in, it had been one of the best days of Emma's life. She'd truly believed she had entered the world of *Star Wars*.

Unfortunately, her mother felt the complete opposite.

Emma hadn't paid attention to the time as she explored the ship and ran from Jabba's guards, but apparently, it had been two hours.

Two hours of her mother frantically searching for her.

So, yeah, she was never allowed to go on one of his ships again.

Abby pointed to the black-and-white photo Emma had seen last night in her dreams.

Now, with it standing in front of her, she examined it more closely.

There was no noose around her great-grandfather's neck, but his eyes stared straight at Emma as if he were alive inside the photo. His slicked black hair, overalls covering his wiry frame, he must have been some kind of farmer, though no one ever spoke of him, so she was only guessing.

But standing next to him was Grandma Virginia in the same twenties-style dress from her dream. Though she'd seen this picture a thousand times, Emma's breath caught in her throat. She really was her grandma's twin. Down to the smattering of freckles across their noses.

Never having seen the photograph, Abby exclaimed, "When did you get these done? Is that from the mall where they do Old West photos? Who's the guy next to you?"

"That's not me. That's my grandma," Emma admitted.

"Like your *grandma*, grandma? The grandma here, this-is-her-house grandma?" Dana obviously needed clarification of the highest order.

Emma nodded, amused at their reaction. Since she could walk, every family member she ever came in contact with would utter the phrase in some kind of variation. "I can't believe how much you look like your grandma."

"So, who's the guy next to her?" Dana asked.

"Her dad. He died when she was young. Supposedly, a few days after this photo was taken," Emma answered.

"Why does that sound so creepy?" Abby shuddered.

"Because it *is* creepy," Dana answered.

She had to agree. She also realized she hadn't told them all the details of her dream. "He was in the nightmare I had last night. Both of them, actually. Dressed just like in this picture."

Abby blinked. "Um, excuse me?"

"Yeah, he had a rope around his neck, like he'd hung himself or something." Emma shuddered at the memory.

"Whoa," Dana responded.

Abby took another gander at the picture. "Well, you guys are twins," she repeated, as if she had to say it again.

"Weird, right?" Emma agreed.

Dana eyed the photo again. "Very." Then she turned to Emma. "No offense, but your grandma smells."

"Yeah, she smells like my uncle Frank," Abby added.

"Mom says it's because she drinks too much alcohol."

"My parents drink wine coolers every night, and they don't stink," Dana said.

Emma shrugged, not understanding it either. "Mom says she goes through at least two bottles of the clear stuff that looks like water a day."

Abby appeared unbothered as she admired another picture. "Well, we can hold our breaths when we're around her. Honestly..." She pulled out the twenty Grandma Virginia had given her. "It's worth it. I still can't believe she gave us so much money."

Emma was used to it. Slipping grandchildren cash was kind of her thing. She was just happy her friends got to partake as well. Picking up her teddy bear, she hugged it tight. "And Grandpa Roy gave us these."

Dana hugged her elephant. "*Santa* gave us these."

Warmth filled Emma. "Same thing."

VIRGINIA

Walking into the bathroom with a plate full of Almond Roca, Virginia sneered. She *hated* Almond Roca. The little logs always reminded her of turds, if she was being honest. She supposed the taste was all right, being toffee covered in chocolate and crushed almond sprinkles, but my god, did they not take an ounce of thought as to how they'd look?

Though she was grateful for them now. It had to be fate her soon-to-be-dead husband's favorite treat was Almond Roca. After all, cyanide powder tasted like almonds, which made it the perfect way to disguise the poison. If he had a suspicion or thought it tasted funny as he gobbled down the little turds, it would be too late. At least, that's what she learned from the Tylenol fiasco a few years ago.

Some psycho had opened the gel caps and replaced the insides with cyanide powder. Seven people had died before they finally wised up and took it off the shelves. They still had no idea who did it. It made Virginia sick a nut job like that was roaming free. But because of said nutjob, and being a national scandal in the news for weeks, it had given her a mini-education on everything she'd ever wanted to know about the poison.

The question had been, where was she going to get her hands on cyanide? Especially in a way that would cover her trail in case the police did a blood test. Nothing could lead back to her.

The risk they might find her garden was too high. She'd have to let the authorities take his body away, never to be part of her bed of wretches.

And he deserved to be there.

Forever rotting.

Forever wiped off this earth.

Truth be told, she had no idea if it was going to work.

Virginia had been collecting apricot seeds, apple seeds, and peach pits for months now since the news said they were all full of the poison. She wasn't a scientist, but she figured if she shaved the seeds and made a powder, it would have to work. And if it didn't, it would at least make his disloyal, cheating ass sick.

She was willing to experiment.

And if that didn't work, Plan B would serve. Originally, shooting him and making it seem like self-defense had been plan A, but cyanide poisoning was better. Safer. Fewer questions from the cops.

Placing the plate of Roca on the counter, Virginia pulled out a small Ziplock baggie of the shaved seeds. Turning on the sink, she put her hand under the running water, then let a few drops of water fall onto the logs from her fingers. Drying off her hands, she reached into the baggie and sprinkled the coarse powder over the wet spots and smiled when it stuck tightly to the surface of the candy.

In a sudden bout of paranoia, she glanced over her shoulder.

Being in the small bathroom, it was obvious no one was there, but she still shoved the shower curtain aside to make sure.

She stared at herself in the mirror. "You can do this."

Why did she need a pep talk? She was doing the right thing.

Roy had cheated on her, destroyed her trust, betrayed her very soul.

Virginia didn't give her heart to many, but she had given it to Roy, told him about Father and what he'd done to her and Rachel as children. Shared her most intimate thoughts. She would have done anything for Roy—stand in front of a train, kill anyone who dared to hurt him.

Over the years, she'd doubted him before, threatened him with baseball bats, chased him with a knife, pointed the gun at him several times, but she never intended to kill him. He'd never done anything bad enough for that. Threaten, yes. Enough to get him back in line.

They kept all this private, of course.

To everyone else, they were the perfect loving couple. And Virginia had thought that, too, despite her occasional temper tantrums toward him.

So, for him to betray in the way he did? Her ears pounded with the blood rushing to her head. Pure rage. *No.* There was no other choice.

He needed to be punished. And death was the only way to satisfy the guttural pain deep inside her.

Did he deny what he'd done?

Of course, he did.

But she had walked into his office to surprise him with lunch and had seen with her very eyes his secretary lunging in for a kiss. If Virginia hadn't busted in at that very moment, who knew how far it would have gone? Roy claimed he had nothing to do with it and fired the wench immediately, but she knew better. Every man she'd ever known was a liar and untrustworthy. She'd thought Roy was different, but it turned out he was like all the rest.

As a young woman, she'd vowed no one would hurt her like that. And yet, here she was, heart wrenched and squeezed until there was nothing left but hate and vengeance.

Her father had been the first to learn not to hurt Virginia. He'd paid with his life.

As if hearing her thoughts, he appeared next to her, identical to the photograph, the noose around his neck flipping wildly.

"You're doing the right thing. He deserves his fate, just like I did," his voice was graveled and rough.

Her younger self appeared next to her. Virginia had to do a double-take.

"Emma?" she asked, needing to make sure. It was confusing having her granddaughter here in the house. Virginia was used to seeing her younger self, but adding Emma into the mix mottled her brain. Virginia shook her head to clear it and stared in the mirror, not looking at either presence.

But then the girl spoke, "You said you'd protect your loved ones, at any cost."

Father growled.

Virginia peered down at the girl. "I am. You know what Roy did to me. He was supposed to love me and be loyal, but you don't do that to someone you love. I *trusted* him!"

Young Virginia glared at her, tears in her eyes. "He said nothing happened."

"I *saw* him," Virginia said a little too loudly, closing her eyes to calm herself. After a deep breath she added, "He's a threat to me and my family, and you know what I do with threats."

Father's laugh reverberated against the porcelain tiles, the tail end of his hanging rope active and loose.

Young Virginia spat, "You're like *him* now."

Virginia's entire body tensed. She was *nothing* like him. Turning to the younger version of herself, she yelled, "Leave me alone!"

Father and Young Virginia calmed down and watched quietly.

Getting rid of Roy for good filled her with determination rather than fear or guilt.

If he were gone, then she'd no longer have to suffer the humiliation of loving someone who obviously didn't love her. It would give her peace.

Killing was therapeutic at this point. But her first kill, Father, had been more terrifying than the exhilaration she experienced today. She still remembered the harmony though that had radiated inside her as he choked on the rat poison she'd slipped into his coffee. Yes, it sounded like a boring and mundane way to kill someone, but back then, the poison was strychnine, not the pansy-ass rat poison they had today. It killed efficiently and violently. It may have been a simple way to kill him, especially after years of fantasizing about new and inventive ways to rid the world of his evil. In the end, she grabbed what she could and got the job done. If she had had the chance, she might have done it differently, mainly because of how she'd taken care of the others in her garden.

But Father? Her first? Virginia had dreamed of murdering him every time he lay with her after her mother died. He had seemed so monstrous, a creature out of one of the wicked fairytales Mrs. Gordan would warn them about in Bible Study.

Glancing to her left, she saw Father standing quietly next to her, the tail of his noose swinging in a nonexistent wind.

She took what both of her ghoulies said with a grain of salt, though.

Virginia did what she wanted.

She always had.

She always would.

Speaking of which...

Virginia pulled out her flask of vodka from the inside of her cardigan sweater and drank heavily. After downing almost half the flask, the familiar warmth spread through her limbs as Virginia placed it back in her pocket.

With one last glimpse in the mirror, she took a deep, calming breath.

Grabbing the plate of Almond Roca, Virginia left the bathroom.

Time to get rid of the vermin.

EMMA

At this point, Emma considered herself a stalker. But how could she not be? The Fair Lady was the most beautiful thing she'd ever seen.

Abby and Dana weren't helping. They were drooling as much as she was. But the three of them kept their distance, sitting at a card table in the living room, playing Go Fish, but also not really paying attention. Abby had asked her if she had any fives, and Emma had said, "Go fish," but afterwards realized she had two of them. But when Emma had asked for Abby's five the next turn, her friend had been so focused on the bike, she'd simply handed the card to Emma without questioning it.

Dana said what they were all thinking. "How are we going to get our hands on that bike?"

It didn't help that Lisa hovered over her prized possession like the dragon Daltorine hoarding her gold. Emma's cousin polished the already shiny chrome handlebars for no reason except to make them jealous—which was working. Then she'd wave her hand over the seat, or the pink metal frame, or the wheels, presenting each part of the bike like she was Vanna White on *Wheel of Fortune.* Any excuse to show off and claim her territory.

The bike was hers, and Emma and her friends were never going to ride it.

Her grandmother walked into the living room, distracting her from the bike. She held a plate in her hands of some kind of...food? Emma couldn't really tell. She wondered where it would have come from, though, since her grandma had emerged from the hallway where only the bedrooms and bathrooms were. Maybe she had a secret stash of candy. It wouldn't surprise Emma in the least. Her grandmother always had some kind of sweets in her house.

As Grandma Virginia headed toward the dining table, Emma did a double take when she saw Great-Grandpa walking behind her, noose tight around his neck, rope trailing after him. Was he a ghost? Was he friendly? His lopsided smile indicated he was pleased about something. Maybe he liked whatever was on the plate she carried.

"My great-grandpa from the picture is here," she whispered. "He's following Grandma Virginia. He has a noose, though."

"Um, *what?*" Dana dropped her cards.

Abby's eyes rounded. "Are you joking?"

"Guys, he's family. He's probably nice." Emma tried to assuage her friends, but Abby's clenched fist and Dana's tensed shoulders indicated it wasn't working very well.

"*Two* ghosts now?" Dana stared at Emma's grandma, squinting her eyes as if trying to see the man as well.

"What the heck?" Abby mouthed to herself.

A pang of guilt rushed through Emma. This was supposed to be a fun getaway, not *Ghostbusters* without the busting equipment.

Her grandmother held the plate high and announced to everyone in the house, "Alright, everyone to the table. But no one touch the Almond Roca except Roy. We all know they're his favorite." She said it with a warm smile and gave her husband a loving wink.

Emma didn't know why Grandma's dad was following her, but she felt her grandmother's genuine desire to give Grandpa Roy his favorite candy.

Sauntering over from her bike like a cartoon bully, Lisa crossed her arms and stared Emma straight in the eye when she said, "*You* should eat one."

Curious as to what other food was on the dining table, Emma ignored Lisa and led Abby and Dana to the dining room area. A large table, at least ten feet long, spread out before them. It was full of every kind of finger food imaginable, from deviled eggs, to rolled sandwich meat on toothpicks, to cheese cubes, to a tray of boiled clams and mussels. Not to mention the pastry selection of cakes, chocolate chip cookies, pies, and donuts. Emma spotted a maple bar with her name on it.

At the head of the table, in a place of honor, her grandmother placed the plate of Almond Roca.

"I *said*, 'You should eat one,'" Lisa repeated as if Emma hadn't heard her the first time.

"She said they're for Grandpa." Emma dismissed her cousin, not bothering to make eye-contact. She edged her way toward the maple bar, almost tasting it in her mouth.

Abby whispered in Emma's ear. "She's just trying to get you in trouble."

"Yeah, don't listen to her," Dana agreed.

"Don't worry, I won't," Emma assured them.

Lisa stepped in front of her, arms crossed. "I dare you."

Dana and Abby groaned.

"Emma, *no*," Dana pleaded.

"You don't have to do *every* dare," Abby argued futilely.

It amazed Emma her friends thought she had a choice in the matter. "It's the rules."

Abby burst with frustration. "What rules? No one has these rules. These are only *your* rules."

Emma didn't want to argue. She wanted to eat the Almond Roca and be done with it. "Grandpa wouldn't mind if I only ate one."

Dana's hands rested on her hips. "You're going to do it no matter what, so just get it over with."

Now that was more like it.

"And share if it's good," Abby added.

The satisfied grin on Lisa's face was almost enough for Emma to break her own rules and leave the dining area entirely, but Emma couldn't fight the compulsion that filled her when she heard the word "dare."

Time to go.

Emma inched toward the Almond Roca, leaving her friends and cousin behind, though she could see them staring with anticipation.

None of the adults paid any attention to her as she slowly made her way to the end of the table. As she shuffled closer, the adults grew in size, taller and wider, and their clothes transformed into guard uniforms of leather and metal. The scenery around her shifted until she was no longer in the dining area, but inside a stone fortress, wet and cold, with moss growing in the corners and through the mortar. Now on her tip-toes, Emma was about to steal the prized jewels from the king himself.

As she approached the jeweled plate full of logs made entirely of gold, Emma glanced at Lisa, dressed in the black-and-white striped onesie of a prisoner. She mouthed, "Double dare."

And in an instant, everything snapped to normal, back in the dining area, the plate of candy in front of her.

Here goes nothing.

Grabbing a log of Almond Roca, Emma took a quick bite and chewed it quickly, swallowing it before anyone could make her spit it out.

Not that anyone had noticed.

She whirled toward Lisa, her smile triumphant, when her stomach turned violently.

Having the stomach flu once before, Emma had vowed she'd never get it again after the days of vomiting, but this? This was as if a freight train had run the entire track of her stomach and intestines. Before she could control herself, a projectile stream of acid and toffee flew out of her mouth and onto the table, completely soaking the plate of her grandfather's favorite candy.

That got everyone's attention.

The room erupted into cacophony of yelling, gasps, and movement, but Emma nearly fell from dizziness.

She wasn't sure if she was going to throw up again, but whatever had triggered the exorcist vomit, seemed to have projectiled out of her system. When Emma looked up at the adult next to her, she saw it was Grandma Virginia. Just like her nightmare, her grandmother stared at her with intense anger.

Great Grandpa stood behind her, arms crossed, the rope flailed wildly around him.

Grandma Virginia raised her right hand and swung down, aiming straight for Emma's cheek.

Before the blow could hit, Grandpa Roy swooped her up in his arms. "Oh my, Emma. Are you okay? You need to lie down?"

All she could think was not only had she eaten one of his candies when she wasn't supposed to, but now she had barfed all over the rest, so he couldn't have any.

"I'm sorry," she sputtered.

Her grandpa kissed her forehead. "Oh, sweetie, I don't care about stupid candy. I just want to make sure you're okay."

Emma hugged him as tightly as she could, then nodded toward Abby and Dana. "I'm okay. You can put me down."

He gently placed her on her feet next to her friends.

"What was in that thing?" Dana eyed the table cautiously, a slight quaver in her voice.

Emma's mom raced up to her, brows wrinkled together to create the 'V' of worry that her daughter always seemed to inspire in her.

She placed the back of her hand on Emma's forehead. "No fever, but let's get you to bed."

Pushing her mother away, Emma stomach contents had calmed almost entirely, maybe a gurgle or two, but otherwise fine. "Mom, I'm okay."

Her mom touched her head once more as if a fever would have spontaneously flared up in the last two seconds. "You sure you don't want to rest? Dana and Abby can play with Lisa for a while."

Emma read the "Please god, no" expressions on Abby and Dana's faces loud and clear. "No really, Mom, I'm good."

Lisa walked over to her Schwinn, opened the sliding glass door, and pushed the bike outside. She was apparently over the excitement.

Puke forgotten, Emma, Dana, and Abby all stared at their dream bike riding away.

Her dad joined her mom's side, placing a hand on her shoulder. "You okay, kiddo?"

Nodding, Emma watched Lisa ride the Schwinn in a circle.

He pointed at the bike. "Don't get any ideas. I can fix your broken one."

Really, Dad? After I just blew chunks? "Duh, I know. Can we go outside?" Her eyes never left the bicycle.

Sighing in unison with her mother, her father nodded. "Go ahead."

Like the stalkers they were, the girls immediately ran outside.

VIRGINIA

Blinking rapidly, Virginia tried to free herself of her tunneled vision. It only happened when she couldn't control her emotions. Heart pounding, she breathed in deeply, hoping to calm herself.

What had that girl been thinking?

She should have known that telling an eleven-year-old she couldn't do something would immediately compel her to do it. Hurting her grandchild would have killed Virginia. And the only person who needed to be dead at the moment was Roy.

Grabbing the edges of the plate so as not to get any of the vomit on her, Virginia walked into the kitchen for privacy. As soon as she stepped foot on the floral print linoleum floor, she tossed the Almond Roca into the trash, plate and all.

Without thinking, Virginia punched her fist against the wall.

I could have killed her!

Sweat beaded down her neck at the thought.

What am I doing?

Father stepped out of the shadows, head raised, eyes defiant, noose tightly secured around his throat. "You shouldn't feel guilty. The little demon did it on purpose. She's on *his* side. Have you seen the way she looks at him?"

No.

Virginia blocked his words from her mind. Not about Emma. Not about Mary's child. "Keep your mouth shut. She's a kid and likes candy. It's not brain surgery."

Father leaned down until his nose was within inches of hers, expression as deadly as she had ever seen. "She's working against you. That's how she found you in her dreams. In your sacred place. She'll destroy you in the end."

Her younger self popped in to give her two cents. "Don't listen to him."

"I'm not," Virginia snapped.

It was impossible not to see Emma in the little apparition that constantly haunted her. She wished she could make Father and her younger self disappear, but no matter how much she tried, nothing worked. Alcohol used to keep them quieted somewhat, but not even that stopped them anymore. But she still *tried.*

Pulling out her flask, Virginia polished it off with four large gulps.

Father stepped away, his image fading slightly. "Emma can see things like you can. If she sees what you really are, it's over. *All* of it. Your beautiful garden discovered and destroyed."

She hissed for him to shut up, then said loudly, "She is my *granddaughter*, and I'd kill for her. For any of my family. *You*, of all people, should remember that."

Father disappeared in a flash, and a thrill of satisfaction filled Virginia.

That's right. He needed to remember who had the power.

Her younger self was still there, staring up at her with approving pride at her protective declaration.

It soured her stomach for a reason she couldn't explain. Was it because her father's words affected her? Would there come a time when she'd have to do something about her flesh and blood?

Father's voice whispered, "She's *his* flesh and blood, too. Who do you think she'll choose?"

"I said, *shut up*!" Virginia yelled.

Mary's voice came from outside the door. "Mom? Who are you talking to?"

Virginia pushed through the swinging door leading to the dining area.

Mary and Doris greeted her, one with furrowed eyebrows and the other fidgeting with her fingers as if their mother were about to explode or something.

"I'm just so upset my little granddaughter got sick. I feel like it was my fault," Virginia said, adding a slight choke to her voice. Knowing full well it was her crushed seeds that caused Emma's "episode," the lie felt easy—true—like every lie she'd ever told. Natural.

Mary hugged her mother. "Oh, Mom, it's not your fault. She's probably allergic to nuts. I'm going to have her tested when we get back."

"You think?" Virginia added a little sniff in there as well. It wasn't as if she had to fake concern necessarily, but she still needed to make sure no one suspected any foul play. But almost killing Emma had shaken her deeply. And yet, there was a slight numbness as well, as she began to believe the nut allergy lie herself. As if she had nothing to do with her granddaughter getting sick. "Well, we better make sure there are no nuts in anything else. I don't know what I'd do if anything happened to that little girl."

Father whispered, "You wouldn't do anything. You'd be safer if she were gone."

Virginia grunted in anger.

"Mom?" Mary turned her head in a way that suggested she was surprised at the sudden mood shift in her mother.

Faking a cough and clearing her throat, Virginia said, "Damn phlegm. The joys of getting older."

Before either of her daughters could interrogate her further, she moved past them and toward her bedroom.

Maybe she needed to lie down for a while.

EMMA

Staring out at the enormous backyard of her grandparents' house, Emma could only focus on one thing.

The Schwinn Fair Lady.

Honestly, she just wished the three of them had their own bikes with them so they didn't have to be tortured watching her spoiled cousin do wheelies, like she was performing in front of an audience. Okay, maybe she *was* performing in front of an audience, but that made it extra annoying.

It didn't help her grandparents' backyard was ideal for bike riding, with an asphalt area very similar to the one Emma had in her own front yard, although this one was much bigger. More room for playing and stunts, though normally her grandparents used it for cars, but Aunt Doris must have talked them into parking all the cars in front so her daughter could ride her new toy. The only vehicle visible was Grandpa's RV parked alongside the house. Beyond the asphalt were a dilapidated doghouse, a metal shed, and a wall of pine trees grown so tightly together, Emma wondered if it was even possible to take a walk or hike in the forest.

"How can you stand your cousin?" Dana mumbled as she continued to stare.

The sun peaked through the clouds, beaming down on the bike's surface, radiating like a cherry pink beacon.

"She's like the girl version of Greg," Abby added.

The three girls sighed in unison.

"I hardly ever see her. They come from Indiana once a year. But yeah, she gets worse every time." Emma could never explain why some of her family was awful and some of them were amazing. Lisa used to be fun. Maybe it was living where she did in a small town? Emma never really liked Lisa's friends the one time she visited Indiana. Maybe popularity and being spoiled were badges of honor where Lisa lived? Either way, her cousin had become another person she wanted to avoid.

And avoiding appeared to be off the table.

Lisa finished a wheelie, then an evil glint twinkled in her eyes. Feet to pedals, Lisa sped toward them, as if she fully intended to run them over with her bike.

She wanted to play a game of chicken?

With the most *beautiful* bike in existence?

Emma wouldn't let her cousin ruin perfection, so she stood aside with Abby, not willing to play Lisa's game.

But Dana? Dana stepped directly into Lisa's path.

If Emma was the queen of "dares," Dana was the queen of "chicken." No one had ever beaten her. *Ever.* They always swerved first.

The only problem being... Lisa didn't act like she was going to back down either.

She was riding fast and unwavering.

Emma gulped.

This was going to be bad.

Right before Emma was about to yank Dana out of the way, Lisa spun the bike hard to the left, brakes screeching.

"What are you doing? You should have gotten out of the way!" Lisa yelled.

Dana shrugged as if what she'd done had been the easiest thing in the world. "That's not how you play chicken, dummy."

Lisa scowled. "Nice friends you have there, Emma."

Emma stepped forward, arms crossed. "Thanks, they're the best."

"You don't deserve the bike," Abby threw out.

Lisa laughed. "As opposed to who? One of you? Face it. My parents are richer than yours, and I get anything I ask for."

Abby pushed forward. "How do you know we don't have the same bike at home?"

"Because I can see how you all drool over it," Lisa accused.

Fair.

But still didn't change the fact Lisa was being the devil incarnate about it.

As if seeing the error of her ways, Lisa's face softened. She scooted the bike the few steps separating her from Emma while still sitting on the banana seat. "You want me to get off and you can ride it?"

Emma saw her cousin-of-old in Lisa's expression. It seemed like she suddenly remembered they used to be friends and was coming to her senses.

"Really?" Emma asked.

"Do *not* trust her," Dana whispered.

But Dana didn't know the old Lisa. Didn't remember sledding down a hill on a SuperTube, laughing all night from trying to scare themselves with ghost stories, playing with Lisa's extensive collection of Cabbage Patch dolls. Maybe the bike would be Lisa's olive branch.

Lisa's eyebrows crinkled. "No, really. I was just messing around with you guys before. Of course, any of you can ride it. Emma and I are cousins, right?"

Emma should be skeptical. "It's a trap!" her brain screamed at her in Admiral Ackbar's voice from *Return of the Jedi.*

Dana mumbled under her breath, “I swear if you fall for her shit...”

But Emma kind of was. Even Abby raised an eyebrow in curiosity, then nodded her approval.

Like a moth to a flame, Emma reached out for the handlebars...

Lisa yanked the bike away, jumped on the seat and sped away laughing hysterically. “Sike!” she yelled behind her.

Dana groaned, “I told you.”

Emma watched her cousin go. She knew better. She really did. But she had wanted to believe. “Screw it. I’m going to try the Force. She’s as weak-minded as they get. It’ll totally work.”

Determined, Emma waved her hand at Lisa in the distance. “You *will* let us ride your bike.”

Lisa performed another wheelie and rode off farther toward the abandoned doghouse.

“Right now.” Emma waved again, mimicking the way Obi-Wan and Luke had used it in the movies.

Lisa rode on, oblivious and apparently immune to the Force.

“You suck at the Force,” Dana said.

“Yeah,” Emma had to agree. “But Luke was bad at first, too. And Leia hasn’t started training yet.”

Abby turned toward Emma. “You’re not going to be her again for Halloween this year, are you? That would be three years in a row.”

Dana laughed. “Better than your old British costume you always wear.”

Abby let out an exasperated sigh. “Elizabeth Bennett. She’s a literary icon. Better than you. What were you last year? Indiana Jones?”

“Yeah, because he kicks ass.” Dana side-eyed Abby.

Crossing her arms, Abby said, “He’s a boy.”

“So?” Dana stepped toward Abby.

Before things escalated further, Emma interrupted, “Guys, can we not talk about our Halloween costumes and focus on how we can ride that bike?"

A hand touched Emma's shoulder, and she jumped slightly. Whirling around, Grandpa Roy stood behind them.

"Hey, Grandpa," Emma greeted him, genuinely happy to see a friendly face.

"Hi, Grandpa Roy," Dana and Abby said together.

Grandpa Roy nodded toward Lisa. "Don't mind her. She's a spoiled brat," he said with authority and an encouraging smile.

Hearing those words from an adult sent the three of them into giggles. Because Lisa was a brat. Everyone, including her parents, wanted to make everything nice and not step on any toes.

But Grandpa said it like he saw it, and Emma loved him for it.

"Follow me. I have something I want to show you girls." He led them around the corner to the side of the house.

Emma rubbed her eyes in disbelief.

Hundreds of rose bushes in full bloom as tall as she was, some as tall as her grandfather, lay in front of them. Reds, pinks, yellows, oranges, and lavenders swirled in front of her eyes like a kaleidoscope of petals.

At the same time, all three girls said, "Winterbrook."

Her grandpa smiled down at them. "Exactly."

"It's beautiful." Emma found it hard to find the right words. The amount of time and work Grandpa Roy must have spent cultivating this rose garden was not lost on Emma. It didn't surprise her either. Ever since she was a little girl, he was always growing something in his yard.

But this?

It was beyond anything Emma had ever seen.

He nodded for them to follow, and they walked deeper into the maze of roses. Blossoms of different sizes and textures bombarded Emma's senses at every turn. Each rose unique in its own way, but all both delicate and strong, as if they were porcelain sculptures and not living, growing, flowers.

Magic.

Pure *magic.*

For Emma, the roses came to life, growing giant and swirling with colors.

Dana and Abby's heads swiveled every which way, taking it all in as well.

"The door has to be here," Abby said in wonderment.

"It's gotta be," Emma agreed. "He basically made the gateway."

Dana turned serious, on a mission. "I'll keep an eye out."

They all were now. Still admiring the beauty around them, the three girls searched for the door they knew in their gut was there somewhere.

Her grandfather smiled at their determination and asked, "Better than the bike?"

Um.

Emma wasn't ready to admit that yet, and at her pause, her grandpa laughed heartily. "Well, maybe for actual Christmas I can at least put in a good word for you three with Santa. How does that sound?"

Whoa.

Maybe Emma was starting to believe in Santa again.

Dana gave Emma and Abby an "I told you he was real" look, and Abby seemed like she may have blown a fuse, being so overwhelmed with the roses and Grandpa Roy's promise to talk to Santa.

Tilting his head to the side, her grandpa turned to the three of them. "Did you hear that?"

Emma strained her ears as hard as she could, but she didn't hear anything out of the ordinary.

"It sounds like a battle." Her grandfather winked at Emma.

"*Ohhhh.*" Emma caught on. They were about to step into Winterbrook. It may not be the actual door, but close enough. She swung her hand and pointed, confident. "Queen Madelis is attacking."

Dana and Abby exchanged excited smiles as they too figured out what was happening.

"We have to fight her," Dana said in a voice sounding like a grizzled soldier.

"I know some magic. I've been training." Abby saluted, then waved her hands together as if she were about to cast a spell.

"I have magic as well." Grandpa Roy nodded. "Come. I'll take you to your weapons."

He led them to the end of the rose garden. Leaning against the side of the house were a wooden sword, a walking stick, and a plastic bow with a quiver full of suction-cupped arrows lying next to it.

Emma grabbed the sword. As she did, the wood transformed into steel, the pommel an intricate design of loops and twists of gold and silver. It was light in her hand, but the blade would serve her well in the battle.

Abby wrapped her fingers around the walking stick, and it instantly changed into a white oak staff. At the top, smaller branches grew out of the wooden base and curved up into a point, creating a gnarled cage holding a bright, ruby red crystal in its center.

And when Dana took the plastic bow and arrows, the bow grew to twice its size, now made of knotted yew, the quiver a hardened brown leather with long wooden arrows inside.

Grandpa Roy rotated his hands together, a ball of red flames forming between them. "The battle is beyond these roses." He wore the blue robes of a wizard, thick wool and embroidered trim on the hem and bell sleeves.

The sounds came into focus now for Emma. The clashing of lightning bolt spells, the rumbling of goblins, Queen Madelis shouting orders and casting more lightning, and then above it all, the cries of a little girl.

Heart pounding in her throat, Emma turned to her party. "I think I hear Olivia! She's in trouble."

"We have to save her!" Abby readied her staff.

"Let's go!" Dana pulled out an arrow from her quiver, preparing to shoot.

"I'll distract them with this fireball, while you go in for the rescue." Grandpa Roy's ball of fire, now fully formed and flickering between his hands.

Emma nodded, sword ready.

Grandpa Roy leapt out of the rose bushes and pushed the fireball toward the sounds of combat.

Emma nodded to Abby and Dana, then led the charge forward.

The landscape fully transformed before Emma's eyes until she stood on a battlefield in the land of Winterbrook. Majestic mountains with snow-topped peaks loomed in the distance. Skyscraper-sized pines surrounded Emma's party where they stood on the bright green grass field where the battle took place.

Glancing down at her clothes, Emma now wore a light suit of armor etched with delicate flowers and vines to match the beauty of her sword. Dana and Abby's clothes had transformed as well, with Abby in a long red dress, tied with a gold sash around the waist, and Dana in archery leathers, forest green and deep brown, her matching quiver now strapped on her back.

Grandpa Roy pushed his fireball forward toward the oncoming goblin army.

Hundreds of white, chalky figures, with gnarled limbs ran toward them, surprisingly fast considering they used both their arms and legs to move. If Emma hadn't fought them before, she might have been more frightened, but goblins were easy to defeat with a good stab to the chest. She'd have to watch out for their long, knife-like claws, though. Emma had seen some goblins with claws over a foot long, and they could do serious damage if they reached her or her friends.

The fireball hit with stunning impact, like a bowling ball hitting a hundred pins. Bodies flew everywhere. Skyward, sideways, and even downwards onto the ground to be trampled by their fellow soldiers.

A familiar cackle rose above the roars of magic and battle.

Emma shuddered. She knew that laugh too well.

Queen Madelis.

In the distance, Emma made out an onyx tower made of smooth stone. Queen Madelis stood on top, watching the combat before her and continuing her triumphant laugh. Behind her and tied to a chair with thick rope, sat Olivia, the main character of *The Chronicles of Winterbrook*.

"Look on the tower. Queen Madelis has Olivia!" Emma pointed. "We have to save her!"

Holding out a strung arrow, Dana searched the area around them. "I don't see the wizard Tovias! Do you think she has him too?"

The goblin horde recovered from the blow Grandpa Roy delivered and scurried forward once more.

Emma's grandfather waved his hands and arms, building momentum for more fire. "I'll use my magic to stall the goblins! You girls try to save Olivia! Maybe Tovias went for help! I'll use my fire wave." Once the fire reached a size larger than his arm span, Grandpa Roy threw his hands forward.

A giant blast of fire flew from his hands and smashed into the goblins, incapacitating almost half their numbers.

"Now! Go!" Grandpa Roy shouted above another blast of fire from his hands.

With the goblins fully focused on him and his fire magic, Emma waved her friends toward the tower.

Screaming in rage, Queen Madelis focused on Grandpa Roy.

Emma knew this would be their chance.

In a matter of seconds, the girls reached the tower, a metal rung ladder bolted to the stone.

Dana readied her arrow. "You two climb up and get Olivia. I'll put an arrow through anyone that comes to stop us."

Emma nodded and started climbing the ladder. Abby was close behind.

Out of the corner of her eye, Emma noticed four goblins run

towards them, drool flying out of their mouths.

Gross.

Dana pulled back her first arrow and let it fly.

The arrow lodged itself in the closest goblin's eye, and he dropped to the ground. This caused the other three to slow their charge, cautious now of the archer with true aim.

Having faith in Dana's skills, Emma hurried up the ladder, finally reaching the top and cautiously climbing onto the platform.

"I'll cast an invisibility spell. Hang on." Abby spoke in the language of Winterbrook. "Done," she exclaimed.

It worked.

Queen Madelis didn't even turn her head as two girls arrived at Olivia's side.

When Emma touched Olivia's shoulder, the girl jumped and rotated her view trying to figure out what had made contact.

Leaning in close as she untied the rope that held Olivia, Emma whispered, "We're here to rescue you. We're cloaked in an invisibility spell. Stand still so Abby can cast it on you, too."

Abby incanted the spell a second time, and Olivia disappeared before Emma's eyes.

As if sensing the magic, Queen Madelis whirled around, sniffing the air, head craning every which way, searching. "I know you're still here! I can feel the invisibility spell."

"I got you, girls!" A roaring voice boomed from the sky.

Tears filled Emma's eyes when she looked up to see Daltorine soaring above them, ready to aid in the battle. Shimmering red scales shifted into stunning gold when the sunlight beamed on her back, while her sparkling red wings flapped magnificently.

"Daltorine!" Emma cried with joy, not caring if Queen Madelis could locate her from her voice.

"Get off the platform!" the dragon called out.

Scrambling to the ladder and still invisible, Emma, Abby, and Olivia began to climb down.

"We're clear!" Emma yelled to her dragon friend.

Queen Madelis threw her hands back, ready to cast a lightning bolt at the building-sized dragon now hovering above her.

But Daltorine was faster.

Fire poured out of her mouth...

"Girls! Dinner!" Grandma Virginia's voice cut through the fantasy battle.

Like water being splashed on a painting, Winterbrook melted before her eyes until she sat with Abby in the tree house Grandpa Roy had built her a few years ago.

Dana stood on the ground below with her grandfather on the patchy grass of the side yard next to the house.

"I'm starving." Abby rubbed her tummy.

After losing all the contents of her stomach earlier, Emma found she was famished as well. "Yeah, let's go."

Climbing down the ladder, they joined Dana and Grandpa Roy and began walking toward the house.

With the sun slowly setting, Emma glanced toward the forest. A salty breeze reached her nostrils and filled her lungs with sweet-smelling air.

But as her eyes came to rest on the patch of trees she'd seen on the drive up, the small square of blackened plant life and ground was still there.

Emma shivered.

Grandpa Roy slowed down to walk next to her. "Sun's almost down. It gets chilly fast. Let's hurry inside." Her grandfather placed his cardigan on her shoulders.

But Emma's chill had nothing to do with the weather.

VIRGINIA

Virginia watched Emma and the others walk toward the house. Father stood next to her, lips drawn into a line. The rope of his noose whipped wildly around him. "She loves him more than you."

Her mind twisted at his words. She didn't want to hear his venom. Ignoring him, she turned abruptly and stormed into the house.

Dinner went as well as it could. Virginia didn't dare try to poison Roy a second time. It would be too obvious. Not that any of her family would ever suspect her. They saw her as a sweet old woman. Sometimes the monster slipped out, but whose monster didn't?

Her daughter Mary had a worse temper than her own, and no one would accuse her of murder.

If any of them actually knew what she was capable of, what would they do? Would they try to stop her? Or would they bury their heads deeper into the sand? Probably the latter. It was human nature after all. To sit idly by and watch the world burn, then suddenly be shocked no one did anything to stop it. Lazy.

But Virginia wasn't. When she saw a wrong, she fixed it. Or eliminated it. Was there really a difference?

Standing in the doorway of the hallway leading to the bedrooms and bathrooms, she watched her family interact with each other. It fascinated her sometimes, the way people disguised how they felt inside with smiles and laughs. They couldn't possibly be that happy. But there they were, her three daughters and their husbands, her two grandchildren and their friends... and Roy. She gagged as he cheered with Harold and Doyle, watching their beloved Indiana Hoosiers playing Michigan State.

Roy couldn't care less about college football, but suddenly he was acting a fool, pumping his arm in the air at a touchdown. He didn't know what a touchdown was before he met her. Roy wasn't much into things normal men were into. It was what drew Virginia to him in the first place. But she also thought he'd never cheat on her, even though she herself was "the other woman" with his last wife. She'd always dismissed the "if he did it to someone else, he'll do it you" mentality. After all, their love had been written in the stars, right?

How could she have thought that? How could her brain have actually believed Roy loved her with all his heart the way she had loved him? *How?!*

Her chest seized with rage and humiliation.

How stupid his secretary must think she was. And, if she truly contemplated the matter, whoever else he probably messed around with. Emotions boiled inside her like a violent storm.

Stop.

Think of the goal.

The mission.

Your purpose.

Roy would no longer be breathing after tonight.

Heart racing now, Virginia pulled in a deep breath, but it wasn't enough to stop the pounding. She needed alcohol. Carefully removing the flask from her back pocket, she gulped half its contents.

There it was.

The calm.

The tension in her neck and shoulders dissolved with this magic elixir.

Focus on the room.

Your family.

Just don't look at him *and everything will be fine.*

A cacophony of talk and laughter overwhelmed her ears, but the alcohol made it bearable. She should rejoice that her family was having a good time.

She didn't.

Virginia didn't feel much of anything anymore except anger. Anger and the calming release that filled her when she'd right a wrong and remove a problem from this world. She wasn't a religious woman, but if there was a god, she was doing His work.

Scanning the room at each cluster of family, she raised an eyebrow when her eyes landed on Emma. Even the kids seemed to be getting along, playing Monopoly.

The girl had landed on Boardwalk, and Virginia smiled to herself. Her granddaughter was so much like her. She loved her more than the rest because of it, but it also scared her.

Father arrived at her side, following her gaze. "Emma is planning something. Have you forgotten that she saw us?"

Her younger self materialized as well. The two could never be apart from each other. "She's playing a game. And you just thought to yourself you loved her the most."

Virginia didn't answer, knowing how she'd be viewed being a seventy-five-year-old woman standing in a doorway talking to herself.

Father continued his train of logic. "Then why did Emma find Virginia's most sacred place in her dreams? She'll find her way back there, mark my words."

Not speaking was becoming increasingly difficult, especially since she agreed with Father. Emma had found her at her old house. Her granddaughter had witnessed her fantasy of killing Roy in the tub. Virginia wasn't sure if Emma remembered any of it. Otherwise, she was sure her granddaughter would have given her side-eye when they'd arrived. But if Emma was anything like her at that age, she'd start remembering dreams like that soon.

Father may be right.

Emma could become a problem.

Her younger self placed her hands on her hips and countered, "It was an accident."

But Father ignored Young Virginia and said, "Emma stopped you from doing what was right with the poison. She risked her own life for...*him*."

Her eyes strayed to Roy, cheering and laughing with her sons-in-law, pretending to care a damn football team was winning.

"Look at him," Father encouraged. "Oblivious to the pain he caused you. Acting as if he's part of this family. He's not. That ended when he betrayed you."

Father was right. Roy wasn't worthy of her. He wasn't worthy of anyone here, including Harold, who was always a bit of an ass.

Virginia's younger self tugged on her cardigan. "Roy loves you."

Father walked behind Young Virginia, placing a warning hand on her shoulder. "True love is loyalty. He has none of that. And neither does Emma."

Virginia's gaze shifted to Emma and pondered how her granddaughter was physically identical to Virginia's younger self. It was almost as if two of them existed in the same room.

Father clamped both hands on Young Virginia's shoulders. "Emma is weak, like this one was." The tail end of the noose's rope wrapped around Young Virginia's body like a vise. The apparition struggled to free herself.

"Let me go!" Young Virginia cried out.

The rope twisted around her so tightly, with a muffled scream, she disappeared entirely. The rope then turned to Virginia, creeping up her leg.

Father stared at Emma as he said, “If you’re not ready to act, then just watch her. You’ll see. She’ll betray you worse than the man you used to call a husband.”

Virginia didn’t respond. She didn’t want to believe that about her granddaughter. But her doubts about Emma grew deeper.

The rope from Father’s noose writhed around her as she watched Emma play her game.

She’d take his advice. She would watch the girl.

And if Emma intended to betray her, Virginia would make sure she’d strike first.

EMMA

Trying to concentrate on the game was almost impossible for Emma due to her father's raised voice on the phone in the kitchen.

She'd even bought Boardwalk! That was her lucky charm, and she had never lost a game of Monopoly in her life. The only time she'd come close to losing was when she and Abby had the stupid idea to play with Greg and Kyle, and *Greg* bought Boardwalk. He didn't even want it. He just knew Emma wanted it.

She would have let it slide. She could win without it after all, but Greg performed a five-minute victory-rub-it-in-her-face dance, and Emma had snapped. Without waiting to see who would have actually won, Emma had flipped the board, finding great satisfaction in Greg and Kyle's shocked faces. Plus, the top hat then smacked Greg's forehead right in the center and left a red mark for at least a couple of hours. It had been gratifying.

The game counted as a draw in Emma's book, not a loss, so as far as she was concerned, she'd never lost.

Her mother stood by her father's side as he talked tersely into the receiver. Emma could tell it was her dad's work. They were always asking him to come in on his days off. And from his slumped shoulders and her mother's crossed arms, Emma could tell today would be one of those times.

Lisa snuck a few five-hundred-dollar bills from the bank, but Emma had an entire stack of them herself, so she decided to let her cousin cheat. With the four monopolies Emma already had, and the seven hotels, she would still win anyway.

The slam of the phone brought her attention fully to her parents, and before she could respond, both of them were by her side, kneeling down to her eye level.

"I'm sorry, kiddos, but they need me at work early tomorrow morning. We have to leave," her dad said, and Emma could hear the tinge of disappointment laced with anger in his voice.

"Tonight?" Emma asked, not prepared to leave so suddenly.

"Afraid so." He put on an encouraging smile, but his cyes told a different story. He was definitely upset.

Dana tossed her money on the game board, fully willing to stop playing, seeing as she owned exactly two properties. Her strategy had been to be picky about what monopoly she wanted, but with three other players, most of the properties were gone before she even landed on her favorite. "Should we call our parents?"

Abby worried her lower lip. "My parents are out of town tonight."

"You girls can still have a slumber party at our house," her mother suggested.

Emma could tell she was trying to make the best out of an uncomfortable situation.

But before anyone could say anything else on the matter, Grandma Virginia stepped in. "Nonsense. They can stay here with us. The whole family flew in from Indiana, and Emma hardly gets to see them. Plus, her friends came up here for some fun."

Heart skipping a beat, Emma found she was conflicted. She had to admit, going home sounded good at the moment, especially since Lisa taunted the three of them with her perfect bike.

"Would you girls like that? Stay here with family?" Her mom asked them.

Um.

Looking at Abby and Dana. They seemed on the fence as well, fidgeting and squirming a bit.

It was Lisa who spoke first. "I swear I'll let you ride my bike. I promise this time."

Desperation fueled her cousin's expression. Emma knew what it was like being the only kid with a bunch of adults. Even the Fair Lady couldn't mask that forever.

"Really? No take-backs?" Emma eyed her cousin suspiciously.

Dana rolled her eyes, fully suspicious of Lisa. "You *know* you can't trust her."

Lisa put up her little finger. The most solid of promises. "No take-backs. Pinkie-swear."

No one, *no one* went back on a pinkie swear. Emma wrapped her pinkie around Lisa's.

Abby obviously didn't trust Lisa either, because she said, "You pinkie swore. We're going to hold you to that."

"Three against one," Dana added for measure.

"I *swear*!" Lisa said with a hint of indignance.

An explosion of desire filled Emma. To simply ride across the asphalt would be a dream. Turning to her parents, she said, "You guys go. We want to stay."

Her dad playfully groaned, "You and that bike."

"All right. I'm going to call your parents to let them know the situation," her mother took charge.

Dana shrugged. "They won't care."

Abby laughed. "Yeah, good luck getting a hold of them."

Emma's mom answered, "Well, we're going to try, anyway. We'll see you in a couple of days. Be good."

She could make no *real* promises on that front, but Emma said, "We will."

Her parents walked toward the hallway leading to their guest room, and a sudden chill coursed through her when her grandmother said, "Don't worry, Grandma will spoil them rotten."

While Grandma Virginia smiled at her parents as they passed, Great Grandfather's lips curved into a grin, making Emma's skin crawl.

Why did she feel like her only protection was about to leave?

EMMA

Dressed in her *Star Wars* pajamas, Emma crawled under the covers of the king-sized bed, Dana and Abby already tucked in. The fact they got the room to themselves was exciting in itself. Before her parents had left, the plan had been to share a bedroom with Lisa in two queen-size beds. But now that they were gone, Emma and her friends were able to take over her parents' room. Her entitled cousin acted as if this had been the plan all along, never deigning to share a bedroom with her cousin scum. Sighing a sigh of relief, Emma snuggled into the comfy quilt and fluffed her pillow.

Uncle Harold and Aunt Doris walked in with a smile.

"You girls ready for bed? No staying up all hours of the night talking. Tomorrow's a full day." Doris gave Emma the "stare." She'd thought only her own mother had that power, but apparently it was hereditary.

"And don't worry," Uncle Harold added, "we'll call your mom in the morning. Let her know you're having fun."

"Thanks, Uncle Harold."

The adults left the room, switching off the lights, leaving the three girls alone in the dark.

"You really think Lisa will let you ride her bike?" Abby asked in the darkness.

"Hell, no, but I'll make her if I have to," Dana said firmly.

"She did pinkie swear, though," Emma defended her cousin, mainly out of hope rather than any real faith she'd let her ride the bicycle.

"I'll believe it when I see it." Dana had the last word.

They each mumbled a "good night," and Emma rested her head on the soft pillow. As she closed her eyes, she wished she'd dream of each of them riding their own Fair Lady.

NOT HERE AGAIN.

Emma stood in front of the dilapidated house from her previous dream.

Freya had warned her this place was more than an ordinary dream, that she was in her grandmother's head, whatever that meant, but it still appeared like a dream to her. She hoped angry-grandma wasn't here this time.

Light poured out from the bottom of the closed door where the base didn't quite meet the floor.

Emma jumped slightly when shadows blocked the light underneath. It was clearly a person standing behind the rickety old entryway.

Please don't be Grandma.

Please don't be Grandma.

Materializing before her very eyes, the wizard Tovias from Winterbrook suddenly stood before her, his long white beard and heavy woolen blue robes a staple from his wardrobe in the books.

Startling blue eyes pierced through Emma when he said, "You need to have your spells ready. We have to fight Queen Madelis."

Dizzy with excitement in this sudden turn of her dream, Emma exclaimed, "Tovias!"

He motioned her toward him with a wave of his hand. "You must..."

Mid-sentence, Tovias's body transformed into a billion flakes of dust, rotating with a speed faster than Emma could follow until he lifted into the air like a tornado and was gone.

Breathing hard, Emma stopped, unsure of what just happened.

The legs behind the closed door shifted slightly, but the barrier stayed shut.

In Tovias's place now stood the younger version of Grandma Virginia, the one who followed her grandmother around and was identical to Emma.

Young Virginia bit the side of her cheek. "He's not real, and neither are his words." She stepped closer to Emma. "Why do you keep coming back here? They're getting suspicious of you."

Heart still racing from the shock of her Winterbrook hero disintegrating into dust, Emma sputtered, "What did you do to Tovias?"

The apparition's eyes slitted as she said, "I told you. He's not real."

A gulp of air calmed Emma down some, and she focused on the girl in front of her. Wait. Were they the same person? Was this her shadow self, like what happened to Olivia in book four of the *Chronicles of Winterbrook*? A version of herself that would attack her in the battle for Winterbrook? But all that came out of Emma was, "You look exactly like me."

"You didn't answer my question. Why do you keep coming here?" the girl asked, arms crossed.

Emma took a moment to think about it. Why did she come back to this place? She hated it the first time, and she certainly didn't want to upset her grandmother again, dream-form or awake-form. "I didn't mean to," she answered honestly. "I fell asleep and ended up here."

Uncrossing her arms, her twin nodded emphatically. "That's

what I told her, but I don't think she believes me. She doesn't like me either."

BOOM! BOOM! BOOM!

The silhouette behind the door pounded on its surface.

Emma jumped a full two feet backwards.

It stopped as suddenly as it started.

"Don't answer it." The girl said, feet solidly on the ground and arms crossed again.

A sudden thought hit Emma. "Is it Queen Madelis? Is she influencing Grandma somehow?" It was the only answer that made sense to her.

The girl from the photo shook her head. "No. She makes her own choices."

Emma stared closer at the girl. The way she held herself, the expression of disgust on her face. "Are you really her? My grandma?"

The girl shrugged. "What's left of her." Arms uncrossed, she pointed at the door. "She's more *him* now than anyone else."

Focusing on the peeled paint of the wood, trying not to think of who stood right behind it, Emma asked cautiously, "Who's *him*?"

The door flew open.

Standing in the doorway was Great Grandfather, just as Emma had been seeing him in waking life, noose around his neck, rope twisting and turning with a life of its own, the tail end of it creeping toward Emma.

Great Grandfather peered down at young Grandma Virginia. "She found her way here again, like I told you she would."

Not in the least bothered by his looming figure, the girl waved him off. "Oh, what do you know? She got here by accident, like *I* told you."

Great Grandfather's gaze turned to Emma, the rope now at her feet. "Accident, huh? There are no accidents. Not when it comes to the gift."

Young Grandma Virginia huffed, "What would you know about

it? You're not even real."

"And you are?" he laughed.

Confusion ate at Emma's mind. "Are you both ghosts?" Though it felt like a reasonable conclusion for Great Grandfather, it didn't quite fit with the younger version of her grandmother.

Great Grandfather's dark brown eyes pierced through her. "No. We're not ghosts."

Emma worked through the logic. "You haunt Grandma like ghosts."

His lips curled as he snarled, "Who are you to judge?"

The rope wrapped around Emma's ankles. She tried to kick free, but it tightened and continued to wrap around her legs.

"You came here on purpose!" he shouted.

Though she was in dream-form, sweat beaded at her neck. Could he hurt her here? Was that possible?

"It was an accident," Emma argued weakly.

"*Lies!*" Great Grandfather stepped closer, eyes alight with fury.

The rope squeezed her ribs as it wrapped tightly around her.

Gasping, her vision blurred, then swirled into dizzying colors. She closed her eyes to steady herself.

Opening her eyes, Emma grabbed onto the back part of a booth to steady herself.

Where was she?

At least she wasn't being squeezed by a rope with her terrifyingly creepy great-grandfather. What had that been? Why had he been so angry?

Her limbs free and clear of any bindings, Emma examined her surroundings more closely, she recognized she was in some kind of restaurant or diner.

It wasn't even a nice one. Ratty vinyl booths, a faded brown color, but in places were still their original red, chipped black and white Formica tile, old '50s mini-jukeboxes at each booth. Giant windows stretched all the way to the ceiling and ended at the booth's height.

They made a U shape that was squared off by the back wall of the diner. It consisted of a room-length bar with bolted-in stools and, behind those, the kitchen.

It was fairly empty. Only a few people sitting at the bar, and a couple of families in the booths. But then a familiar face caught her eye in the back corner of the restaurant.

Grandma Virginia.

A man in his twenties sat across from her, hands fidgeting under the table, but his eyes open and eager.

Emma walked over to them. “Hi, Grandma.”

But her grandmother didn’t respond. And neither did the man.

Oh.

Emma sighed.

She was in her grandma’s dream, or memory, or whatever this was.

Emma had done this before with her parents and friends. Her mother found it amusing, but her dad did not. He didn’t like anything science or facts couldn’t explain. And telling him about his childhood memory of playing on the docks and getting stuck in-between the planks until the fire department had to pry him out could not be explained by science. He, of course, mumbled that he must have told her that story, but Emma and her father both knew it wasn’t true. She never pushed him, though. She’d had many dream-memories of her father since, but she kept them to herself.

Emma wondered how she could go from confronting her great-grandfather and the younger version of her grandma at the dilapidated house to a diner. But since current-grandma wasn’t responding to her, Emma figured it was safe to say this was a memory.

At this point, having no control over anything so far in this dream adventure, she figured she’d watch and see why her grandmother was meeting up with this strange, shifty fellow.

“I’ll give you ten grand to leave Mary alone and move back to... where are you from again?” her grandmother said tersely.

Leave Mary alone? Who was this guy? And what was he doing to bother her mother? Emma was on her grandmother's side. The fact that she was willing to pay this guy to stay away from Emma's mom, said volumes about how good of a mother she was.

"I'm from Kansas," the man answered.

"Kansas. You know she's married, right? With a kid?" Grandma wasn't playing around.

Emma even wanted to help, though this was only a memory. She tried kicking this guy's shins just for measure, but her foot passed through him.

"Love is love," he said with a smile that made Emma's skin crawl.

"Grandma, you better get him arrested or something." Emma had had enough dreams of killers to know there was something seriously wrong with this man.

"Except she doesn't love you," Grandma responded.

Go Grams!

"She will," he said with confidence.

Emma's hands trembled. The man terrified her.

But her grandma simply sat back, oozing confidence. "Money or Mary? What will it be? Alex, is it?"

There was only one answer this Alex could give, or Emma was sure her grandma would call the cops.

But after a long moment, Alex finally nodded. "Money."

Grandma Virginia's mouth curved into a satisfied grin. "Great. I've got the cash in my car." She stood up and began to walk toward the exit, expecting Alex to follow.

He leapt to his feet and hurried after.

Emma followed as well, eager to see how this exchange would end.

As she exited, she noticed the beat-up neon sign: Joan's Diner. The small building was nestled far off the main road, amidst a clutter of trees. Making their way through the parking lot, it was small, maybe fifteen total spots and only three of them were taken.

Grandma Virginia continued past the cars, farther toward the edge of the tree line. "There weren't any spots when I got here, so I had to park in Timbuktu," she laughed.

Alex shrugged, but Emma suspected Grandma parked her car away from the diner on purpose. Maybe she was going to punch the guy, to really scare him into leaving her mother alone.

At last, they arrived at the car. It had been backed in, so the trunk was almost entirely immersed in the trees. "It's in the trunk. I assume twenties are good with you?"

Alex reminded Emma of the Joker, his smile wide and hideous. He obviously cared more about money than his so-called love, and Emma was grateful for that.

Walking to the tail end of the car, her grandma used her key to unlock the trunk. As the trunk door swung up, Alex turned the corner to receive his payday.

Grandma Virginia thrust a large knife directly into Alex's neck all the way to the other side.

Emma screamed, though no one heard her.

Yanking out the blade, Alex clutched his throat, uselessly, but his eyes turned lifeless before he fell. Her grandmother guided his body into the trunk of the car lined with plastic.

Emma's throat tightened at the sight. Maybe this wasn't a memory. Maybe it was a nightmare of her grandmother's.

"Can I leave now? Please let me leave!" she screamed into the air.

Her grandmother leaned down with a bottle of bleach and poured it onto the cement where a few drops of blood had hit. Satisfied with her cleanup, Grandma Virginia placed the bleach into the trunk, then slammed the door shut.

"Please, let me leave." First the crusty old house with her great grandfather trying to crush her with a rope, then this? "I just want to wake up!" she yelled.

Her grandmother's head swung toward her.

Grandma Virginia could *definitely* see her now.

Emma stepped back. Her grandmother didn't have a rope to attack her with like Great Grandfather, but in dream-land, Grandma Virginia might be capable of far worse.

"I told you I didn't want you here!" she yelled.

"I didn't mean to," Emma stammered, but she began to doubt. Maybe she *had* meant to. But why?

"Father warned me about you, but I didn't want to believe him. I wanted to believe you loved me. That you are loyal to me." She clenched her fists.

"I *do* love you, Grandma."

"Then why are you here!"

A swirl of color blinded Emma, her surroundings changing once more until she was at the rundown house again.

Great Grandfather stood over her, nostrils flared. He leaned down, eyes wild and bright. "She's seeing things we don't want her to! I told you she was dangerous!"

A tight squeeze reminded her that in this dreamscape, the rope from his noose wrapped around her like a boa constrictor. When Emma tried to speak, the rope tightened further, and the words stuck in her throat.

"What did you see?!" Great Grandfather screamed.

Two arms climbed out of the very air behind Emma, bodiless, but moving with purpose. They grabbed onto Emma's shoulders. She had no time to be afraid as the vise-like rope threatened to pop her out of existence.

"Grab her!" Great Grandfather yelled at Young Virginia, but Emma's twin folded her arms in defiance.

Leaping toward her, Great Grandfather reached out toward Emma...

Yanked from the dreamscape as his fingers touched her arm, Emma gulped in air, now free of the strangling rope, coughing uncontrollably.

How could this still be a dream?

Was she now coughing in bed while Abby and Dana watched unable to help her?

The arms, now attached to a body, belonged to Freya.

Her hand rested on Emma's back, comforting her. "Breathe. You can breathe. You're still sleeping."

Her calm demeanor and soothing voice helped Emma regain her composure, but she was starting to think Freddy Krueger might be involved in all this.

Dana had forced her and Abby to watch *Nightmare on Elm Street* by sneaking into the movie theater after it started. Until this day, Emma's mom thought she and her friends had seen *Ghostbusters* for the tenth time. And with Emma's "normal" nightmares, her mom hadn't noticed the uptick every night after she saw the film.

Once Emma had visibly calmed down, Freya stepped backwards a step.

"What was that? They said they weren't ghosts, but what are they?" Emma's heart thudded against her chest at the thought of her great-grandfather reaching for her.

They stood along the winding road leading up to her grandparents' house. Though still a dream, it was nighttime. A full moon lit the sky, casting beams on the blackened part of the forest. Even from here, the ground shifted and vibrated, looking as if thousands of insects crawled in its topsoil.

Freya nodded toward the road, and the two walked in the direction of the house. "I still don't know. Not spirits like me. They're a part of her."

"So, she made them up? Like imaginary friends?" Emma tried to process.

Freya shrugged. "I really don't know. They seem to be her conscience...I'm not sure."

"But if they're not really there, how can I see them?"

"Because some part of her wants you to, I think," Freya said.

"I dunno. He didn't seem too happy I could see him. He tried to crush me with his rope."

Freya bent her head as she walked, the seaweed surrounding her crawled up her arms and legs as if energized suddenly. "Just be careful. Promise me."

Emma's eyes met hers and she nodded, though deep down she knew it was a promise she couldn't keep. Not if her grandmother planned to hurt anyone else. "Did Grandma really stab that man?"

Freya nodded.

"Why?" Emma croaked in disbelief.

"She thinks she's protecting her family." Freya peered at the blackened part of the forest as they walked.

"But *I'm* her family."

"You're *his* family, too."

"I don't understand."

Freya pointed to the dark trees.

"Can you tell me what that is?" Emma asked, hoping Freya would answer this time.

"Death," Freya whispered.

Emma's bones chilled, that one word vibrated with power.

"What happened to you?" Her body shook as Freya reached down and touched her forehead.

"I'll show you."

It was suddenly daytime, and Emma stood in the front yard of her grandparents' house.

Freya was there, long black hair full and shiny, no seaweed, but wearing the same bell-bottomed jumpsuit, alive and healthy. She pounded on the front door, frantic. "I know you're in there, Mrs. Wilson, and I know what you did to Alex Kriston! I've already told my FBI friend!"

Alex Kriston.

Alex.

The man Emma witnessed being stabbed by her grandma.

Freya knew about it? How? Emma hadn't seen her there.

Freya waited a moment longer, but no one answered the door.

As Freya still faced the door, Emma watched as her grandmother stealthily came from the side of the house carrying a wood-handled shovel with a shiny new bladed head. She held the shovel in the same way she had held the knife before she killed Alex. Calculated.

"Run!" Emma screamed, though past-Freya couldn't hear her.

As Freya turned to leave, Grandma Virginia hit Freya so hard with the shovel, her entire body flew backwards and slammed against the door. She slumped to the ground, unconscious.

Grandma Virginia stood above Freya's body. Her lips curled into a genuine moment of amusement. "Not much of a psychic, are you?"

Dropping the shovel, her grandmother lifted Freya from the ground and threw her small frame over her bulky shoulder.

The scene blurred until Emma could no longer distinguish her surroundings, then just as suddenly everything blinked into focus, back to the winding road with Freya, palms sweating.

"Your grandmother drowned me in the Sound after that." Freya motioned to the seaweed crawling on her body. "Hence the seaweed."

Was this all true? Had her grandmother killed two people?

"Freya..." Emma stuttered, not sure what to say.

Freya sighed, "I think she hoped my body would wash up on shore and they'd think it was an accident. The currents are strong where she dumped me, and lots of rocks to explain my head injuries. But the seaweed pulled me in. I'm still down there, Emma. No one except you knows." Freya's nostrils flared. "And *her*."

"I can tell someone. Your FBI friend you mentioned?" She offered, desperate to do anything to help her new friend. If her grandma had killed two people, Emma didn't care what happened to her at this point.

Opening her mouth to speak, Freya turned her entire body toward the house. "Your grandpa's in trouble." She pointed to the house looming in the shadows in front of them. "He needs you." Freya leaned in close to Emma, inches from her face. "Wake up!"

EMMA

Jolting awake, Emma held her chest.

"What was that?" Abby whispered in the dark.

"Bad dream," Emma answered, catching her breath.

"No," Dana said. "There was a loud *boom*, then you woke up."

"Oh," Emma responded. "What did it sound like?" She couldn't think straight, her mind cluttered with everything she had witnessed in her dream. Her grandmother murdered a man named Alex. She murdered Freya. Grandma's father and some child version of her were living, breathing, entities scaring the bajeezus out of Emma.

Freya's words, *He needs you.*

Emma leapt out of bed before waiting for their answer, ear to the door. "Freya warned me Grandpa Roy is in trouble."

"Whoa," Abby's voice had a slight shake to it.

Dana jumped up to join her, while Abby stayed in bed.

Actively listening now, Emma heard the faint sounds of arguing.

Dana whispered, "It sounded like something fell before."

"Not a gunshot?" Emma asked, scared of the answer.

"No, it sounded like a book or some kind of heavy object," Dana observed.

A muffled yell.

"That has to be your grandparents then, right? If Freya said Grandpa Roy is in trouble?" Dana shifted her weight from foot to foot.

"Must be." Emma's eyes met Dana's, unspoken words between them. If her grandpa needed saving then, they were going to save him.

"What are we doing?" Dana asked, no fear in her voice at all now.

"I'm going to check it out." Emma couldn't let her grandma do something to Grandpa like she did to Alex and Freya.

Abby huffed, throwing the blanket aside, feet slapping on the floor. She was at their side in seconds. "Fine. Do we have a plan? Aside from 'checking it out'?"

Grandma Virginia's voice boomed louder, more intense.

Emma paused, took a deep breath, then plowed forward. "Guys, the dream I had...if it's true...Grandma Virginia is a...killer. I'm scared she wants to kill Grandpa."

Dana's shoulders set in determination, hands already in fists ready to fight.

Abby took a couple of deep breaths, but she grabbed her copy of *Pride and Prejudice* from the dresser, holding it like a weapon. "Seriously, what's the plan?" She hefted her book for emphasis.

"Spy, then do something if we have to?" Not the greatest plan, but they'd had worse. Like the time they sledded down Tuskee's hill on a piece of cardboard before taking the giant staples out of it. Dana had to have six stitches from that "plan."

Dana and Abby nodded in agreement, though, so Emma creaked the door open and the trio made their way to her grandparents' room. As they neared, the voices grew louder. The door was cracked open by a sliver, but it was enough to see through.

"I'll look first." A shock of panic hit her brain like a lightning bolt at the thought of possibly putting her friends in danger.

Dana and Abby each took one of Emma's hands and held tight.

With a final nod, Emma peeked through the door.

VIRGINIA

Standing about ten feet away from Roy, Virginia held her revolver steady. Father stood on her right side, younger self on the left. Excitement and glee radiated from him.

But her younger self stared up at her, eyes welled with tears. "You don't know what you're doing. Please stop."

Virginia ignored her.

This would be the moment.

She'd tell everyone he was an abuser, and she'd had enough. Virginia needed bruises for that, of course. The police always needed proof. Carefully, while still holding the gun in place, she punched herself in the gut. Almost doubling over, she regained her composure. It would definitely leave a mark.

Good.

Roy raised his hands in the air in supplication. "Virginia, you've got to stop this!"

"Me?! You're the one who has to stop!" She punched herself in the arm as hard as she could, impressed she didn't flinch.

Father laughed. "That's it. Make everyone believe it's self-defense. Who would hurt a sweet old lady?"

"He loves you," her younger self pleaded.

The words made her skin crawl. He *didn't* love her, and he probably never did. He was a liar. He was a *man.* "Stop hitting me! Please!" she yelled at the top of her lungs so the whole household could hear.

That they all stayed tight in their beds instead of helping their mother wasn't lost on Virginia, but she couldn't blame them. Fear was a powerful motivator. And so was not getting involved.

Seeing the realization on Roy's face of what she had planned was delightful. She hoped his internal organs were squirming. He'd always know she was better, smarter, and he'd never pull one over on her again.

"Virginia, I told you nothing happened with Sandra." Roy almost looked like he meant it.

But liars were like that. They'd make you believe anything. She would know. She could do it better than anyone.

Father whispered, "You know he's deceiving you. Think of how I used to lie."

Exactly.

Virginia cocked the gun. "Never say her name. You claimed to love me more than anything, but you can be with another woman like it's nothing?"

"I told you. She made a pass at me. I was about to push her away when you walked in. You're all that matters to me. Virginia, I love you more than my life." Roy's shoulders crumpled.

"He's desperate to make you believe," Father hissed. "Desperate to convince you what you saw with your own eyes wasn't real."

But she knew better.

Father continued, "His words are sweet, but it's all deception."

Virginia laughed at Roy's attempt to convince her. "Well, that's good, because you're dead to me now, anyway."

Young Virginia wrung her hands together. "No. *Please.*"

The trigger warm against her sweating finger wanted to be pulled. She could feel it. One small movement, and justice would be done.

All she had to do was *squeeze.*

EMMA

"She's lying about him hitting her," Emma said.

Dana stuck her head in the crack next to hers.

"What's happening?" Abby asked, standing on her tiptoes to peek herself, *Pride and Prejudice* gripped in her free hand. "So, he's not hitting her?"

Emma whispered, "I see Great Grandfather and the young version of Grandma, just like the photo you guys saw. In my dream, my great-grandfather is scary, not nice like I thought he might be. And he still has a noose around his neck. She was there, too, but they both said they weren't ghosts. Freya says they're somehow parts of Grandma. They're both talking to her, but I can't hear them." Straining her ears as hard as she could, Emma desperately tried to hear what the strange spirit-thingies were saying.

"Whoa," Abby whispered. "How can you see them if they're not actually ghosts?"

"Freya thinks it's because part of my grandma wants me to, but I honestly don't know," Emma confessed.

She pushed the questions aside. It didn't matter. She had to protect Grandpa Roy at all costs.

Little Virginia suddenly faced Emma. "Help her," she said, fading into the scenery.

Freya appeared next to Emma, Dana, and Abby. She placed a hand on Emma's shoulder, nodding. "It's time."

As if proving her point, Grandma Virginia re-aimed her gun. "Goodbye, *husband*."

Without thinking, Emma pushed the door open wide, Dana and Abby still grasping her hands, followed her lead.

"Grandpa, we can't sleep. Can you read us a story?" Emma blurted loudly.

Lowering the gun and immediately tucking it into the back of her pants, her grandmother focused solely on Emma. In unison, Great Grandfather's head also snapped to her, eyes round with rage, the tail end of the rope from his noose, flicking wildly.

She jumped at the intensity, trying to avoid the rope flapping near her. Emma couldn't read her grandmother's expression. Confused? Frustrated? Angry? With almost blank eyes, it was impossible to tell.

If Freya was right though, and Great Grandfather was an extension of Grandma Virginia, then the only conclusion Emma could reach was that her grandmother *hated* her.

But why?

For trying to protect her grandfather?

Emma and her friends walked over to Grandpa Roy. She grasped his hand for reassurance.

"Of course, girls. Let's get you back to bed." Her grandfather's shoulders relaxed, his smile genuine and tinged with relief.

Freya stood in the doorway, guarding them as they left the room.

But as Grandpa Roy ushered them out of the room, Emma stared at her grandmother one more time.

This time she wasn't looking at Emma.

She was looking directly at Freya.

Grandma Virginia could *see* her.

VIRGINIA

What was that woman doing here? Damn ghoul. And was she talking to Emma?

"Friends with another enemy. How much more proof do you need?" Father whispered, the rope from his noose dancing around her arms and legs.

Virginia watched as Roy led the girls to their room, her chest twisting with betrayal.

"You, see? The girl chose him. She'll never choose you now. She sees you're a monster." Father pushed his point further. "It'll be the end of you."

She didn't want to see her granddaughter as the enemy, but how could she not? She had foiled her attempts at finally getting rid of Roy not once, but twice now. And to befriend a has-been psychic who had tried to destroy her? Had she told Emma about her FBI friend?

Virginia had spoken to him soon after she'd drowned the bitch. He'd been suspicious. It didn't take a psychic to decipher that much. But there had been no body. And, judging from all the seaweed covering her skin, it didn't take a rocket scientist to figure out that ghoul was still at the bottom of the Sound.

She might as well have put the damn psychic in her garden if she didn't have the decency to wash up on shore and clear Virginia's name.

That ghost could have told Emma everything.

Her own granddaughter was a threat.

A threat to her. A threat to her survival.

There was no other way to look at it.

Emma was a witness.

The girl had watched her point a gun at her husband and punch herself. Plus, she'd figure out the poisoning attempt at some point, if she hadn't already. And Emma had the gift, which had been a source of pride for Virginia, but now it was quickly becoming a hindrance. The girl was too clever for her own good.

If Virginia were to kill Roy, then there was only one way she could get away with it.

She had to kill Emma first.

The dead psychic still stood in the doorway, no doubt trying to read Virginia's mind. "Go away, ghost. Go back to the water where I drowned you."

But she stood her ground. "I won't let you hurt that girl, and I won't let you hurt Roy."

Fire burned in Virginia's veins. "Are you making threats? To *me*? I figured you'd learned your lesson the first time."

"I'm still here for a reason, and I'm thinking that reason is to protect *your* loved ones." The seaweed wrapped around her limbs, twisting around her body as if they'd turn into some kind of praying mantis or something.

"Love is loyalty." Virginia didn't feel like she needed to explain this to a ghost, but apparently, she did.

"Is that really how you see it?" The dead psychic's shoulders caved. "You'll eventually have to kill everyone."

Father whispered, “No one understands you. No one understands what true love is.”

She’d had enough of this ghost.

Without having to command it, Father’s rope chased the woman draped in seaweed, wrapping around her legs and body, squeezing the nasty spirit until she screamed.

Virginia cackled with satisfaction.

The ghost’s mouth opened, her eyes widened unnaturally, then she disappeared before the rope could pinch her out of existence.

Good riddance.

Virginia slammed her door. She had a lot of planning to do.

First, she had to get everyone out of the house tomorrow, except Emma.

As she walked to bed, she ignored the low chuckle of Father and the quiet whimpering of her younger self.

Tomorrow, her granddaughter would be the victim of a horrible accident.

EMMA

Her grandfather's hand clasped hers tightly, and Emma never wanted him to let go.

Freya had been right. Her grandmother was trying to hurt him. And if everything she saw in her dreams really happened, then her grandma needed to be stopped.

But how could she possibly do that?

Entering their guest room, the girls all crawled into bed, but Emma couldn't let go of her grandfather's hand. "You should sleep in here. Don't go back there."

Dana and Abby nodded frantically in agreement.

"Yeah, stay here," Dana pleaded.

Her grandpa sighed heavily as he took his free hand to cover Emma's, making her hand a sandwich between his. "Girls, Grandma Virginia is a passionate woman and sometimes does crazy things like you saw, but I promise you, she'd never hurt me or anyone else. She never has before, and I know in my heart she never will. Okay?"

How could he say that? "Grandpa, please, don't go to her."

He patted the top of her hand. "I'll sleep in the camper. How's that sound?"

Emma wasn't sure.

Couldn't Grandma walk outside and shoot him there? Couldn't she come in here and shoot them *all*?

A deep shaking fear rattled through her entire body.

But then Freya appeared behind her grandfather, her expression calm and reassuring. "He'll be safe there tonight."

Relief washed through her. "That sounds good."

Turning to her friends, she gave them a reassuring nod. "Freya says he'll be fine."

The tension in their faces and bodies relaxed in relief.

"Who's Freya?" Grandpa Roy asked. "Is she from Winterbrook?"

Emma trusted her grandfather, but something held her back from telling him about Grandma's victim, so she nodded. "A character we made up. She's a protector."

Patting the top of her hand again, Grandpa Roy said, "Trust me. I'll be fine. Freya can look after you and not worry about me." Her grandfather released his hands and stood up, seemingly doing his best to appear calm and unaffected. "You three get some sleep."

But before he left, his eyes welled up slightly as he regarded Emma and her friends. He tipped an imaginary hat with a solemn smile. "Good night, girls."

"Goodnight, Grandpa Roy," they said in unison.

With one last nod, he shut the door.

Abby dropped *Pride and Prejudice* on the bedside table, then turned to Emma and Dana. "What in the *hell* was that? What happened?"

Adrenaline pumped through Emma. "She was going to kill him."

Her friend's hands fidgeted with the blanket. "She looked like she was going to kill you when we walked in there."

Dana placed her own hand on top of Abby's to calm her. "But she didn't. And she won't." She turned to Emma. "We won't let her touch you, okay?"

Love surged through her. Emma would do anything for her friends, and from the determination in their eyes, she knew they'd do the same.

It was time to tell them the details of her dream.

She told them everything. Every detail, down to the bleach, the blood, and her great-grandfather yelling at her that she was seeing too much.

Abby whimpered, "We should have left with your parents."

"If we had, Grandpa Roy would be dead." Saying the words curled her intestines. This was about saving her favorite person in the entire world.

Abby was scared. So was she. Dana was her usual see-no-fear self, but Emma also didn't want her friends in danger.

"You guys should definitely leave in the morning. I can call my mom, and she can meet you guys at the other end of the ferry—"

"No way," Dana said before Emma could even finish. "We're not leaving you alone with her."

Abby tugged on a strand of her curly hair. "This feels crazy, doesn't it? What are we saying? We keep forgetting Grandma Virginia has always been the best. Maybe those were *just* dreams, and we totally misunderstood what was happening between the two of them right now. Some people like weird things in their bedroom. I walked in on my mom and dad once, and my mom was in handcuffs, and my dad was wearing some kind of leather bikini or something."

Emma's hand flew to her mouth to cover the explosion of laughter. "Abby! You never told us that before!"

Dana laughed too.

"Well, it was *weird*. But it felt appropriate to bring up right now. Do you think you could have been mistaken? About your grandparents?" Abby's eyebrows were raised so high they practically disappeared into her hairline.

"Maybe. But either way, I think it'd be safer if you guys went home. I need to stay here to make sure Grandpa is safe." Emma tried to influence them once more.

"I said no." Dana huffed. "We're in this *together.* Maybe Abby is right. *Maybe* you just had a nightmare and your grandparents are kinky freaks, but either way, we're not leaving you."

Abby, though her eyes screamed she was still terrified, nodded all the same. "We got your back."

Warmth spread through Emma.

She hoped it would be enough.

VIRGINIA

Waiting in the kitchen, Virginia wondered how long it would take for one of her daughters to walk in. Before she'd gone to bed, she'd unplugged the refrigerator to make the food rot. There was no way she could get rid of Emma with everyone in the house, so she needed a reason for them all to leave.

A shuffling outside the door, then Doris strolled in mid-yawn. "Oh, Mom, good morning."

About time.

Tears. She needed tears to pull this off.

Virginia's eyes welled up instantly, secretly impressing herself, as she pointed to the fridge. "Don't open it. It smells to high heaven in there. I'm a goddamn idiot. I came in here last night for a cup of milk and tripped on something. I figured it was something the kids must have left out, but it was the plug to the refrigerator. All the food's gone bad." As the plug had been secured to the back wall, there was no way this could have happened as she said. She'd had a devil of a time yanking it out, but she hoped her daughter wouldn't think about it too hard.

Doris's face fell, and she immediately pulled her mother into a comforting hug. "Mom, don't cry. It's just food. I'll go to the grocery store now before everyone wakes up."

Heart dropping, Virginia pulled away from the embrace. "No. I can't have you do that. Not alone. Why don't you wait for everyone, and we'll make a trip out of it? Get the girls their favorite cereal? The sugary kind that Mary never lets them eat."

Doris's mouth crinkled with disgust. "That's true. Mary said she's been giving Emma wheat germ shakes in the morning because she read it was healthy." She shuddered. "You're right. They deserve something with some kind of marshmallows in it."

Voices and movement sounded from behind the door. Relief rushed through her. "Sounds like everyone is up, anyway. Let me go get my things." She had no intention of going with them, but she had to make Doris think she wanted to. She hoped this would be easy and Emma would be asleep.

That girl slept like the dead, and good luck to anyone who tried to wake her. But she had a backup plan if it didn't happen. Virginia had already come up with the perfect lie, which would be that Mary had called an hour ago and wanted to talk to Emma. She'd volunteer to stay behind so her granddaughter could call her mother.

Stretching her arms wide and yawning a second time, Doris headed to the door. "I'll go get everyone ready." Pushing open the swinging door, her daughter left the kitchen.

Her younger self materialized next to her, staring at the now-closed door. "Just yesterday you thought it would kill you if anything happened to Emma. Now you want to hurt her?"

Father materialized next to her, rope whipping against the counter. "Don't listen to her. You're protecting yourself."

Young Virginia scoffed. "That's rich. How is killing her granddaughter protecting family?"

Not bothering to glance in Young Virginia's direction, Father crossed his arms. "If anyone were to find out what my baby girl has done, the family would be ruined." He peered down at the girl. "Emma has seen too much. She knows too much. If she tells her parents, it's over."

"She's a kid. No one would believe her over her grandmother," the young girl retorted.

"And you can guarantee this? Swear to all that's holy, Emma's mouth won't get us killed?" Father said, his rope inching its way to Young Virginia.

Virginia forced herself to block their voices out of her mind. They were both right of course. Yesterday, Emma being poisoned by her hand had almost destroyed her. And yet, today, after her granddaughter had not only thwarted her attempts to rid the world of Roy twice, but had dreamed of things no one else but Virginia and her little garden knew? There didn't seem to be any other logical choice.

Avoiding her younger self's disapproving glare, Virginia pulled out her flask and drank the rest of the contents. She'd need liquid courage to do what she must. The familiar ease of the alcohol numbing her emotions and thoughts gave her peace. It wouldn't be hard. It would have to look like an accident.

Grabbing a full bottle of vodka from the cupboard, Virginia filled up her flask. She'd need to keep this state of acceptance for at least the next couple of hours or she wouldn't be able to go through with it otherwise. Taking a swig from the bottle itself, the calm and determination grew stronger, and more sensible. She was doing the right thing.

Yes.

It would hurt.

But it would fade.

Swinging the kitchen door open, Virginia entered the dining area.

Harold and Doyle walked out the sliding glass door toward the RV parked by the side of the house.

Gertrude led Lisa by the hand, following behind them. When she saw Virginia, she stopped. "You coming, Mom? Doris is getting the girls. Looks like Dad was already in the RV, so he's driving."

A flush of adrenaline coursed through Virginia. They were all leaving, and Emma could go with them before she could stop them. She'd drunk too much. Her head was fuzzy. She shook it to try to clear it. She needed to casually mention Mary wanted her daughter to call her.

Doris's voice boomed from the guest room. "Come on, girls. In the RV. We're getting food."

Emma must be awake.

Gertrude and Lisa exited the house through the open sliding glass door.

Virginia was about to call out to Doris and tell her Emma needed to stay home, when one of the little ones asked, "What about Emma?" It was probably the lanky worrywart.

Father appeared next to her, grinning like a cat that ate the canary. "Fate is on your side. She's meant to die today."

Virginia couldn't argue with him. Her best-case scenario had been for Emma to be in one of her sound sleeps. And that her friends weren't able to wake her? It was a gift. One she wouldn't squander.

Joining Doris in the guest room's doorway, she said, "I'll stay with Emma. I'm not feeling too good, anyway. You girls go ahead."

"You sure, Mom?" her daughter asked.

Dana stepped forward, arms crossed. "We're staying, too." What a brave girl for being that short. Virginia rather liked her.

Her daughter discreetly took a whiff of her. From the crinkle of her nose, Virginia knew she smelled the alcohol.

Turning to the girls, Doris said sternly, "With your parents not here, I'm in charge of you two, so no. Come on."

"Both of you wait out there. I have to change my pants. We'll be there in a sec," said Abby, the worrywart.

Doris acknowledged this with a grunt, and both she and Virginia walked away from the door as Dana shut it.

Virginia fought the rising bile in her throat.

If they woke the girl up...

Their muffled voices carried all the way to her ears in the living room.

"Emma, wake up. Come on, wake up!" she heard Abby beg.

Dana said, "They're forcing us to leave, and you're going to be alone with insane-o grandma. Get *up*!"

Insane-o, huh? Well, the girl didn't understand how life worked yet. Virginia couldn't blame her. And she felt a pang of guilt at how her little friends would react when they came home from grocery shopping to find Emma dead. Not enough to derail her plan, but it still stung a little. They were loyal. A trait Virginia held most dear.

It was why Emma had to go. If only her granddaughter had taken her side and not Roy's, things could have been different.

"Emma!" the frail one yelled.

"This is ridiculous," Doris groaned, then yelled, "*Girls!* RV! Now!"

Virginia smiled as the two girls tromped out of the room, shutting the door behind them. As they approached Virginia at the sliding glass door, Dana slitted her eyes. "Anything happens to Emma, we'll know who did it."

"Dana!" Doris gasped. "That will be enough."

"You smell her. She's drunk!" Abby said in a rush, obviously terrified. "You're really going to let a drunk woman take care of your niece?"

Doris ducked her head down, avoiding eye contact with Virginia, embarrassed. Through her teeth she scolded, "Get in the RV right now."

Just in case her daughter got any ideas, Virginia said, "I did have a small sip this morning in my coffee, but don't you worry, I'm absolutely fine." She prayed she hadn't slurred any of those words.

"Of course. We'll be back in an hour." Doris still hadn't met her eyes. She ushered the two girls out of the house and toward the RV.

Father stepped next to her, chuckling as he said, “It’s time.”

Virginia had been so sure only a second before, but now that she was alone in the house with Emma...was she really going to do this?

Taking out her flask, she drank it to its last drop. Her entire body swam with comforting numbness.

Yes.

She could do this.

She needed to do this.

Her younger self materialized next to her. “I’m begging you. Please don’t hurt her.”

Father cut her off. “The time for debate is over.” His rope spun around her other half at a frightening pace, constricting the girl’s body.

Through gritted teeth, Young Virginia pleaded, “You claim Emma isn’t loyal...where’s *your* loyalty?”

Virginia placed the empty flask into her pocket, shutting out her words until the rope popped her out of existence. “He’s right.” She spoke to the empty space. “Emma’s a liability. And she’s not my family anymore. She stopped being that when she took his side. And the ghoul’s.” She and Father walked toward the kitchen.

Virginia needed a weapon before her granddaughter woke up.

EMMA

Standing next to the long wooden table in the dining area, every square inch of it was covered in tiny logs of Almond Roca. Either her grandmother was making up for the plate of candy Emma ruined, or she was in a dream.

Jennifer Thatcher entered the room, wheeling the Fair Lady next to her.

Definitely a dream, then.

The bike glowed like a pink diamond as Jennifer leaned it against the wall next to them.

"You got your bike," she said as she abandoned the bike and walked over to Emma.

"It's my cousin's," Emma corrected her. She wished it were hers, but at this point, all Emma wanted to do was kidnap her grandpa and get home safely.

Jennifer gave her signature head tilt and commented nonchalantly, "Not for long."

What did that mean? Emma wondered, but her attention was brought to the mounds of Almond Roca on the table. "I'm allergic," she let Jennifer know.

The older detective picked up one of the chocolate-covered toffee logs and smelled it. "Do you remember the episode where I caught a man trying to kill his boss with poison?"

"Not really," she admitted. There were a lot of *Murder in the Margins* episodes, and she couldn't remember them all in detail.

"Well, he used something called cyanide. And he mixed it in an almond-flavored cookie because cyanide tastes and smells a lot like almonds." Jennifer Thatcher tapped her chin with her finger. "Do you understand?"

Peering up at her mystery television hero, Emma wasn't sure what Jennifer wanted her to think. Was she saying the candy was poisoned? Was that why she threw up? Her mom said it must have been a nut allergy, but Emma had eaten an entire can of Planters salted almonds at Abby's house a while ago and nothing had happened to her.

The Almond Roca had been meant for her grandfather.

Was this her grandma trying to hurt him like she'd hurt Alex Kriston and Freya? Like she tried to hurt him last night?

Before she could draw any more conclusions, the scenery swelled into a tornado of black and dark green until everything came into sharp focus.

She stood at the center of the small patch of blackened forest she had been seeing this entire trip. Moonlight filtered through the pine needles, giving her some light, but mostly it was difficult to differentiate any kind of detail.

Stepping toward the closest tree, Emma reached out to touch the branch. The texture was like any other pine tree, not charred like she'd wanted. Because if there had been a small fire here, then it would give some kind of explanation for why everything was so pitch-dark. Everything from the dirt and rotted leaves under her feet, to the bark on the giant boles, was enveloped in the blackness.

Perfectly lit by a single beam of moonlight, Jennifer Thatcher stood outside the blackened area. "You found something?" she asked.

Emma fully took in her surroundings. "I don't know what this place is," she admitted.

"You're the detective. Time to do your job," Jennifer said with some authority.

The ground began to rumble.

Emma searched the dirt beneath her with what little light she had.

It was moving.

Something was *underneath* her.

She had to get out of there.

Preparing to run toward Jennifer Thatcher, Emma's legs rooted in place. No matter how hard she tried, it was as if her feet were cemented to the forest floor.

"Help me," she called out.

The detective raised her signature eyebrow as if fascinated by Emma's request. "I am helping you."

A dozen hands and arms burst out of the ground, reaching wildly.

Emma screamed, clasping onto her legs, desperately trying to force them to move.

The hands stilled as one unit, then turned toward her, palms facing her, as if sensing her movement and desperation.

Emma stopped, and the appendages slowly began to sway, as if waiting for her to try to run again.

Keeping her eyes glued to each and every arm, time slowed as she wondered what she should do next.

An owl hooted above her, and she glanced up.

Glowing in the moonlight, the owl perched on a branch a few feet above Emma's head. His eyes met hers. It screeched.

Throwing her hands over her ears, the bird's blood-curdling shriek shredded her nerves until her teeth began to chatter.

The arms and hands shook violently at the owl's scream and bolted toward Emma at a frightening speed. Grabbing her ankles and legs, they pulled her down into the ground.

Heart pounding, the last thing Emma saw before she was swallowed by the soil was the owl, screeching stopped, staring at her with large, sad eyes.

Blackness surrounded her as the hands yanked her deeper and deeper into the ground. Dirt filled her mouth, her eyes, her nose.

Her scream transformed into strangled choking.

Panic set in as Emma clawed at the soil surrounding her, trying to hold on to anything to stop her descent, roots, rocks, anything. But the harder she struggled, the farther she was yanked down.

She was going to run out of air.

Buried alive.

Could she die in a dream?

"Getting all worked up won't help you at all," Jennifer's voice echoed through the blackness.

Pausing only a second was enough for Emma to realize she could still somehow breathe, the dirt no longer invading all her senses. Or, at least, she simply existed within the soil.

Finally, the hands stopped her from sinking deeper.

A light from an unknown source lit up the area around her. In front of her were hundreds of tunnels ranging in size. Her dad had told her animals liked to burrow underground and create tunnels like these.

Emma's body quivered. Dream or not, she didn't want to run into some kind of creature with teeth and claws.

As the hands let go of her legs and feet, she attempted to dig upwards using roots for purchase, but made no progress.

Jennifer Thatcher walked through the dirt like a ghost, the walls of soil passing through her. *She had a flashlight.* It illuminated the surface of the surrounding ground, and the detective moved as if she weren't under a pile of dirt, but simply walking in the open air.

It strangely calmed her enough to focus on what Jennifer was trying to show her. Lifting her foot off the ground, Emma found she could walk through the earth as well. Relief washed through her.

It was only a dream.

In dreams, anything was possible.

She wasn't being buried alive. She wasn't going to die.

Emma walked toward the woman, passing through roots and dirt with ease.

Five silhouettes of large lumps wrapped in burlap spread out every few feet, resting within the ground at Emma's waist level. The closer she walked toward them, the better she could see how the hands and arms clasped onto the burlap.

She gazed at Jennifer, but the older detective only nodded her forward.

Though she could move, it was still discombobulating moving through the soil, but Emma inched forward until she finally arrived at the jagged row of silhouettes.

Jennifer Thatcher waved her hands over the burlap lumps, and the burlap tore open enough to see through.

A grotesque display lay out in front of her.

The lumps were dismembered *bodies*, all in different states of decay. Their rotted eyes staring at her through the torn fabric, frozen in an expression of terror, mouth agape, eyes open wide.

Emma kicked and moved her arms, desperately trying to dig her way up again, to get away from this nightmare. But the body in the middle shoved their arms through the tear in the fabric, reaching out toward her.

The corpse's face became visible, suddenly alive and screaming.

Rearing back as far as she could, Emma recognized him.

It was Alex.

Emma woke with a start and found herself staring into Freya's eyes.

A scream almost escaped her lips, but Freya put her finger to her mouth, eyes full of concern.

Emma squeezed her hand to stop herself and obeyed.

"That's where she put him?" Emma whispered. She didn't know why, but the dream, then with Freya motioning her to be quiet, it somehow felt appropriate.

"That's where she'll put you too if you don't get up and hide." Freya waved her hand for Emma to hurry.

Jumping out of bed, Emma reached for her suitcase.

"No time, you have to get out of here now." Freya examined the door, as if waiting for it to burst open at any second. "There's an empty doghouse up past the asphalt in the backyard. Hide inside there." With that, she disappeared.

Emma didn't take the time to think. She trusted Freya.

Grabbing nothing, not even her shoes, Emma carefully opened the door.

VIRGINIA

Thundering into the kitchen, Virginia wasn't sure how long it would take the family to go grocery shopping. Knowing her daughters, it could be hours, giving her ample time to make Emma's death seem like an accident. Rummaging through the knife drawer, she found the perfect weapon. A butcher's knife.

Definitely something a kid would find and play with. Right? Didn't kids play with knives? Virginia had. Sometimes, having a knife under her pillow was the only way she could get to sleep. She never used it back then, but simply holding the wooden handle as she slept gave her comfort.

Besides, Emma was always pretending she was some kind of hero in a story, using those strange plastic...swords? She wasn't really sure what they were, her and her friends smacked them about like swords, but where the blade should be was a cylindrical stick lighting up like a flashlight. Mary had told her they were called light swords or other such nonsense, but last time Virginia had spent time at their house, it was all her granddaughter went on about.

Playing around with weapons wouldn't be questioned.

Not with that girl.

She had thought about using scissors. Kids often ran with scissors and met with deadly fates. But Virginia didn't have the heavy-duty kind that would finish the job. If Emma lived, she'd blab to everyone Grandma had stabbed her. *No.* She needed the girl to be gone before they returned.

Gripping the wooden handle of the butcher knife, Virginia headed toward the door.

Young Virginia materialized in front of her, blocking her path. "You're honestly going to kill her? Your *granddaughter*?"

Virginia walked through the little girl without a word.

Father trailed behind and answered, "She's doing what she must."

Walking through her didn't stop her from existing. Young Virginia reappeared where she'd been, placing her hands on her hips, staring down Father. "I wish you'd butt out. She didn't listen to you when you were alive. She shouldn't listen to you now."

Virginia stopped in her tracks. Her cheek twitched in response. "I don't listen to either of you. I do what my conscience tells me."

Her younger self hurried to Virginia's side. "Since when is killing your own family listening to your conscience?"

Virginia nodded toward Father. "I killed *him*, didn't I? Didn't see you complaining about that."

Young Virginia crossed her arms, pouting.

Father breathed in deeply through his nose. His lips tightened in a line. "I betrayed her, so she did what she had to." He raised an eyebrow as he spoke to her younger self. "You betrayed her, too, young lady."

"*Me?*" Young Virginia said with genuine surprise in her voice.

"You're the one who hurt her," Father replied, his mouth curled into a sinister smile.

But Virginia had heard enough. She rushed toward the door, trying to block out their voices.

"You tried to stop me back then, and Emma is trying to stop me now. She picked her side, and I won't let her take me first." Virginia wasn't sure who she was talking to at that point. She'd already killed them both, after all.

Father's familiar chuckle reverberated through her skin.

Young Virginia ran in front of her as she pushed the door open. "What? You really think they'll believe she accidentally stabbed herself while playing?"

"I can't help it if a dumb little girl plays with knives." Saying it out loud caused her to stumble forward slightly. Thinking and saying seemed to be two different things.

Pulling out her flask, she grabbed the closest bottle of vodka and refilled it to the top. Then decided to drink straight from the source and gulped down a third of the bottle.

Satisfied, Virginia, tucked the flask into her back pocket and this time walked through the door, heading toward Emma's room.

EMMA

Quietly shutting the sliding glass door, she scanned the backyard searching for the doghouse Freya told her about. About a hundred feet away, she spotted the small structure. It looked like the cartoon Snoopy's house, all wood, painted bright red. Without waiting to see if her grandma was behind her, Emma headed toward it.

It took her only seconds to get there, and she immediately dropped to her knees and crawled through the arched opening. Scooting as far as she could go inside the small mini-house, Emma thanked her lucky stars Grandma and Grandpa's dogs weren't around anymore. Caesar and Taco. She remembered when she was five and her grandmother thought it would be funny to have the dogs chase her.

News flash, it wasn't funny.

They didn't attack her or anything. Just tackled her to the ground, growling.

When Grandpa Roy realized what was happening, he had rushed over.

Emma had been scared of dogs ever since. She had to admit she had been relieved when both dogs passed away a couple of years ago.

The wood was old and faded inside the doghouse. How long was she supposed to stay in here? Where was Freya? Though she quickly remembered the ghost couldn't just appear since Grandma Virginia could actually *see* her. Emma hated to admit how much like her grandmother she actually was.

"Emma!" her grandma's voice yelled from inside the house.

Wrapping her arms around her knees, she tried to make herself into a ball as if it would help her hide more.

"Emma! Come on out! I have something for you!" Virginia shouted, still inside.

But the *shunk* of the sliding glass door opening and closing caused Emma's hairs to rise on her neck and arms.

"Emma!" she snipped, obviously irritated.

And a little slurred, Emma noticed. Grandma would get like that when she drank too much. "Didn't your mother ever tell you not to play with knives?"

Her voice was close now.

Too close.

Emma breathed hard and fast, trying to calm herself, but it wasn't working.

"Emma." No longer yelling, her grandmother was much closer.

Staying as still as possible, Emma's hands shook.

What was she going to do?

"I can't believe how irresponsible your mother was in not telling you to stay away from sharp objects. I bet she didn't even tell you not to run with scissors. Not with the way this knife is sticking out of your gut."

Great Grandfather chuckled. He was there too.

Before she could stop herself, a small whimper slipped out of Emma's mouth. Slamming her hands against her face to prevent any more noises that might spill out of her, Emma saw her grandmother's legs walk into view, a butcher knife held loosely at her side. She was about twenty feet away, Great Grandfather trailing next to her, his hanging rope dangling behind.

Emma squeezed her hands tight to control the shaking.

Her grandmother stopped, then turned so her feet now faced Emma.

Slowly, her grandmother bent down until...

...her eyes met Emma's.

Time stopped.

Emma's heart stopped.

Her breathing stopped.

A smile spread across her grandma's face.

Freya appeared in the doghouse directly in front of Emma. "RUN!" she yelled.

Emma's mind froze, but her body responded. It was as if she were on autopilot, scrambling to her feet, fast-shuffling out of the doghouse, only able to avoid her grandma because of distance.

That didn't stop Grandma Virginia from trying, though. Lunging toward her, the woman missed Emma by a few feet.

Still struggling on the ground, Emma half-ran, half-crawled away from the looming monster barreling toward her. Finally gaining purchase with her bare feet, she ran.

Ran as fast as her legs would carry her.

A quick glance over her shoulder and her grandmother charged toward her, butcher knife leading the way.

And she was coming fast.

Surprisingly fast for a woman in her seventies.

But Emma saw her salvation.

The Schwinn Fair Lady.

A beam of light hit it from the clouds, as if it was sent from the heavens.

Grabbing the handlebars, kicking up the kickstand, Emma ran with the bike until she was able to jump on. Her bare feet pedaling as fast as she could, quickly widening the gap between her and her grandma. Through rough grass and dirt holes, she thundered through the rocky patches until the wheels finally hit the smooth asphalt of the road.

Where she was going, Emma had no idea.

Away.

She needed to get away.

Pajamas whipping in the wind, Emma flew down the winding road.

Her grandmother was coming.

Her grandmother wanted her dead.

VIRGINIA

Emma rode away from Virginia as she hurried to her car.

"The girl is getting away. She'll tell everyone what you tried to do," Father said frantically.

"Not if I get to her first," Virginia growled. She opened the car door.

Young Virginia formed next to her. "You're not going to hurt her."

Ignoring her, Virginia was about to slide into the car, but her younger self refused to be disregarded. I said, "YOU'RE NOT HURTING HER!"

Virginia's eyes widened at seeing Young Virginia so enraged. The girl's hands reached outward. "Remember the day you killed us both!" She slammed her hands directly into Virginia's temples.

The car and house disappeared and transformed, the trees swirling into another space and time. Virginia had enough wherewithal to grab the car's roof for balance as her mind was now locked into the vision her younger self wanted her to see.

Virginia's feet hit the ground, and she noticed they were the feet of a child.

Her mind struggled to get to the car, to her mission, but her younger self held her hostage in what Virginia now recognized as her memory.

She was in the old farmhouse she grew up in, or really more of a shack. The dilapidated house Emma kept finding her way back to. Sometimes, she wondered who built this dump with its grey wooden walls that had never been sealed or drywalled, with exposed two by fours and outer walls. There were cracks in the wood where weather and woodpeckers had used the house as a feast. The surface beneath her feet was the subflooring, cold as ice from the Indiana winter. The entire house consisted of one large room acting as the living room, dining room, kitchen, and three closed doors. Two leading to the bedrooms and one to the bathroom.

Virginia was in her child self's body, and nothing she could do mentally could break her out of it. She was forced to live out what was about to happen. Walking past the torn cotton upholstered couch, Virginia made her way to the old wooden table that served as the dining area, four mismatched chairs tucked underneath. The kitchen made up the back wall of the house, but it was no more than a cast-iron stove, a used refrigerator her dad had stolen from the Harrison's side porch, a sink with chipped porcelain and rusty handles and spout, and a smattering of cupboards haphazardly nailed onto the exposed studs.

Flinching at the sound she dreaded hearing from this memory, Virginia allowed herself to go through the same motions.

But the screaming.

It was almost too much to bear.

Her sister Rachel.

The piercing scream ended with the sound of a loud punch, then grunting.

Even in the memory, Virginia's teeth gnashed, her jaw clenched at having to listen to her sister being beaten and worse. Her father had been doing this to Virginia for years now, as she remembered she was eleven during this memory. Ravaging her, then cuddling and fondling her afterward. A never-ending cycle he had decided to pass on to his youngest daughter.

Their mother had killed herself when Virginia was five and Rachel was two. Left them really. Left the world because Father had abused her as well. Virginia often wondered if her mother ever thought or cared that Father would simply switch his focus to the two little girls she left behind.

If she were still alive, she would have added Mother to her garden. No one deserved it more.

Except Father.

Knowing what came next, Virginia relished the next part of the memory as she calmly walked to the kitchen. Pulling down a mug, she placed water in the kettle, lit the stove and heated it up.

All as the screaming, punching, and grunting continued.

But Father had no stamina. It would end soon.

And Virginia would end *him* soon.

The kettle whistled, and Virginia poured the water into the mug, with a couple of scoops of instant coffee. Opening up the bottom cupboard, she pulled out a box of crystallized powdered rat poison and, as calmly as she'd been so far, Virginia stirred a few spoonfuls of the stuff into the drink. Just as carefully, she placed the poison in its spot under the cupboard. Taking the milk out of the fridge, she mixed it into the deadly concoction.

Door flying open, Father stumbled out, drunk as usual. He zipped up his fly, and Virginia felt the memory of her hands shaking with rage.

She tried not to see Rachel curled into a ball on the bed, sobbing. But she hid her fury, handing him the cup of coffee. "I made you coffee." She tried to sound as pleasant as possible so he'd drink it.

But this was a memory so internal she nearly giggled with delight as he gulped the whole thing down in one go. "Tastes awful," he complained.

He wouldn't be complaining about anything ever again.

"Maybe the milk is a little old," she offered.

Father backhanded her.

Her frail little body hit the floor, the taste of iron in her mouth, fresh as if she were there again.

"Get my keys. I'm going out," he barked.

"Yes, Father," Virginia said, but she didn't move.

Her father stumbled into one of the chairs, his arms spasming violently. He clutched his throat, eyes bugging out, more from the shock than the poison. Virginia had killed enough rats with the strychnine to know what to expect next.

As if his spine snapped in two, her father's body arched unnaturally, crashing on the wooden floor with a satisfying thump.

As she watched her father seize painfully, a satisfied smile pulled at both young and old Virginia's lips.

Father's trembling hands reached out, panic-stricken, desperate for any kind of help.

"Sissy, come out and see." Virginia wanted Rachel to know she'd killed the monster once and for all.

Rachel limped out of the room, face and body badly beaten, dress torn.

Father gasped for air as his body convulsed at odd angles.

Virginia leaned in close, making sure he heard every word. "You could have kept doing what you wanted with me. I can take it. I'm strong. But then you hurt Rachel, and now you have to take your punishment."

Gently taking her sister's hand, Virginia squeezed it with love.

Virginia barely noticed Rachel's wide eyes and terrified expression. She was too busy enjoying watching her father take his last breath and die on the floor in front of them.

"Go get a rope. We'll hang him from the rafters. Everyone will think he killed himself like Mamma."

Virginia finally broke out of the vision, Father twisting his hanging rope around Young Virginia's hands, pulling them out of Virginia's head. The force of it flung the young girl's body across the backyard.

Father yelled, "Leave her alone!"

Young Virginia cowered on the ground, but her eyes sparkled with satisfaction. She'd done her job. Stalled Virginia enough Emma could get away.

Sighing, Virginia gained her bearings and walked toward the house.

Emma would have either met up with the RV, or made it to the grocery store by now.

She'd have to come up with a new plan.

EMMA

Screeching the bike to a halt before she spun out of control, Emma stared at nothing. *What she had just seen?*

One minute she'd been flying down the winding road of Bentmer Island, the next she was in the decrepit house watching the younger version of Grandma Virginia poisoning her father. And the noises from inside the closed door...

The bruises on Great Aunt Rachel.

Emma never met her great aunt. The woman had died before she was born. But she'd spent an entire day with her ghost when she was younger. It had been magical, and Rachel had cemented herself as her favorite aunt that day by playing the part of Daltorine from Winterbrook, the two of them defeating Queen Madelis. Grandma Virginia had been so happy when she'd told her.

It was one of Emma's fondest memories.

No one talked about Great Aunt Rachel much, but one time Emma overheard her dad say she'd killed herself.

Gulping in air, Emma tried to gain her bearings.

The vision had been so real. So vivid.

Grandma Virginia had killed her father.

Then hung him to make it look like suicide.

That explained the noose.

Sweat beaded on Emma's back through her T-shirt.

If it were true, then her grandmother had been killing for a very long time.

Acid crept up her throat, and Emma almost threw up, but she swallowed it down.

Her great-grandfather was an evil man. She knew that now. Twisted and demented like a monster in a horror movie.

But so was her grandmother.

No wonder he creeped around her. She was exactly like him. Wasn't she?

Veering around a corner, Emma's heart soared in her chest.

Grandpa Roy. The RV. Driving up the winding road, coming straight toward her.

The squeaky sound of the large vehicle's brakes sounded like heaven to Emma. She couldn't wait to dump the bike and race inside to the safety of her grandpa's arms and the RV. Emma jumped off the bike and pounded her fist on the flimsy metal door of the RV as it came to a full stop.

It opened wide, almost hitting her, but in the doorway was the best thing she'd ever seen.

Abby, Dana, and Grandpa Roy, all looked down at her with worry and concern.

Abby was the first to cross the space between them, jumping off the rubber-lined steps and into her arms. "Are you okay?" she asked.

"What happened?" Dana was close behind, her body turned toward the road.

But no cars were coming.

She'd seen Grandma Virginia racing to her car, but maybe the vision had stopped her, too?

Emma whispered to Abby and Dana, "She came after me with a knife."

Telling the adults was too much of a risk. No one ever believed her, anyway. Maybe Grandpa Roy could, but he loved Grandma so blindly, she doubted he'd be different. She needed to re-group with her friends and figure out what to do next.

Abby and Dana squeezed her tighter in their hug.

With the chaos being too much to ignore, everyone in the RV filed out of the vehicle.

Lisa was last, but when she saw her bike leaned up against the RV she screamed, "You stole my bike!" Racing to it, she grabbed the handlebars and yanked it close to her as if Emma would somehow try to take it away.

Pulling away from the hug, Dana rolled her eyes. "Relax, she just borrowed it."

Abby crossed her arms. "You pinkie swore she could ride it, so what does it matter?"

Lisa backed up out of arm's reach, as if she were afraid Dana would attack her, then admitted, "I was crossing my fingers!"

Under her breath, Dana exclaimed, "I knew it. Asshole."

"It's mine, and none of you can ride it! Ever!" her cousin screamed.

Aunt Doris pivoted to her daughter. "*Lisa!* Apologize to Emma and her friends!"

"No!" Lisa jumped on the bike and pedaled toward the house.

Dana snickered, "At least it's all uphill."

Uncle Harold eyed Doris. "She needs to learn to share."

His wife gave him a look that would kill most humans where they stood. "You think?"

Grandpa Roy motioned to the door with his head. "Let's get back in and go to the house. We'll pick her and the bike up along the way."

Piling into the RV, Emma stayed close to her friends. All she wanted to do was call her mother and go home.

VIRGINIA

What was that girl going to tell everyone? Would they arrive at the house with accusations and yelling?

Virginia yanked the flask out of her pocket and drank deep.

It helped.

A little.

But not a lot.

She'd have to drink an entire gallon of the stuff to feel nothing, but she needed her wits for whatever was about to come her way when the RV arrived. All she had to do was make Emma sound like a kid with an overactive imagination. Shouldn't be too hard. She actually *was* that kid.

"Just like I used to be." Young Virginia had recovered from Father's scolding and stood next to her.

"Go away," she said, though there wasn't much conviction to it. Truth be told, her other self was a comforting presence, which she didn't quite understand.

As she walked toward the kitchen's back door, her legs wobbled. Was she that drunk?

"It's relief." Her younger self's eyebrows lifted, her face a perfect frame of hope.

She stared at the girl for a moment, her insides battling a mix of emotions.

Was it relief?

Did she really *want* to kill her granddaughter?

Taking another step toward the door, Virginia kicked something on the asphalt.

The butcher's knife. It had fallen to the ground from being forced to re-live the memory of her father's death. Normally, she savored remembering his bugging eyes and reddened face as he suffered. But her younger self had made her watch *all* of it. Rachel's screams, her whimpering, and his grunts...

Virginia downed a few more gulps from her flask.

No.

It wasn't *relief*.

It was disappointment.

She'd failed in killing Emma. Just like she'd failed in killing Roy.

It wouldn't happen again.

Virginia grabbed the blade off the pavement by its handle, then rushed into the kitchen.

The phone rang, but she ignored it as she placed the knife in its rightful place in the drawer.

It kept ringing.

She didn't have one of those answering machines so whoever it was could let it ring all day as long as no one picked it up.

As the sound of the RV reached her ears, Virginia realized she didn't want anyone else to pick it up either, but she needed to do damage control. She couldn't do that if she were on the phone.

The door opened. The voices of her daughters and their husbands filled the kitchen.

No one sounded angry.

No one said her name.

They were discussing groceries and the pink bike.

"Are you going to get the phone, Mom?" Gertrude asked.

Taking a calculated risk. Virginia grabbed the receiver. "Hello?"

Mary's voice greeted her. "Hi, Mom. I wanted to check in on the girls. How's everything going?"

Her stomach wrenched. On some level, Mary must have picked up on Emma's fears and decided to call. At least she didn't sound panicked.

Father appeared next to her. "Don't lose resolve. You know what you have to do."

Young Virginia kicked Father in the shins, then asked her, "Why do you always listen to him? You *hate* him."

Turning away from them both, Virginia said, "We just got back from the grocery store. I think she's playing." She was stalling. What would Emma would say to her mother?

Virginia would do anything for Mary. She *had*. She'd killed a man for her. Now, she herself was a threat to Mary's own child.

Father stood in front of her. "Emma is far too dangerous now."

Her younger self was right. Why *was* she listening to him?

"I'm *you*, remember? Not him. And haven't I always steered you right?" Father grinned as if he were encouraging a toddler.

She stumbled forward slightly, and Gertrude caught her by the elbow.

"You okay, Mom?"

Not wanting to deal with any of it, Virginia handed the phone to her daughter.

"Whoa, Mom. Who is this?"

Virginia didn't want to answer. She left the room and made her way to the living room where there was another phone. Because her next move depended on what Emma had told everyone. Very carefully, she picked up the receiver and listened in.

"Gertrude? Where did Mom go? How are the girls?" Mary's voice was agitated, but so far not too concerned.

"I think the girls are playing. Look, Mary, we just got back and Emma was in a state. She stole Lisa's bike and rode it down those winding hills to find us in the RV..." Gertrude began.

The sound of shuffling, and through the door Doris whispered harshly, "Are you crazy?! She'll be on the next ferry up here if you tell her that!" Then Doris was on the phone. "Mary, Gertrude is being a drama queen. Emma was playing around. She had permission to ride Lisa's bike. We're all fine here."

A loud sigh from Mary. "She gets like this. She gets homesick then either makes up stories or does something to force her way home. Remember when she faked food poisoning to leave sleep-away camp? Could you just put her and her friends on the five o'clock ferry?"

"Hold on. Let's not go crazy," Doris said. "Why don't I put Emma on the phone and you can talk it out with her?"

Virginia held still, not wanting them to hear her on the other side, but she couldn't let Emma leave. The first thing that girl would do would be to tell her parents everything.

"Fine," Mary conceded.

"I'll go get her," Doris said.

Another shuffling sound, then Gertrude's voice was on the other end again. "Doris is going to get her, don't worry."

Virginia placed the phone on the cradle as Doris hurried out of the kitchen.

Surveying the living room, Doris's eyes met hers. "Have you seen Emma?"

"Out back." Virginia nodded toward the sliding glass door.

She watched Doris set her eyes on Emma.

Her daughter's frown said it all. She saw what anyone with sight could see.

Emma was scared.
And she wanted to go home.
Virginia couldn't let that happen.
Not alive, anyway.

EMMA

"She's really milking it. You'd think you'd stolen her dog or something," Dana grumbled under her breath.

Emma agreed.

Lisa rode the Fair Lady in the backyard as if it would somehow reverse time so her cousin would have never touched it.

"Okay, what happened?" Abby asked, her face all business.

Emma told them everything. From her dream about where Grandma Virginia buried her victims, to Freya waking her up and telling her to hide, to her grandmother chasing her with a butcher knife, to the vision of Grandma Virginia killing her dad as a kid. No secrets. Not from her friends.

Dana's mouth fell open. "Shit."

"We gotta get out of here." Abby blinked slowly, squeezing her eyes extra tightly each time. She only did that when she was really scared.

The sliding glass door slid open, causing all three of them to jump.

But it was just Aunt Doris.

"Hey, girls. Emma, your mom is on the phone. She wants to speak to you."

The words sent a thrill through every part of her body.

Knowing her mother was on the phone gave Emma a sense of relief she was very aware was missing. Protected.

Apparently, her aunt didn't like the expression on Emma's face because she said, "Hold on. What are you going to tell her?"

Emma said frankly, "That we want to go home."

Abby and Dana emphatically nodded in agreement.

Aunt Doris sighed heavily. "You can't say you're having a great time? You don't want to worry her."

A pang of guilt knotted her stomach. Emma hated worrying her mom, let alone her Aunt Doris, who she rarely visited.

She could only imagine what her mother would do if she knew Grandma Virginia had been chasing her with a butcher knife.

But her family never believed her, and they didn't like talking about things, didn't like admitting things, and never ever made drama. It was a suck-it-up kind of household.

She could be honest with Abby and Dana. They were a circle.

Aunt Doris crossed her arms, disapproving of her hesitation. "What can I do to get you guys to tell your mom you're having fun and stay one more night?" the woman pleaded.

Wow.

Her aunt was *desperate.*

Dana seemed to be deducing the same thing as she glanced over at Lisa riding the Schwinn. "Um, Emma's bike recently...uh... broke. And she needs a new one."

Emma drew her head back, mouth agape.

Her friend was a brave badass.

"Done," Aunt Doris said as if she were bargaining at a swap meet.

The three girls stared at each other in shock, not sure what was truly happening.

But Doris waved her daughter over. "Lisa, get over here. You're giving your bike to your cousin."

Lisa screeched to a halt in front of them. "*WHAT?!* Never! Mom! You can't give her my bike!"

Emma was pretty sure this would break her cousin.

And she was *here* for it.

"I can and I will. How did you really think we were going to bring this thing back to Indiana, anyway? I honestly don't know why your father bought it for you in the first place." Aunt Doris seemed like she hadn't even wanted to buy Lisa the bike. She also didn't seem to care her daughter's red face was on the verge of exploding.

"Mom!" was all that came out of Lisa's mouth.

"Oh, relax. We'll get you a brand new one when we get home." Aunt Doris rolled her eyes.

Lisa appeared to ponder this, then after a moment, shoved the bike at Emma. "You got your cooties all over it, anyway."

Holding the rubber gripped-handles in her hands, excitement rushed through her despite the horrors she'd just survived.

"We have a deal?" Aunt Doris asked, hands on hips.

A bike for silence.

Was that what she was doing? Could she live with herself? Her bike was broken back home, and her dad would never buy her a new one. He'd just fix the old one, like he'd said. Not only was she holding her dream in her hands, but the old bike would be the only chariot she'd have if she didn't take this.

Her mind was fraught with indecision.

Everyone was safe, right?

No one had gotten hurt, not even her.

Maybe her imagination had played tricks on her and everything was fine? It was possible. Wasn't it?

Why shouldn't she accept the bike?

As if hearing Emma's internal struggle, Abby pulled them aside, almost knocking over the bike when she whispered, "Wait. Are we sure we should do this?"

Dana's eyes pleaded when she said, "If we can get Emma one good thing out of this trip, isn't it worth it?"

"Yeah, but her grandma was pretty much trying to stab her, and we saw her with a *gun* last night." Abby crossed her arms. The magic of the bike had obviously worn off for her.

Dana added, "Look, I get it. But we're talking about a bike Emma's parents would never buy her in a trillion years. Doesn't she deserve it? After everything she just went through? It would only be one more night."

Abby shifted her feet, obviously moved by this argument. Turning to Emma, she asked earnestly, "What do you think about it?"

What *did* she think about it?

Maybe she should trust her grandfather's words last night about Grandma being harmless. Her dreams could simply be fictional nightmares. And Grandma Virginia had possibly just been chopping up...something in the kitchen, then went to find her. Maybe witnessing Grandma poisoning her father was the first and only time she'd ever hurt anyone. That it was her protecting Great Aunt Rachel.

She also *really* wanted the glorious bike currently in her grip.

"Maybe my imagination got the best of me." Emma said it out loud only to feel the hollowness of the words.

"You believe that?" Abby asked, hope in her eyes.

"Not really, but I *want* to believe it," Emma answered honestly. "And we need to look out for Grandpa Roy as well." It wasn't just herself she was worried about, after all.

After a moment of reflection, Abby nodded. "Okay, but no more being separated from each other. We have to be each other's bodyguards."

"Agreed," Emma said.

"Duh," Dana answered.

Abby seemed satisfied as she straightened herself, nodding to the Fair Lady. "Right. Screw your cousin. Let's take her bike."

Emma and her friends moved to Doris.

"We're in," Abby spoke for the three of them.

Emma could see the visible relief on her aunt's face. "Go on inside and talk to your mom."

Dana took the reins of the Schwinn from Emma. "We'll protect it with our lives."

Emma nodded and ran inside.

Passing by her grandmother in the living room, Emma didn't make eye contact, especially since Great Grandfather sat next to her, staring Emma down. Keeping her head down, she walked into the kitchen, grateful a door now separated them, even if it was only a swinging one.

Upon seeing Emma enter the room, Gertrude handed the phone receiver to her with a smile. "Here you go, sweetie."

Placing the phone to her ear, she tried to sound as chipper as she could muster. "Hi, Mom."

"Honey, are you okay? You homesick?"

That was an understatement.

Part of Emma wanted to tell her mother everything, but the deal was to make her mom think she didn't want to leave. And she didn't want Aunt Doris to take back the bike. "Not at all. We're having the best time." She didn't know if she was pulling off the role of a lifetime, but she hoped it would be enough to convince her mother.

There was a pause on her mother's end, and Emma sensed she was trying to read her daughter. She needed to sell this more. "Really, Mom. We're having fun here." Or at least they would be now.

After a long pause. "Are you sure?"

Not really. "Yeah, I'm positive."

Then Emma's heart dropped. What if her parents wouldn't let her keep the bike? What if when she showed up with it at home, her dad would make her send it back? Keeping her voice as excited as possible, she said, "Cousin Lisa decided to give me her bike!"

Pause.

Emma felt a trickle of sweat bead on her forehead.

Oh god.

Her mom was going to make her return it. She just knew it.

"Really?" was all her mother said.

This was bad.

Really bad.

Be convincing! "Yup! We're going to ride it right now!"

"Put your Aunt Doris back on." Her mother's words were quick and terse.

Emma flinched. "Kay."

Aunt Doris stood next to her. Emma hadn't noticed her coming in, but when she handed over the phone, she covered the mouth-piece. "She's suspicious, so you better sell it."

Doris let out a small chuckle. "I will, now go play."

Emma didn't know why her aunt was laughing. Her mom was about to give the third degree.

Crossing her fingers the conversation went well, she ran outside. She really didn't want to lose the bike.

VIRGINIA

After watching her granddaughter speed outside, Virginia carefully picked up the receiver once again to hear if Emma convinced Mary to let her stay.

Doris's voice filled her ear. "See? Everything is good. And we'll bring her home tomorrow, a day early."

Boy, she was laying it on thick.

"Did you bribe my daughter to tell me everything is okay with a bike?" Mary asked.

Virginia detected a hint of amusement and had to fight the urge to laugh, a swelling of pride. Mary saw through Doris's schemes every time.

"You better hope she never sees through *you*," Father chastised as he leaned on the couch, the tail end of his rope flipping on the floor.

Swatting his words away with her hand, Virginia continued to listen.

"It worked, didn't it?" Doris said with a tinge of annoyance.

"Doris, just put her on the five o'clock ferry tonight." Mary, apparently, had decided to put her foot down.

Virginia's heart jumped.

She'd have to let the girl go.

Unless an opportunity presented itself.

But could she do it?

Could she really kill Mary's child? Disloyal as she was, she was still a *child*.

Father whispered in her ear, "You were a child when you killed me."

True.

What did being a child really mean? Virginia couldn't remember a single memory of herself being an actual child. She was forced into being an adult at five when her mother killed herself and her father replaced her with Virginia.

No.

Life was unfair.

Emma, unfortunately, had to pay the price.

Virginia held the receiver away from her ear from the blast of Doris's raised voice. "*Tonight?* Can't you give us one more night? We'll leave first thing in the morning."

"If they're not on the five o'clock ferry today, I'll be on the seven." Mary wasn't messing around. And she only thought her child was homesick. She had no idea she was in *danger*.

Her chance to get rid of Emma was slipping through her fingers.

"Fine. They'll be on the five."

The click of Doris hanging up the phone was the cue to replace the phone on the cradle.

Just in time, too, as her daughter stormed out of the kitchen. "Mary wants the girls home tonight!"

She forced her face to contort with surprise.

Her younger self appeared on the couch next to Father, a wide grin mocking her. She might as well be taunting her with "nanny nanny nanny goat," the brat glowed with happiness. "Good. Maybe

Emma can escape from *you*."

Virginia ignored her, though inside, the words stung. But she answered Doris, "The girl was always a worry-wart." Standing with a huff, she brushed past her and headed toward her bedroom. She needed to regroup.

"I'll go tell the girls," Doris said at her back.

"You do that," she grumbled.

Opening the bedroom door, she shut it behind her.

It wasn't over yet.

And she still had until five.

EMMA

Holding her prize by the handlebars, Emma admired her new bike. The sun hit the pink metal frame at exactly the right angle, making it glow. "I can't believe it's mine."

"After all is said and done," Abby lifted her chin with approval, "good negotiating, Dana."

Their friend beamed. "Can I ride it as a reward?"

Emma laughed and rolled the bike to her. "Of course."

Without another word, Dana leaped onto the bike and pedaled fast, making sure to do a wheelie in front of Lisa.

Glancing up from drawing hopscotch on the asphalt with chalk, Lisa gave Dana the bird.

Emma and Abby laughed, which immediately earned them the double bird from Lisa, which made them laugh harder.

Turning to watch Dana, Abby said with wonder in her voice, "You'll definitely be able to ride the seat with no hands on Suicide Hill with this bike."

Emma had to agree as she watched Dana ride the Fair Lady,

cheeks burning from grinning.

But her smile faded as blood began to pour out of the bike's wheels, seat, and handlebars.

Neither Abby nor Dana seemed to notice.

Everywhere Dana rode, she left trails and puddles of blood, creating a canvas of red in the backyard. Soon Dana's entire body was soaked in it, with streams of red flying in the wind behind her.

Emma backed up a few steps from the onslaught of visuals.

Just as suddenly, the blood was gone.

Dana continued to perform tricks, eyes sparkling, and Abby stared at her with giggles. Though, at this point, the laugh seemed a bit twinged with envy.

But Emma had to ask, "Do you think I should have told my mom about what we saw last night? About Grandma chasing me? Is the bike really worth not saying anything?" Why did taking the bike suddenly feel like Judas and his thirty silver pieces?

As Dana rolled past them and pulled up into the perfect wheelie, even Lisa seemed impressed, which only caused Emma's stomach to turn more.

Abby shrugged. "I was on the fence before, but Dana was right. You deserve it, not your bratty cousin. We can always tell your parents when we get home. And besides, we're leaving today, anyway. You got the bike, and we get to leave. Win, win." Abby seemed to have thought this through, and from the way she stood, chin up, arms crossed, Emma could tell she believed it.

"Yeah, I guess," she reluctantly agreed. "I'm just worried about Grandpa Roy."

Her friend frowned. "He said that he had it under control. I feel like he has a better chance of defending himself than you do. We're just kids."

As if hearing his name, Grandpa Roy walked out and waved at her and Abby as he headed toward the rose garden armed with a hose.

"I'm going to talk to him real quick, but you can ride it after Dana." Emma put her friend's jealous mind to rest.

And from the gleam in Abby's eyes, she'd made her day.

As Emma headed toward the garden, Abby's yell reverberated through the entire backyard. "It's my turn!"

Entering the rose garden, Emma was swallowed up by its beauty. She saw Grandpa Roy ahead of her, watering the soil. The sun beamed on his white hair making him glow like an angel. He noticed Emma and nodded for her to come over. "I hear you're leaving early?"

"You should come with us," Emma said impulsively. And she meant it. Maybe if he stayed at their house, she wouldn't have to worry about him anymore.

Her grandfather scuffed her head. "You don't need to worry about me. I'll be okay. Your grandma has always been like this. She thinks I did something, so she's going to be mad at me for a while until I can convince her I didn't do it. But she'll be fine. I know her."

No, he didn't. Of that, Emma was certain. "I don't think you know her very well."

Grandpa Roy laughed, which made Emma's chest tighten. She was losing him.

"I know her better than you think," he said kindly.

Her stomach sank.

Grandpa Roy was going to stay no matter what.

She suddenly remembered the time Grandma Virginia had taken her out for ice cream after they went to Great Aunt Natalie's funeral. It had been such a sad time, but her grandma had made sure Emma was taken care of. "She's always been so kind, but I don't think she likes me anymore."

Grandpa Roy turned off the spray nozzle on the hose, bending down to Emma's eye level. "Oh, that's not true. She loves her family more than life itself. There's nothing she wouldn't do for you."

Emma stared at him, not sure how to respond, not sure if she should tell him what her grandma had done and said to her. But if pointing a gun at Grandpa Roy last night was normal for her and he was alive and well, maybe running around with a knife was normal, too? Maybe Emma *didn't* have to worry?

The dirt.

The bodies.

Freya.

Poisoning her father.

Grandpa Roy placed a hand on Emma's shoulder. "I know it's hard to see, but she's had a rough life. We just have to love her extra hard."

She hesitated, remembering the vision of Grandma Virginia's father and what he'd done to her and Great Aunt Rachel. But could she simply understand and look past everything to love her extra hard? "But the gun," she stuttered, her mind desperately trying to process the last couple of days.

"And did she hurt me?" he asked.

No.

But would she have if Emma and her friends hadn't interrupted?

She took a moment before she shook her head.

"She's never hurt me, Emma. I truly believe she never will. Doing things like pretending to point a gun at me is the way she learned as a child from her abusive dad. Like I said, she's had it rough," he said, his expression full of compassion and love for his wife.

And she had seen firsthand that what Grandpa Roy said was true.

Emma *did* love her grandma. It had only been during the last couple of days, with her dreams and her grandmother's strange and scary behavior, that she had felt any differently for her. "And we should love her extra hard." She said it as a statement. A mantra she could use to help her.

Grandpa Roy straightened up and squeezed her shoulder before releasing it to pick up the hose and nozzle head again. "That's right." He motioned to the hose. "Now, you want to help me water these roses? I'm pretty sure I saw a door to Winterbrook here a minute ago."

Excitement shot through Emma, and all she could manage to do was nod.

Her grandpa laughed, then furrowed his brow, concentrating. "It comes and goes though, so you gotta keep an eye out."

"I will," she uttered, voice shaking from the thrill of possibilities.

Grandpa handed her the hose. Upon taking it into her hands, she pulled the trigger of the spray nozzle and water flew everywhere.

They both laughed.

As Emma watered the roses, she glanced up at her grandfather with as serious a face as she could muster. "Just promise me if you're ever scared of Grandma, *really* scared, you'll find the door and hide in Winterbrook?"

From the way he slightly pulled back, she could tell she surprised him, but he quickly smiled and placed his hand on her head.

The sun rose behind him as it had earlier, but this time his entire body became a silhouette with the sun's glow behind him.

"I promise," he said solemnly.

But Emma couldn't fight the feeling he'd never make it to the door.

EMMA

Standing on the ferry dock, Emma was antsy to get on the boat and leave Bentmer Island. The wet and cold of the early evening air chilled her to the bone, her hands numb as she clenched onto the handles of her new bike. With her friends by her side, she viewed her family one last time, though only her grandparents and Aunt Doris had come to send them off.

"Your mother will be waiting on the other side."

"Thanks, Aunt Doris," she replied.

Her aunt smiled warmly. "Give me a hug."

Emma handed the bike to Dana and gave her aunt a hug, followed by Grandpa Roy, and then Grandma Virginia.

As she cautiously hugged her grandmother, Virginia whispered in Emma's ear, "Sweet dreams, baby girl."

Quickly pulling away, Emma took the reins of her bike from Dana.

The smile on her grandmother's face distorted suddenly, and Great Grandfather materialized, the end of his hanging rope snapping at Emma's feet.

Not showing her reaction, she turned quickly, nodding to her friends to follow her onto the ferry. She carefully steered her bike toward the entrance over the rain-soaked walkway with Dana and Abby on each side of her.

The three girls maneuvered past the lines of parked cars and arrived at the stairwell that led to the belly of the ship. The wind whistled through the small hallway, and the biting cold caused Emma to shiver. Lifting the front of her bike by the handles, she rolled it up the stairs one at a time. The steps were wet from people's shoes, so she had to go slowly. Her friends acted as her backup in case she slipped.

Finally reaching the top, a warm blast of heating hit Emma in the face. Her body instantly relaxed as it started to thaw.

"Let's stay in here," Abby said aloud, obviously worried her friends might want to go outside with the bike.

"Agreed," Dana concurred. "Why is it so cold in summertime?"

"It always gets cold on the islands," Emma reminded them. "Let's get a booth before anyone else does."

Abby ran ahead to claim the booth, sliding in on one side. The large window with curved edges perfectly framed the Puget Sound and its dark waters. A slight tug and the ferry began to move.

They were going home.

Carefully leaning the bike against the booth table, Emma let Dana climb into the booth opposite Abby, then Emma sat next to her.

Dana and Abby gazed out the window.

Emma kept staring at her bike, not sure how she felt about it. On one hand, she was thrilled. On the other, it felt as if she'd given something of herself to get it.

Freya materialized in the distance, near the restroom, where it was empty of people. She motioned for her to join.

Now that they were finally free of the island and her grandmother, Emma didn't want to drag her friends back into potential drama, so she said, "I'm going to go to the bathroom. Watch my bike?"

Dana's shoulders lifted, her eyes twinkling. "Gladly."

Both girls ogled the Fair Lady as Emma walked toward Freya.

Once at her side, they both moved into a corner of the ship, where no one could see them.

Freya's seaweed crawled around her arms slowly. "I can't go past a certain distance from the island. I've tried. When I was alive, ghosts seemed to travel long distances, but I think I've somehow bound myself here. I'm getting weaker the farther we go."

Emma shuffled her feet. "Can you protect Grandpa?"

Freya shook her head. "Let's pray he can protect himself."

The pit in her stomach contorted. "What about you? You're saying you're stuck there forever?"

Freya reached over and touched Emma's cheek, though it passed through. "I don't know. I hope not." Her body began to shift in and out of view. "My time's almost up."

"Maybe you can find me in my dreams." Emma wished it could be true.

"Maybe," Freya answered, her smile small, kind. Her body, like static, fluttered in and out of view. "If you're ever in trouble, I want you to call Lewis Jackson. He's an FBI agent," Freya paused, tears welling up in her eyes. "He was a good friend." Freya straightened, serious. "You can trust him. Say his name back to me."

"Lewis Jackson," she repeated. Emma wouldn't forget.

"Good." Freya nodded.

Her body shifted out of existence, then materialized fully again. "I gotta go."

Emma stepped toward her. "Thank you." She paused, knowing those two words would never be enough. "For everything."

"Stay safe." The ghost's seaweed moved toward Emma lovingly. "Goodbye, Emma."

“Goodbye, Freya.”

Freya’s body translucent now, almost gone, but before she disappeared entirely, the woman warned, “She can still get to you in your dreams, so stay on guard.” Freya’s expression was serious, like she was giving orders to a soldier.

“How?” Emma whispered in desperation. How in the world could she protect herself from her dreams?

But Freya disappeared, unable to answer her question. Not like she could have, anyway.

Emma walked out of the corner and turned toward the booth with her friends.

Queen Madelis appeared next to the Fair Lady, black gown and hair flowing from an invisible wind, back again from Winterbrook. Her bony hand pointed to the bike, eyes slitted. “You left him there.”

Dana and Abby continued to talk to each other, also admiring the Schwinn, oblivious to Queen Madelis looming tall next to them.

Emma closed her eyes, then opened them fast, hoping to stop this vision of the queen.

“You could have saved him. But you sold him out for this bike,” Queen Madelis condemned Emma with every word.

The handlebars began to bleed, then the seat, then the pedals, until the entire floor of the ferry flooded with blood.

“Was it worth it?” The queen floated over the blood to Emma, arms raised as if she were about to cast a fireball at her.

And Emma wished she would.

Because the queen was right. Emma had left Grandpa Roy alone with her grandmother. Though part of Emma still held out hope that Grandma Virginia was good, that Emma had misunderstood somehow, most of her knew what she saw was real.

Her grandma was a killer, and Emma had left her grandpa at her mercy.

Emma squeezed her eyes shut, praying the queen and blood would go away.

"You okay?" Abby's voice rang out from a distance.

Opening her eyes, Emma sighed in relief.

No blood.

No Queen Madelis.

Emma walked over to Abby and Dana, forcing a smile, trying desperately to recover from what Queen Madelis accused her of. "I'm good. Just tired."

Abby didn't seem to notice Emma's struggle, too focused on the Fair Lady. "Greg is going to flip when you do the stunt down Suicide Hill. I bet you could toast him in a race too."

Dana shifted to face them as well. "Yeah, we should dare him to a race."

Emma pushed down her thoughts of her grandparents and brushed her hand on the pink flowers printed on the banana seat, thinking of all the possibilities. Grandpa would be okay. She had to trust him. Trust he'd find the door to Winterbrook if things got bad.

Fully taking in that the Schwinn Fair Lady was truly hers and no one else's, she breathed in deep, then said, "I can't wait to see the look on his face."

With Dana and Abby excitedly talking about how they were all going to humiliate Greg, Emma stared out at the departing dock. Her family was gone, but in the far distance, the dark patch of woods in the forest hills stood out like a black hole waiting to swallow her.

EMMA

A rush of icy wind cooled Emma as she flew in thc open night sky.

Whoa.

Normally, she loved flying dreams, especially ones like these where she was conscious of it, but the chill in the air was deeper than the temperature. It resonated within her bones. Though her body was safe at home, her racing heart predicted grave danger ahead.

Soaring across the Sound, the wind bit deeper into her skin. The moon hung behind Bentmer Island, like a giant sentry trying to wave for help with only its bright glow casting the island into silhouette. Dread tangled into knots in her body, and she feared they'd never come undone.

And before her was the destination. The target.

Emma's nightmare.

Her grandparents' house.

The only beacon of light in the dark was their nestled home.

Emma flew toward the windows, eardrums pounding with terror. Flying through the panes of glass as if they weren't there, she arrived in the living room to a familiar scene, robbing her of breath.

Grandma Virginia leveled a gun at Grandpa Roy.

Great Grandfather stood next to her grandmother, laughing gleefully as his rope wrapped around Grandpa Roy's legs.

Emma's insides recoiled in helplessness.

Grandpa Roy held his hand out, pleading, "Virginia, no!"

BAM!

Emma screamed.

Everything slowed down to a snail's pace.

The bullet left her grandmother's gun and soared toward her grandfather.

Able to move in real time, Emma floated her body in front of her grandfather, hoping she could somehow stop it.

But just as she reached him, time snapped back to normal. Her grandfather clutched his chest, blood pouring out of his wound, dropping to the floor.

Emma forced her dream body to kneel on the floor next him.

His breath was shallow, gasping for air that wouldn't come. She sat beside him, desperately trying to hold his hand, but it kept slipping through.

She choked on her tears.

Then something happened, making her gasp.

Grandpa Roy's eyes met hers.

And he saw her.

He really *saw* her.

A smile tugged at his lips. "Emma?" he coughed, blood coming up with it. Grandpa Roy reached up to touch her cheek, hand passing through her. "I don't want you...to worry...about me..."

Her grandmother walked calmly up to her husband, gun aimed at his head, Great Grandfather with her, his rope billowing behind her. "Mumbling to your girlfriend? She can't hear you."

Grandpa Roy coughed up more blood.

Tears streamed down Emma's face. "Grandpa, you have to run! You promised!"

His eyes sparkled. "No, it's okay...Emma...I found...the door..."

BAM!

Straight through his forehead.

Eyes that were twinkling lights of love and beauty only moments ago were now empty glass.

He was gone.

Rage coursed through Emma like a living poison as she whirled toward her grandmother, her fury overpowering. "You *killed* him!"

But her grandmother didn't see her. In fact, she thundered through Emma's incorporeal form, grabbed her husband's arms and dragged him toward the bathroom.

Anger quickly switched to panic. Emma didn't know what to do.

Watching her grandfather's body being pulled across the floor, leaving large streaks of blood in his wake, left her breathless.

When Grandma Virginia turned out of view down the hallway, Freya materialized, standing in the pool of blood left from her grandfather.

"She killed him." Emma's chin trembled.

Nodding, Freya's seaweed drooped and began to shrivel and die. "She killed me, too. You saw the others."

Even though Emma was only there through her dream, the tears on her face felt real. "I was supposed to protect him."

Freya's head turned to the window. "You should leave now. You shouldn't see what happens next."

But the thought that her grandmother could be any worse only fueled her anger. "What happens next?"

Reaching out, the ghost tried to pull her toward the window, but the woman's hands kept slipping through Emma's dream form.

Giving one last glance at Freya, Emma ignored her ghost friend and followed the streaks of blood.

The once familiar hallway now appeared dark, dingy, and unfamiliar to her. It was as if she'd never stepped foot in the house.

It wasn't the same house anymore.

It never would be.

Grandpa Roy had been its light, and now her wretched grandmother had snuffed it out, leaving only darkness.

Entering her grandparents' bedroom, she followed the blood to the bathroom.

It was the same bathroom as the one in Emma's dream before coming to Bentmer Island.

But now, her grandfather was in the tub.

It was *his* blood she'd seen.

She had been watching her grandmother's plans, which was why Grandma Virginia hadn't wanted Emma there.

And she'd succeeded.

Great Grandfather stood next to Grandma Virginia, his hanging rope seemed tame now, only wistfully playing with her grandmother's arms and legs.

More tears flowed down her cheeks, and she stood frozen, unable to leave, but also unable to fully comprehend what she was witnessing. If throwing up had been possible, Emma would have.

Freya ran into the bathroom. "Emma, please. You need to leave."

Emma gagged as her grandmother's hand gripped a metal saw and tore into Grandpa Roy's shoulder until his arm separated from his body. She tossed it out the window, landing in a large barrel as if it were simple garbage she was disposing of.

Her grandmother's head snapped toward her. Or not to her... to *Freya.*

"Emma? Where?" she asked the ghost.

Freya's eyes rounded.

"Where is she? Is she here? Can she see me?" her grandmother's words were frantic. Then she turned to look at Great Grandfather. "You were right."

Though she was in a dream, Emma felt as if she were suffocating.

Freya stepped forward protectively in front of her. “Your time has come, Virginia. You won’t be able to hide this one.”

Saw still in hand, her grandmother walked over to the ghost. “We’ll see.”

Great Grandfather placed a hand on Freya’s chest, and his rope whipped around her neck as if she were cattle on a farm. “OUT!”

The rope squeezed fast and tight, popping Freya out of existence.

Emma was alone with her grandmother. She carefully took a few steps back, hands shaking.

But Grandma Virginia’s eyes roamed the room aimlessly. She spoke to the air, however, assuming her granddaughter still stood there. “If you’re here. Enjoy the show. Because you’re next.”

Emma’s surroundings morphed around her until she sat at the bottom of the oversized metal drum, amidst her grandfather’s body parts. She screamed and struggled to climb free, but every time she gained purchase, another limb fell on top of her. Liquid was next, noxious and strong, causing Emma to choke uncontrollably, but she kept climbing, desperate to break free.

As she was about to reach the surface, a lit match flew toward her face. Looking up, she saw her grandmother and Great Grandfather standing there, watching.

Emma screamed as flames engulfed her.

EMMA

Emma woke up screaming unable to stop herself.

It's my fault.

It's my fault.

It's my fault.

The thought repeated over and over in her head. She could have saved him!

I left him.

I left him.

I left him.

And still she screamed, hoping to drown the guilt pushing down on her body.

"I'M SORRY!" Emma yelled. "I'M SORRY! I'M SORRY!"

Every part of her body shook. Hands, arms, legs, even her teeth chattered uncontrollably, tears pouring down her face.

It wasn't until her mother's voice yelled through the wall of her room, "I'm coming!" that she finally stopped.

Emma had no idea how much time had passed by the time her

mother hurried into the room, racing to her bedside.

"What is it? Oh my god. You're shaking. What happened?" Mary couldn't hide the quaver in her own voice, her hand immediately checking her daughter's forehead. "No fever."

Emma vomited on her quilt.

"Oh, god," her mother gasped, immediately pulling the quilt off, careful to not spill anything on the floor. After wadding it up quickly and placing it on the ground, she pulled Emma onto her lap, rocking her gently.

Through chattering teeth, Emma sputtered, "Grand...pa...murder...ed."

Her mother's arms wrapped tighter around her, pulling her closer against her. "Oh, honey, you just had a nightmare."

Pushing out of the embrace, Emma stuttered, "N...n...no...I *saw*....it." Her heart sank. Not telling her parents what had happened earlier was a huge mistake. Now they'd never believe her. "Grandma... shot him... and ch...ch...chopped him up. She...she....said I was...next." Emma managed to get out.

Would her mother believe her?

Did taking the bike for silence seal Emma's fate?

What had she been thinking?

Racing thoughts threatened to overwhelm her.

Her mother's eyes were round as if she were horrified.

Maybe she *would* believe her?

"Oh, Emma. What a horrible dream."

Emma's chest caved into itself.

Her mom thought this was all fiction, a simple nightmare.

Cupping Emma's tear-stricken face, her mom said, "I promise you it was only a dream. We'll call your grandparents in the morning, and you can talk to Grandpa yourself. Okay?"

No. It *wasn't* okay. Nothing was okay. Grandpa wouldn't be on the other end of the phone. He was gone. Dead. *Murdered.*

Emma needed to calm down, needed to re-group. Feeling warm

arms around her, grasping her tightly, helped her shaking slow down. "It was s...so...scary," was all she could utter.

Too scary.

Too *real.*

Part of her desperately wanted to believe her mother's words, that it had been a bad dream.

Kissing the top of Emma's head, her mother rocked her gently. "I know. But you're safe now. Everything is going to be all right."

She listened to her words and took them in, but she knew nothing would ever be all right ever again.

VIRGINIA

Watching Roy's body burn in the metal barrel, Virginia's body and clothes were covered in his blood. And yet, she struggled to feel anything.

Content? Satisfied? Justified? All the emotions she had expected to feel were just...*missing.*

"How about guilt? Do you feel that?!" Her younger self stared at the flames with tears in her eyes.

"Nope," Virginia answered honestly. No guilt. Simply *nothing.*

"You're in shock. You'll regret this forever, eventually!" Young Virginia screamed.

Taking a deep, calming breath, Virginia kept her eyes on the fire, the body parts, the way Roy's face began to melt down to his skull.

Flesh was so fragile.

It was a wonder anyone lived more than a week.

Grabbing the metal lid, Virginia topped the barrel so the fire could get hot enough to burn the bones. No body. No evidence.

Virginia's body convulsed, and she fell to her knees.

What was happening?

Young Virginia touched her cheek. "You *do* feel something."

A guttural scream ripped out of Virginia, disintegrating her younger self where she stood.

No.

"I feel nothing."

"Nothing?" Father cocked his head to the side. "Not even the satisfaction of righting a wrong?"

Virginia rose to her feet. "Yes. Satisfaction," she lied to Father, essentially lying to herself.

A kill had never felt like this before.

The hollowness threatened to swallow her.

No.

Virginia stormed back inside the house. She needed to get this blood off her body and clean up. Clean up *everywhere.* There'd be no sleep tonight.

But first, she needed a drink.

RUBBER GLOVES COVERED IN BLOOD, VIRGINIA USED HER ELBOW TO LIFT the faucet handle as water poured out of the spout. Water mixed with blood drained down the sink until her gloves were clean.

"Was it worth it?" Young Virginia asked. She stood in the corner, face wet with tears.

Virginia ignored her as she opened the cupboard doors under the sink, pulling out a gallon of bleach.

"Of course it was worth it," Father answered, his rope flapping as he spoke.

"He loved you," Young Virginia whispered.

Virginia set the gallon container on the counter, then reached into her front pocket, pulling out her flask. Taking a quick swig, her shoulders relaxed as the burn of vodka coated her throat.

Taking a deep breath and stuffing her flask in her pocket, she grabbed the bleach once more. When she moved to leave the kitchen, the phone rang.

With an exasperated sigh, she picked it up. “Hello?”

“Hi, Mom. Listen, Emma had a bad dream last night about Dad. Can she talk to him?” Mary’s voice had a ring of concern in it, but Virginia was willing to bet it was for Emma and not from any real fear of something happening with Roy.

Father stepped close. “You, see? She’s already turning you in. It won’t be long before the police are involved. Or the FBI agent who has it in for you.”

Her younger self walked over to her side with wide, pleading eyes. “You scared her. It’s still just a dream to her.”

Virginia turned away from both of them. “Oh, poor thing. Well, I’d love to, but he left for work. They’re shipping off to Norway, so it’ll be a few weeks. Do you want me to talk to her?”

Father grumbled, “I bet the ghoul showed her everything. Even where you put the bodies.”

Young Virginia stamped her foot. “You don’t know that.”

Father crossed his arms, the rope whipping violently now. “It won’t be long now. If you do nothing, you’re finished.”

Though Mary had obviously tried to cover the receiver so Virginia couldn’t hear, she could still make out what she said.

“Sorry, sweetie, he’s gone on a trip. You know he’s a shipping boat captain. But he’ll be back soon, I promise. You want to talk to Grandma?”

Virginia rolled her eyes as Mary’s next comment indicated Emma’s refusal. “Are you sure? Hearing her voice might make you feel better? Remember how much she loves you?”

“No way,” Emma spat.

Virginia could imagine her stomping her foot for emphasis.

Mary’s voice was clear now, no more muffled hand. “Sorry, Mom. She only wants to talk to Dad. Will you give us a call when you hear from him?”

Father’s rope writhed and curled, mirroring Virginia’s conflicted thoughts. She couldn't let the girl spout theories about her. Eventually, Mary and Derrick would listen. Especially when Roy never showed up again. They'd remember this. They'd remember what Emma accused her grandma of.

Virginia needed to take care of Emma once and for all.

"Actually, I have a better idea. I'm feeling a bit fragile up here by myself," she said as she gripped the gallon of bleach. "Maybe I could stay with you for a week or so? Keep an old lady company? Then I can spend some time with Emma and ease her mind."

Father chuckled while her younger self scowled.

Virginia needed to protect herself. Protect her family, even if it meant some sacrifices.

"That sounds really nice, Mom. We'll get the guest room ready for you." Mary had a renewed hope in her tone.

Poor girl thought Virginia would help her daughter.

A deep weight pushed on Virginia's chest at the thought of hurting Emma. Shoving the bleach away from her, she pulled out her flask once again and drank deeply. Sometimes the alcohol could numb her mind of her guilty thoughts.

Sometimes not.

Today, it didn't seem to be working.

"Maybe because you killed the love of your life," Young Virginia spat at her.

Virginia turned her back, closing her eyes, concentrating. She had to do what she had to do. "I'll be on the next ferry over. I'll see you this afternoon."

"See you then," Mary said cheerfully.

"She won't be so happy when you murder her daughter." Young Virginia appeared in front of her again, narrowing her eyes. They were Emma's eyes. Which made her goal easier in a way. She'd killed that part of herself years ago. Now she was going to do it again.

Virginia grunted. "Shut up, you little ghostie."

Father watched her, anticipation in his eyes.

Virginia hadn't been lying when Emma's dream-self had visited her last night.

Her granddaughter was next.

EMMA

Emma's mom hung up the phone with a satisfied smile, which only made her blood boil. "Mom! You can't let her stay here! Didn't you hear what I said last night? She *killed* Grandpa! She said she's going to kill *me*!"

She recognized the patronizing look on her mother's face. Wait, no. More like irritated.

"Emma, your grandmother wouldn't hurt a fly. She's had a very hard life and is extremely protective of her family. You had a bad dream. That's all it was."

Love her extra hard, Grandpa Roy had said.

It didn't feel right at the moment, especially with the looming dread of her grandmother coming to stay with them. How could she go from complete trust and love of her grandmother to total terror? Maybe it *was* just a nightmare. Maybe everything that had happened on Bentmer had creeped into her brain and created the worst dream of her life.

"You're probably watching too much TV," her dad chimed in.

Yeah, Dad, that's it. I'm dreaming of my grandpa being chopped to pieces because I watch too much Murder in the Margins.

Emma hoped her eye-roll wasn't too obvious since she tended to get grounded for the major ones. But part of her didn't care. Part of her *wanted* to get grounded. Maybe then, she'd be sentenced to her room and she wouldn't have to see her grandma at all.

It was time to tell the truth. The *whole* truth.

Aunt Doris was already back in Indiana, so she couldn't take the bike away now.

"What does TV have to do with it? And she chased me with a knife over at Bentmer, and she had a gun pointed at Grandpa. You still think she's not a murderer?"

Emma metaphorically patted herself on the back. How could they argue with that?

But her mother's nostrils flared larger than Emma had ever seen before. "Emma, what did we say about making things up? Why would you say that?"

Okay, maybe Emma had *exaggerated* some things in the past, but how could her parents not see she was telling the truth now? "Because it's *true*."

But her mom took a deep calming breath. "Emma, what you're saying is very serious. Do you realize what you're accusing your grandmother of?"

Emma wanted to scream at her mother for refusing to believe in her. Crossing her arms, she spouted, "Yeah, murder. She's a *muurrd-derreeerrr*. I dreamt it. I saw all of it." Why wouldn't they believe her?

Her parents made eye-contact at the word "dreamt," and Emma knew she was toast.

Her mom's eyes softened. "You dreamt it?"

One word, and they now thought she'd dreamt *all* of it.

"Yes. But not the knife stuff, or the gun stuff. Just the murder and, oh yeah, the bodies she has buried in the forest stuff." Emma thought she'd throw that in there for more credibility. "Oh, and her dad with the creepy rope around his neck. And her younger ghost thing said Queen Madelis wasn't involved, but I'm not so sure anymore..."

"That's enough," her mother said in her clipped, angry tone Emma hated. From the pinched eyebrows and glare her mother now aimed at her, she realized she may have said too much.

She couldn't give up yet, though. Maybe she could reach them. "Ask Abby, ask Dana, they'll tell you." They always believed her friends more than her, anyway.

Her dad shook his head. "Your friends do everything you say. They're not exactly reliable."

Desperation infected her blood like poison. "Fine, then call Aunt Doris. She'll tell you about the bike, at least."

Her mother had had enough, her eyes penetrating deep into Emma's. "I already know about the bike and how she gave it to you because you were homesick." Taking a deep breath, she continued, "We'll sit down when your grandmother gets here and sort everything out. You'll see. You had a bad dream, and your imagination took over."

Her mother's tone said that the argument was over.

A sudden fury raged through her. "I knew you guys wouldn't believe me. That's why I didn't say anything. And now she's going to come here and murder me. You'll feel like shit later."

It was Dad's turn to be angry now. "Language!"

But Emma didn't care. She wasn't sorry at all. She had been honest, and they were choosing to ignore it. "I'm going to stay in my room the whole time." Then she threw out for good measure, "Just to stay alive."

With the "mom" look fully activated, Emma shrunk a little in her chair.

"Go to your room. We'll discuss this later."

There would be no "later." Not if she intended to survive her grandmother's visit. Grabbing a pancake off her plate, she slid out of her chair, slamming her feet on the carpet. “Gladly,” she huffed, then walked to the hallway leading to her room.

She stopped in the middle to listen to what her parents had to say, and her insides turned at her mother’s words. “She has one bad dream and her grandmother is suddenly a villain? Why does she continue to do this? Remember her first grade teacher, Mrs. Gordan, and how she had us convinced she was locking her up at recess? But, really, she just had to stay at her desk because she had been talking to Abby during class?”

Emma could hear her father’s exasperated sigh from there. “Yeah. I still think she watches too much TV.”

Not wanting to hear anymore, she quietly entered her room and shut the door.

They didn’t believe her.

Emma was in big trouble.

She needed her friends to help her come up with her next move because she was about to spend the next week with a killer who wanted Emma to be her next victim.

EMMA

It didn't take long to gather her little gang. The three of them now congregated in Abby's bedroom. Emma figured it was better to be out of her own house in case her parents tried to listen in. She was planning her grandmother's demise, after all.

Abby's room reflected her friend's personality to a T. From the canopy bed with floral bedding, to the antique furniture looking like it belonged in a Jane Austen movie. Laura Ashley could have designed it, all light greens and blues, with white accents.

Sitting cross-legged on the light green carpet, Abby organized her Sasha doll clothes into small piles.

Dana slumped into a wooden rocking chair, and Emma sat on the edge of the bed.

Abby placed another pair of doll pants into the pants pile. "They really didn't believe you? After you told them everything? Even about the gun?"

"Yup. They think it's all my imagination," Emma said, still feeling the sting of her parents not taking a second to consider she might be telling the truth. So what if she had an imagination? It didn't change the fact her grandmother was a homicidal maniac.

Dana said what Emma was thinking. "What assholes."

Groaning loudly, Emma fell onto the bed with a thump.

Abby took a miniature cardigan sweater and began placing it on her Sasha doll. "You do make up stuff a lot though, so it kind of makes sense."

"Abby!" Dana gave a pointed look. "You're not helping."

Tugging the cardigan to fit properly on the doll, Abby's cheeks flushed. "Sorry."

"No, she's right. I do...exaggerate things a lot," Emma admitted, though she didn't want to. She couldn't help how she saw the world. Sometimes there were ghosts, and sometimes there were giant asphalt mouths trying to eat her bike. It was honestly the same to her. "But what do we do then?"

"Call the cops?" Dana suggested.

Emma sat up. "You think?" Heart thumping, it was one thing telling her parents, but to inform the actual police? It somehow made it more real. But Emma knew what she saw. And her grandma wasn't right in the head. Grandpa Roy told her to love her extra hard, but it still didn't feel like the right thing to do. She needed to be put away so she couldn't hurt anyone.

Namely *her.*

Abby glanced up from her Sasha doll. "If she murdered him, then yes. You really think she killed him?"

Emma did. It may have been a dream, but she didn't doubt herself this time. She wouldn't let herself. Doubting her dreams led to Grandpa Roy dying in the first place. Emma nodded, short and quick, before the tears formed in her eyes.

Dana yanked herself out of the rocking chair and walked over. "Then let's call. We can pretend to be an adult. Make it anonymous."

Emma planted her feet on the carpet right as Abby stood up. The three girls shared an unspoken air of determination and loyalty.

"Let's use the phone downstairs so my brother won't bother us."

Dana crossed her arms. "Can't the cops trace phone calls? We should go to a pay phone."

"Four Tree Mall?" Emma suggested.

A quick nod from her friends, and the girls were out of the room, heading for the front door.

Swinging the front door open, Abby yelled over her shoulder. "We're going to the mall!"

From somewhere in the kitchen, her friend's mom shouted, "Be home before dark!"

Without another response, the three left the house.

Pedaling fast, the girls arrived at Four Tree Mall on their bikes, braking in front of the payphone. It was situated between Payless Drugstore and Albertsons. Luckily, no one was using it. Abandoning their bikes in a heap against the cement wall, Emma took the lead and stood in front of the public phone.

Abby's nostrils flared. "I can't believe it's a *quarter* now."

Dana rolled her eyes. "'Cuz you make so many phone calls."

"Shut up." Abby lightly nudged her arm.

This was it.

Emma was going to call the police on her...*grandmother.*

Flipping through the phone book, Emma found the number for the Bentmer Island's police department. "Got it." Pulling out the quarter, Emma paused a moment before she placed it in the vertical change slot.

"I'm nervous," Emma admitted.

"You're doing it for Grandpa Roy," Abby encouraged.

"What if my mom is right?" Emma's doubts reared their ugly head again. It was simply too horrible to be true.

And the way he looked at her, knowing he was dying, telling her he'd found the door to Winterbrook...

But then Grandma dashed all her hopes of him escaping, by shooting him a second time before he could escape...

Dana stepped toward her, eyes finding hers. "We know your dreams happen. We've seen it over and over again in the news. We believe you." Nudging Abby, she added, "*Right?*"

"As Dana would normally say, 'duh.' Plus, I'm still not over Mr. Waller." Abby said, then quickly glanced over her shoulder as if he'd be standing there.

Dana rolled her eyes. "Abby."

"Sorry," Abby said.

Seeing her friends next to her, faces so full of faith in her and her dreams, filled Emma with confidence. It was nice to be believed, especially when she knew how it sounded.

This would all be a lot easier if her parents would have as much faith in her as her friends did.

"Okay. I know what I'm going to say." She dropped the quarter in and dialed the number.

Through the phone a female operator answered, "Bentmer Police Department, how can I help you?"

Clearing her throat, Emma threw her voice to sound lower, like her mother. "I heard gunshots from my neighbor's house. They fight a lot, and I'm worried something horrible happened."

Abby and Dana's thumbs were up and they nodded in approval.

The operator asked, "What is your neighbor's address?"

"5522 Wrentley Road," she answered.

There was a typing sound through the phone. Emma was sure they were tracing her call. The overwhelming urge to hang up and bike out of there was so strong, she almost slammed the receiver down right then and there, but the operator said, "We've had calls for that address before. We'll have a unit check it out."

A mixture of relief but then also anger rushed through her. What did the woman mean? *They'd had calls there before?* Had her grandpa been dealing with her grandmother for years? Emma held the phone receiver away from her mouth, covering it with her hand. "They've had calls from other neighbors before."

Both Abby and Dana's eyes rounded.

"See?" Abby pressed her lips together.

Dana nudged her head toward the phone. "Tell them about the backyard."

Emma uncovered the phone receiver. "Thank you. And you might want to check the backyard. That's where it sounded like it came from."

"Can I get your name?" the operator asked.

Emma's stomach plummeted. She quickly hung up. "She asked my name, so I hung up. But they're sending someone now."

Dana shifted on her feet. "You think the barrel is still there?"

Emma shrugged, unsure. "Grandma is on her way to my house now, so hopefully they can find something without her there."

"Let's get out of here in case they traced the call," Abby suggested, forehead lined with worry.

But she could be right.

Grabbing their bikes, the girls hopped on and pedaled toward home.

Emma had no idea what to expect, but she hoped the police would find *something* to incriminate her grandmother.

Now she only had to worry about Grandma Virginia staying in her house for the next week.

VIRGINIA

Virginia waited at the front door of her daughter's house, suitcases next to her. She'd had a bad feeling ever since she drove onto the ferry. Not being able to place what it was, she had stayed in her car rather than join the others up on the upper decks.

I killed Roy.

Virginia shook the thought from her mind. What was done was done, and he'd deserved it.

Staring at the small rectangular stained-glass window of a sunflower embedded in the oak door, Virginia found she couldn't reach over to ring the doorbell.

What was wrong with her?

Thinking about her intentions toward her granddaughter took her breath away for a moment and she found it difficult to breathe.

Her younger self formed next to her. "You came here to do bad things."

"Shut it, you little monster." Virginia straightened her windbreaker, taking a deep breath. Before she could think further, she slapped the doorbell with her hand.

Through the stained glass, a moving silhouette walked toward her. She pulled out her flask and took a few swigs. The heat quickly turned to relief as the alcohol numbed her thoughts, numbed her memories of what she'd done, of what she intended to do.

Everything felt right again. Justified. *Yes.* Killing Roy was supposed to give her peace, but only the liquid in her flask could truly do that.

The door opened and her beautiful daughter Mary stood in front of her with a welcoming smile.

Virginia's heart swelled at the sight of her. It had only been days since she last saw her, but it had felt like months.

Young Virginia eyed Mary. "She has Roy's eyes."

The moment of happiness deflated in an instant, and Virginia desperately wanted to empty her flask, but she tucked it away in her pocket and threw her arms out wide. "Give me a hug."

Mary fell into Virginia's arms and squeezed her tight. Virginia wished she could hold on forever, but her daughter pulled away with a smile. "Come on in."

Taking Virginia's suitcases, Mary led the way inside the house.

Closing the front door behind her, Virginia surveyed her daughter's home. The living room, dining room, and kitchen made up the first floor, with a small hallway to the left leading to the floor's bathroom and Emma's room. To the right was a doorway that led to the guest room. Good. She liked she'd be on the same floor as Emma. She could keep an eye on her. Farther off to the left was a dual staircase, one ascending to Mary and Derrick's room, and one descending to the basement where Emma had a playroom the size of the entire floor. The girl was spoiled.

"She's not *spoiled.* You're trying to make excuses," Young Virginia corrected her.

Virginia ignored her and turned to Mary with the biggest smile she could muster. "Where's my granddaughter?"

Mary tugged at both suitcases, half-dragging them to the guest room. "Out playing with her friends."

As if the stars aligned, Emma swung the front door open and walked inside, almost tripping on one of the suitcases.

Mary stumbled forward from the sudden force. "Emma, be careful," she scolded.

From the girl's furtive gaze at Virginia and the immediate step back, her granddaughter was clearly frightened of her.

As she should be.

"There she is!" she exclaimed, watching Emma shrink farther away from her. She was almost out the door at this point. "Give your grandma a hug."

Emma stayed where she was, folding her arms in defiance, her eyes moving back and forth between Virginia and her little ghostie.

She hated Emma had the ability to see Father and her younger self. Father wasn't there at the moment, so at least she could only see the one. They weren't real. None of this *psychic* stuff ever had a rhyme or reason to it. Otherwise, she'd have predicted the winning lottery numbers by now and been a *rich* old lady.

"We *are* real," Young Virginia kept her stare pointed at Emma.

Emma huffed. "I never said you weren't real."

"Who are you talking to?" Mary rolled her eyes, exasperated.

"I told you. Grandma always has this weird ghost-thing around her that looks like me. She's better than Great Grandfather and the noose he always wears, though," Emma grumbled.

Laughing inwardly, Virginia thoroughly enjoyed Emma talking herself into a corner. The more she spouted about ghosts, the less Mary and Derrick would believe anything she had to say.

Emma's eyes flew to Virginia's. "I'm watching you."

My god, she looks just like me.

Out of the corner of her eye, Virginia spied her daughter giving Emma a glare that would shrivel anyone into submission.

"Enough with your imaginary friends," Mary said in a strict tone.

Uncrossing her arms, the girl grumbled as if she were an eighty-year-old man. "Fine." With the quickness of a rattle snake, Emma leaned into Virginia and gave her a squeeze, then yanked herself away as if she'd touched fire. "I know what you did, and you're not getting away with it."

Virginia almost grabbed her granddaughter's throat. The impulse was so strong, but she held in her anger and hid it with a smile. "Your mom told me about your dream, sweetie. But that's all it was. Roy is safe and sound, captaining a freighter to Norway."

The stare this girl had, eyeing her with invisible daggers. "I'm going to my room."

"Emma!" Mary dropped the bags, her hands now on her hips.

Father appeared next Virginia. "You see the way she yells Emma's name with anger? That's loyalty to you," he said with pride.

Virginia agreed. Her daughter would always take her side.

Emma faced Father, brows furrowed. "She won't be loyal for long! My mom will believe me once she gets her head out of her ass."

"*EMMA!* GO TO YOUR ROOM NOW!" Mary yelled, face red. She pointed to the hallway as if it were a punishment, but the flood of relief on the girl's face was obvious to everyone.

Father chuckled, then stuck his tongue out at Emma as she ran down the hallway.

With the shutting of Emma's door, Mary turned to Virginia. "I'm so sorry, Mom. That nightmare has her convinced of terrible things. I wish Dad would call already so she can see he's okay."

He's exactly where he belongs.

Father's rope crawled toward Mary. "The girl may start convincing her."

Virginia smiled again at her daughter. "He will. Now show me where I can freshen up."

Mary shoved the suitcases the rest of the way to the guest room. Virginia followed, Father and her younger self close behind.

EMMA

Sitting on her bed, Emma read the second book from the *Chronicles of Winterbrook*. It was her favorite, and she'd probably read it over a hundred times. She couldn't explain it. She just never got bored or tired of it. Most of the book was a big heist, which was her favorite kind of story. She'd always imagined herself being the best and quietest thief no one could ever catch.

The main character, Olivia, had to go undercover and pretend to be a castle maid so she could steal back the jewel of Anar. Queen Madelis kept it in her castle after she'd taken it from Prince Rayland over a hundred years before because she needed the jewel to keep herself young, though she was immortal.

That was the only thing she was jealous of Queen Madelis for.

Immortality.

Life felt too short, and she was only eleven. Maybe it was because of her dreams, the ones where she saw people being murdered. Maybe it was the fact she saw and talked to ghosts. Emma would rather have nothing to do with any of it, and that meant living forever if she could. It was her deepest darkest desire she never told anyone, not even Abby and Dana.

And now her grandfather was dead.

She knew it in her soul. Emma had enough dreams to know how to tell the difference between a normal dream and a dream that was actually happening. She couldn't save him. And she was terrified she wouldn't be able to save herself. Or her parents. Or her friends. What if her grandmother went on a murder spree? She shivered, placing her book down.

Grandma Virginia was *in her house.*

The thought paralyzed her.

A knock on her window caused her to jump.

Dana and Abby peered through the window with expectant eyes. They'd go to Mordor with her if she asked. If she was Frodo, then they were her Sam.

Rushing to the window, Emma slid it open.

Abby nodded toward Emma's closed bedroom door. "Is *she* here?"

Nodding, Emma filled them in. "Arrived yesterday, but I've locked myself in my room since then. I only came out for dinner since my mom made me."

Dana's eyes screamed approval. "Smart. Did the cops show up or call at all?"

"Not a peep. They must not have found anything," Emma admitted, defeat crushing her optimism. She hadn't known what to expect, but part of her imagined the entire Seattle police force tearing down her front door and dragging her grandmother away.

She'd hoped anyway.

Abby scratched her head. "We have to do something."

Dana straightened herself, full of confidence. "She's guilty. We saw her with the gun. And I've been thinking about it, too. I think she was planning to kill him when we were all there on the island. That's why she was punching herself. To make it look like self-defense. She didn't plan on us ruining her plans."

Abby pressed her elbows into her sides. "Maybe you should spend the night at one of our houses? To be safe?"

Glancing over her shoulder, the outside air chilled her. Her grandmother's presence alone was enough to give her shivers. "Yeah, I'll ask my mom. Grandma is all sweet and smiles, but the way she stares at me when my parents aren't watching scares me."

Dana balled her left hand and punched the palm of her right. "Actually, no. You're not coming to our house. We're staying here."

Abby stepped back as if this was the last thing she'd ever volunteer to do. "We are?"

Dana continued, "Yes, fraidy-cat. I've got a plan."

It was enough for Emma.

Whatever plan Dana had, Emma was in.

Five hours later, it was midnight, and all three girls snuck up to the guest room door.

Emma mouthed, "Look for anything suspicious."

Dana nodded.

Abby's hand trembled as she reached for the doorknob.

Emma and Dana knew their friend would not be able to handle what they were about to do next, so Emma made sure her eyes met Abby's as she mouthed, "Stand guard?"

Abby dropped her hand and relaxed. She nodded, grateful.

Now the mission was down to her and Dana. "Ready?" Emma mouthed.

"As I'll ever be," she mouthed.

Carefully turning the knob, Emma slowly opened the door leading to her grandmother's room.

Tip-toeing inside, Emma motioned to Grandma Virginia's suitcases, then pointed to herself.

Dana took Emma's cue and pointed at the closet.

Both with their assignments, Emma slowly walked toward the suitcases.

Dana's plan had been simple. Search Grandma Virginia's belongings, hoping to find something to incriminate her. They needed proof because a dream wasn't enough to convince any type of law enforcement.

Virginia snored softly, creating a sense of calm for Emma. If she was snoring, she was asleep. Emma hoped her little ghost-girl wouldn't wake her up, or Great-Grandfather-rope-guy. She wished her friends could see what she could see because even thinking it made her feel a little crazy. And crazy led to doubt. Something she needed to push down if she was going to put her grandmother away for good.

Emma gently rummaged through the bigger suitcase, feeling around for anything suspicious. She honestly didn't know what she expected to find, but she had to do *something*. Glancing over at Dana, she saw her friend was doing the same with the clothes hanging in the closet.

Virginia's snore suddenly changed to a mumble.

Emma and Dana froze, waiting for either another snore, or the old woman possibly waking up.

Their eyes met as the mumbling turned to shifting.

Dread seized Emma.

Should they run?

They hadn't found anything yet.

Dana inched toward the door, obviously getting the same feeling Emma had.

But as suddenly as the mumbling happened, her grandmother was snoring again.

It was difficult not to let out a giant breath of relief, but the moment served as a countdown.

Emma searched once more, this time the smaller suitcase.

Dana did the same, going through each pocket, of each shirt or jacket, until she pulled out a crumpled tissue, immediately gagging.

Abby cringed with grossed out sympathy from the doorway.

A snort from Virginia caused Emma and Dana to freeze again.

"Who's there?" her grandmother called out in the darkness.

Emma stood as still as possible, trying to blend into the wall itself, while Dana moved into the closet hiding among the clothes.

Only the sound of Virginia's breathing filled the room. Emma couldn't tell if she was awake or not, the breathing was so loud. She didn't remember her grandmother ever breathing that loud when she was awake.

As if in answer, Virginia began to snore again.

Another wave of relief, but Emma began to wonder if she could handle much more of this.

Dana walked over to her. "Nothing," she mouthed.

Heart sinking, Emma didn't think she could leave this room empty-handed. Not after the roller coaster of emotion she'd been through.

Quietly rummaging through her grandmother's purse, Emma felt every inch of thc intcrior.

And then she found something.

She didn't want to get too excited before she saw what it was, but pulling it out, her head swum with triumph.

A ring.

Grandpa Roy's *wedding ring.*

"It's Grandpa's," she mouthed to Dana, and her eyes widened to saucers accompanied with a large grin.

Virginia shifted and grumbled again.

This time, Emma and Dana hurried to the door, quickly exiting.

Abby stood just outside, obviously hiding more than taking watch, so she jumped when the two of them reached her side.

Emma showed Abby the ring and grinned. "We got her," Abby whispered.

"Emma? Is that you?" Virginia called from inside the guest room.

None of them had to speak. They ran as fast and as quietly as they could to Emma's room.

But they had it.
Grandpa Roy's ring.
There could only be one reason he wasn't wearing it.
Because he was *gone*, and Grandma Virginia took it.

EMMA

Tucked into her sleeping bag, Emma woke to the sound of movement in the darkness.

Heart pounding, her first thought was Grandma Virginia had come to take back the ring, but only the sleeping bag lumps of Abby and Dana were on either side of her.

About to go back to sleep, Emma glanced briefly at the window.

Silhouetted from the night sky, Great Grandfather towered over Emma from the foot of her sleeping bag.

Jolted fully awake now, Emma scooted up to a sitting position, pulling her knees into her chest so he couldn't grab her feet. "What do you want?" her voice shook.

"Now, that's no way to talk to kin." Great Grandfather attempted a smile, but it twisted in the wrong angles, displaying more of a distorted frown.

"I saw what you did to your daughters."

Great Grandfather paused, staring at Emma.

Was he going to attack?

Could he attack?

Why was he staring?

Questions raced through Emma's brain as she pulled the sleeping bag in closer for protection.

Finally, he nodded. "I thought you might have." He kneeled to one knee to be at Emma's eye level. "I only did what was taught to me by my father. I knew it wasn't right, but I couldn't stop. Do you know what that's like?"

Emma shook her head, reminding herself this man in front of her wasn't a man, wasn't a ghost, but some kind of manifestation of her grandmother. But what did that really mean? Would Grandma Virginia remember this conversation? Could Emma close her eyes hard enough and make him disappear?

"What about you and your dreams?" he interrupted her thoughts. "You know they're not right. Not natural. Yet you keep having them." Great Grandfather raised an eyebrow as if Emma had been sneaking cookies from the cookie jar.

"I can't control them," Emma said defensively. What was he getting at?

Great Grandfather's rope crept toward her. "Can't you, though?"

Emma's teeth began to chatter as she followed the oncoming rope with her eyes.

"Because I think you can," he said as he stood up. "Now, I got what was coming to me. My baby Virginia took care of that. But if you keep trying to hurt her, you'll get what's coming to you, too."

The rope swung wildly, then wrapped around Emma's neck, squeezing tight.

"Understand?" Great Grandfather tugged his mouth into a satisfied smirk.

Emma clawed at the rope, throat too tight to even choke out a gasp as she tried to breathe.

WAKING UP, EMMA CLUTCHED HER NECK, DESPERATELY SUCKING AIR INTO her lungs. Tears streaked down her face.

It was a dream.

It was a *dream.*

Breathing slower now, Emma finally calmed herself down enough to stop shaking.

The sound of a television reverberated from the living room. Abby and Dana snored softly in their sleeping bags.

Recognizing it was a news station on blast, Emma wondered how the noise wasn't waking her friends up, let alone her gasping awake from the nightmare.

Fully able to take normal breaths now, Emma reached under her pillow, pulling out her grandfather's wedding ring, holding it up to the early morning light. Racing emotions ran marathons inside her mind. Emma couldn't tell if she actually remembered Grandma Virginia pulling the ring off his finger as she chopped him up in the bathtub, or if she was imagining it now.

"What's that noise?" Abby moaned as she slowly came to.

"The TV. Grandma must have the volume turned all the way up," Emma said.

Dana rubbed her eyes, waking up as well. "I bet she's doing it on purpose, just to wake us up."

The thought hadn't occurred to Emma, but she acknowledged Dana was probably right. "Yeah, she never seemed to be hard of hearing before."

"Asshole," Dana grumbled as she stretched.

"We should get to one of your houses so we can hide the ring somewhere safe." Emma had been thinking about what she wanted to do with the ring. Their original plan had been to go to the police, but Emma's gut warned her she'd need something more than only the ring. Would the police care what a kid had to say? Adults only believed adults, she'd seen it with her parents, though mostly it was her dad they'd believe, her mom almost had as much credibility as a child if she was being real about it.

"Let's go to Dana's. Greg will try to sabotage anything we do if we hide it at my house," Abby offered wisely.

And she was right.

Greg would torture them any way he could.

"Dana's it is. Now, let's get dressed and go."

A few minutes later, the trio walked out of Emma's room.

The blare from the television was louder than Emma thought possible from their twenty-four-inch TV. They loved television in their house so getting a TV so big was a no brainer. Only Abby had one bigger at thirty-six inches, but her family had way more money than Emma's.

"Oh, did I wake you girls? Sorry, I'm an old woman, but no one likes to be woken up when they're sleeping soundly. Isn't that right?"

The pit in Emma's stomach grew five sizes.

She *knew*.

Of course she knew. Why else would she send Monster-Gramps to Emma's dreams?

But did she know they had the ring?

Every instinct in her wanted to run for the door, but her mother walked in from the kitchen saving her from having to answer her grandmother.

"What's on the agenda for today, girls?" her mother asked in a friendly tone.

Emma played along, smiling big, feeling the ring in her pocket as if her grandmother would suddenly turn into Gollum and steal it from her. "Nuthin'. Just going to play outside, then go to Dana's. Maybe look for the door to Winterbrook." Saying it out loud made Emma realize Winterbrook would be the perfect place to hide the ring. There was no way her grandmother would find the door.

As if reading her thoughts, her grandmother said, "I have a feeling you three will find it this time."

Never in Emma's life had she thought of finding the door as a *bad* thing, but the way Grandma Virginia said it rose the hairs on her arms. Maybe the ring wouldn't be safe in Winterbrook. Back to the "Dana's house" plan.

Quickly studying her friends, Abby fidgeted with her fingers, eyes not blinking, whereas Dana stood like a cowgirl, ready for a showdown.

Emma's mom kissed the top of her daughter's head. "Well, have fun and good luck."

She couldn't get away fast enough. Emma led her friends to the front door and swung it open.

Standing there was a man about six feet tall wearing a brown suit and tie with a white dress shirt. He had short black hair and though his expression appeared serious, his eyes had a sparkle to them. An overwhelming sensation of trust hit Emma. This man was a complete stranger, but he felt so familiar.

Wait.

Was he a ghost?

"Hello, there. Is your mother home?" he asked.

Emma swiveled her head toward her friends. "Can you see him?"

Knowing Emma and why she'd ask something like that, both Dana and Abby nodded.

"Oh," Emma jumped, a little surprised he was real, but she answered his question. "Yeah, she's home."

"Better have her come to the door. I'm sure she wouldn't want you inviting a stranger inside," he said with a warm smile.

But he wasn't a stranger.

Emma felt it instinctively.

What was it about this person that made her feel like she could trust him with anything? She almost handed him the ring but stopped herself. She yelled over her shoulder to jolt herself out of her feelings. "Mom, someone's at the door for you."

Her mom walked to the door. "May I help you?"

The man pulled out a very official looking badge with his picture on it and three giant letters next to it: FBI. "I'm Agent Lewis

Jackson. I have a few questions for you and your mother, Virginia Wilson. Is she here?"

A sensation Emma never felt before rushed through her. This was him. The man Freya told her she could reach out to.

"Did you say Lewis Jackson?" she asked in disbelief.

A curious expression danced on Lewis's features. "I did," he said.

And before Emma could stop herself, she said, "She said I could trust you."

His forehead crinkled in confusion. "Excuse me?" he asked.

Hope sprung within her at the thought of Freya's FBI friend standing in front of her. She had to know why he was here. "Are you here to arrest my grandma for murder?"

"Emma!" her mother yelled with anger. Apparently, it was one thing telling her parents in the privacy of their own home she thought her grandmother was a murderer, but entirely another to say it front of an FBI agent. Her mother turned to Lewis. "Sorry, she had a bad dream and now she thinks her grandma is a murderer."

Lewis turned his attention abruptly to Emma. "You had a dream?"

Her mother apparently didn't like the way Lewis observed Emma because she snapped her fingers to pull his attention on her. "What's this about, Agent Jackson?"

Lewis focused on Emma's mom. "Your father, Roy Wilson."

"But he's on a shipping trip to Norway." Mary folded her arms.

"He never reported in to work," Lewis said carefully.

He never reported in because her grandmother killed him. This was proof enough. Her parents had to believe her dream now. Part of her waited for her mother to connect the dots, but seeing the utter denial in her mom's face, Emma stepped in. "I told you! She killed him. And we have this..." Emma pulled out Roy's wedding ring and handed it to Lewis. "It was in Grandma's purse." There. No one could deny the proof now.

Freya had been right. Lewis was a friend, and he was about to take her grandmother in.

Her grandmother walked over. "Because Roy can't wear any rings as a shipping captain, not with the heavy machinery. He's been giving me his ring to hold onto for forty years now."

Emma's mom nodded, throwing an irritated glance in Emma's direction. "He's been giving her his ring since I was a kid." She whirled on Emma. "You have got to stop this. You girls go and play."

"Mom. You *have* to listen to me. She murdered him." Emma turned to Lewis ready to plead her case to him, but her mother snapped her fingers again, this time in Emma's face.

"Now! Go to Dana's!"

Emma couldn't win this battle, but she was determined to win the war. With a quick disappointed look to Dana and Abby, she led them toward the sidewalk. But she couldn't let it go entirely. Not when she was so close to someone who would actually listen to her seriously. She said to Lewis, "You were friends with her, so you can trust me."

"Emma!" her mother yelled and pointed her finger toward Dana's house.

"Fine." Emma walked to the sidewalk, Dana and Abby following.

She could hear Lewis ask her mom, "Who is she talking about?"

Shoot. Emma never said Freya's name! She was about to yell it at him, but Dana pulled her forward by her t-shirt sleeve. "Let's find a place to listen."

Her mother answered Lewis, her voice dripping with annoyance, "Agent Jackson, I have no idea. To say my daughter has an overactive imagination is an understatement. She's probably referring to one of her many imaginary friends. Now can we please get to why you're here. Where's my father?"

Great.

Now Lewis would think she was crazy because her mother did.

Emma guided them past her house, stealthily slipping behind the large hedge of blackberry bushes surrounding the side yard. With a slight "ouch" from Abby as one of the hundreds of thorns pricked her, the three of them moved in to listen. The blackberries were always delicious, but they came at a cost, and so did spying on her mom and Agent Jackson. It would be worth it, though.

Carefully nestling farther into the bush closest to the front door, Emma made sure to avoid all the thorns from the branches. It was difficult but going extra slowly made it possible.

The view wasn't great, but Emma could at least see all three of the adults.

Her grandmother stepped forward, next to her mom. "Yes, Agent Jackson. What are you here to blame me for this time? How did you even find me here?"

"You weren't at home. Your car was gone, and this is the only other known address on file for you. Let's just say, it was worth a shot." He tilted his head with a smile.

Great Grandfather stood next to Grandma Virginia as she spoke, but no one noticed per usual. Ping-ponging between Grandma and Lewis, her mother asked, "You know each other?"

Lewis nodded. "Your mother has been connected to two missing persons cases. We've talked before."

Emma turned to Dana and Abby. "He's onto her," she whispered.

"Thank goodness." Abby tensed her shoulders.

"How many do you think she's killed?" Dana whispered.

"I saw at least five at the bottom of the forest," Emma whispered.

Abby shushed them with a finger to her mouth, then shifted to get a better position. "Let's hope they don't go inside."

Emma focused on the front porch.

She hoped that, too.

VIRGINIA

Doubt danced in Mary's eyes. Emma's damned words were getting to her. Father had been right. She should have gotten rid of her granddaughter before she ever touched Roy. Then there wouldn't have been any doubts. But Virginia kept her face even, didn't make any sudden movements, breathed slow and deep, all to show how calm she was. She had to with this joker.

He'd been on to her since she'd taken care of that psychic. The damned ghost refused to wash up on shore and clear Virginia's name. A thorn in her side from the moment she knocked on her door. The psychic had said this guy was her friend, but Virginia suspected there was more to their relationship. Either way, the man had been relentless. Virginia shouldn't be surprised he'd show up after Roy went missing.

But the fact he was *already* reported as missing? It didn't make sense. His work never reported him missing when Roy had genuinely skipped a shipping trip. They'd simply assigned a new captain and waited to hear from him. Why were they concerned now?

Glowering at him, Virginia said, "You've *accused* me of being connected to two missing person cases. We haven't exactly talked."

"Mom, he says Dad didn't check in for work."

"Act surprised," Father said calmly.

Virginia made sure to open her eyes wide. "What do you mean? He left early in the morning. I saw him leave. He gave me his ring. Maybe he's home? And if you wouldn't mind?" She placed her hand out to collect the jewelry.

Agent Jackson watched her carefully as he handed her the ring.

"He can see right through you. You should take care of him, too," Father warned.

Young Virginia materialized next to her. "You're going to kill *everyone* now?"

Virginia knew enough not to answer her devil and angel and waited for Agent Jackson to speak for fear of slipping and saying something foolish.

"I went to your house, and no one is there." Agent Jackson kept his eyes locked to hers.

"Of course he did," Father grumbled.

Pursing her lips, just like she'd practiced in the mirror. "Then where is he?"

"I was hoping you could help me out with that. So, you're saying you saw him the morning he was supposed to check in for his trip?"

Those damn eyes, trying to read deep within her soul. "That's what I said, yes. Why exactly is the FBI here? If he's a missing persons shouldn't the police be involved?"

"Oh, the cops *are* involved. They got an anonymous tip a neighbor heard gunshots."

"Impossible," Father responded. "No neighbor is close enough to hear anything. You shot up half the backyard when Roy was on one of his trips to test it. He's lying. He's fishing for information. Don't give into the bait."

"The Bentmer police called me since they know my history with you and your connection to other missing persons cases. Which is why I'm here. Again." There was a slight upturn of his mouth as he stared her down.

He was enjoying this, wanting her to slip.

Mary's eyebrows furrowed. "You mentioned that before. What other missing persons cases?"

Virginia wanted to kill Agent Jackson now, knowing he was going to tell her daughter about Alex. Every part of her wanted to reach across the three feet separating them and slam his face into the side of the house.

He pulled out a picture of Alex Kriston, showing it to Mary and herself. As if she couldn't remember how easily the knife slid into Alex's throat until it hit the spine and she had to shove it through. The satisfaction was similar to popping a really big pimple.

Mary's words brought her out of her reverie. "My ex-coworker? He was stalking me but stopped a year ago. What does he have to do with Mom?"

"A witness places Virginia as the last person to have met with him at Joan's Diner," Agent Jackson's eyes flashed at Virginia again, gauging her reaction.

Her daughter's surprise was almost too much to bear. "Is that true, Mom? Did you meet with Alex?"

Virginia shifted her feet, trying to control the rage boiling up inside of her.

"Stay calm. He's trying to provoke you," Father advised.

Of course, Virginia knew this and wanted to scream at Father. No one liked a know-it-all. She softened her face as she answered her daughter. "He was putting my family in danger. I told him to move back to Kansas." Which was partially true.

"Except he didn't move back to Kansas. No one's heard from him since." Agent Jackson pulled out a picture of the psychic. "And this woman?" He pointed it at Virginia, then turned to Mary. "Freya Lee."

Mary shook her head, no.

Virginia waved the picture away. "You've showed me her already. I told you I've never met her in my life."

"Look at Mary. She's breathing hard. You've got to stop her mind from spinning." Father observed.

"Are you accusing my mother of something?" Mary's voice was barely above a whisper.

The urge to kill Agent Jackson overwhelmed her, Virginia didn't know if she'd be able to stop herself. She needed him to leave. Now.

"If you're going to arrest me, do it. Otherwise, I suggest you leave." *Because if you don't, I will murder you.*

Agent Jackson paused for a moment, then slowly nodded. He handed a business card to Mary. "If you can think of anything that might shed light on these missing persons cases, please call me."

Stepping forward, Virginia slammed the door in his face.

It felt good.

Relieved.

It had almost been too difficult to stop the urge. She'd wanted to destroy him, to stop him from talking, thinking, breathing. Thank goodness for doors.

Walking into the living room, Mary's shoulders drooped. "Mom, what was that all about? Where's Dad?"

Coherent thought wasn't happening for Virginia because all she could think about was Agent Jackson and him potentially ruining her life.

"Don't let Emma get that card," Father warned. "She'll call him first chance she gets."

Snatching the card out of Mary's hands, Virginia tore it into tiny pieces. "How should I know? Do I look like a psychic?"

Father chuckled.

"Aren't you worried about Dad?" Mary watched her mother for some kind of emotion.

She had to give it to her.

Biting her lip and gasping a sob, Virginia answered with a crack in her voice. “Of course, I am. I’m rattled at being accused of having anything to do with these missing people.”

Mary obviously wanted to believe her, Virginia could see it in her eyes. This gave her hope.

“What exactly did you say to Alex?” Mary asked.

With a deep sigh, hoping to sell her mock-concern about a man who deserved his death, Virginia brushed past Mary to the wastepaper basket against the wall. She dumped the remnants of the business card inside. “It was so long ago, Mary. I probably said something like get lost or I’ll call the police.” Hoping it would be enough, Virginia headed to the kitchen with her daughter following. “I’m hungry,” she said and meant it.

The urge to kill always brought out her appetite.

EMMA

The coast was clear.

Mom and Grandma were inside.

Emma hurried down the path to free herself from the sticker bushes to catch Lewis before he could get in his car, Abby and Dana close behind.

As she rounded the last of the bushes and hit the concrete of the sidewalk, she called out, “Agent Jackson?”

He startled a little at her voice, obviously not expecting them to still be nearby. “Girls. You hear all that?” A small smile formed on his lips, almost like he was proud.

“And saw,” Emma answered, slightly breathless. “That Alex guy is buried in the forest near Grandma’s house.” She figured she’d come in swinging, telling him everything she knew.

The surprise on his face was palpable, but his expression also showed interest. “Have you seen this?”

Dana answered for her, in protective mode. Emma may trust Lewis, but Dana apparently was testing the waters. “In her dreams.”

Lewis paused, and Emma had flashbacks to her parents disbelieving her as soon as she said the word "dream."

The FBI agent sighed deeply. "Look, I can't talk to you about this case without your parents present."

Crossing her arms, Emma's heart plummeted. "They'll never agree to that. They don't believe my dreams are real."

Dana stepped forward, hands on her hips, and maybe a little scowl. "Do you?"

Lewis paused again, then nodded. "I do."

The relief was so intense Emma thought she'd collapse right there. He believed her. Believed her dreams.

Then why wasn't he arresting her grandmother right now?

"Who were you talking about before when you said 'she' told you I could be trusted?" His eyes sparkled with hope.

Emma remembered how Freya looked when she mentioned Lewis, and his expression was almost identical.

They had loved each other.

"Freya. The woman from your picture," Emma answered.

Was there a tear in his eye? She couldn't tell, but his shoulders caved in sadness.

"Do you see her? Freya? Is she here?"

"No, not here. But on the island, yes. She's not sure if she'll be stuck there forever."

"And you think your grandma killed her?" he asked, but she could see he already knew the answer.

"I know she did. And she killed Grandpa, too," Emma answered.

After a moment of staring at each other, Lewis took another deep breath. "I need proof. *Physical* proof. Unfortunately, no one else will believe your dreams either." Then he turned away slightly as if ashamed of what he had to say next. "I didn't believe Freya when she warned me about Virginia, and it got her killed."

He immediately straightened his suit jacket, looking more like an FBI agent. Reaching into his pocket, Lewis handed Emma his card. "I'm sure your grandma burned the one I gave your mom, but call me if you're scared or you think you're in danger. You can call any time of day."

The card felt like she'd won the Golden Ticket from Willy Wonka. It was her salvation. Her security. The escape plan if her grandma got crazy.

She tucked it into the back pocket of her jeans.

"I'll keep searching for proof. Any help you can give me?" Lewis raised an eyebrow.

"She burned his body in a barrel. I'm pretty sure it's in her backyard." Saying the words creating knots inside her, but she was glad she could finally tell someone who would listen.

Lewis's eyes rounded, but he didn't contradict her, he simply nodded. Pointing to her pocket, he said, "Remember, I'm only a phone call away."

Nodding, Emma, Abby, and Dana watched Agent Lewis Jackson slide into his car and drive away.

Emma felt a mixture of happiness at finding an ally, but also terror he couldn't stay at her house.

She'd have to go inside and pretend her grandmother was normal. And not the killer she knew her to be.

VIRGINIA

Did she really have to eat this? *My god, Mary is a terrible cook.* But she'd never taught her how, so she had no one to blame. Meat shouldn't be this chewy, though.

Her daughter was loyal to a fault, thankfully. There'd been no talk of Agent Jackson, not even when Emma came home this evening. But Mary was the queen of denial. Virginia took some responsibility for that. Growing up with a mother like herself, she had drilled in the lessons of no drama, hide how you feel, and full loyalty. She might not have been the best mom, but it wasn't as if she had an example to pull from. Honestly, she let Roy handle a lot of the parenting responsibilities.

A pang in her stomach.

What was that?

Roy.

Another twist and ache.

Discreetly, she pulled down her glass of milk from the table, then dumped the remaining vodka from her flask inside. Mary and

Derrick were in a fully engaged conversation about the price of gasoline going up they didn't pay attention.

But Emma did.

Virginia kept her eyes on Emma at all times, but only her granddaughter seemed to notice.

And Emma stared right back, judging and condemning Virginia as if she were the angel of death herself.

Putting her flask away, Virginia took three large gulps of her milk and vodka cocktail. Wasn't the best tasting, but it'd make this baked chicken go down easier.

She needed to get rid of her granddaughter, but she'd never be able to with Mary and Derrick around. An idea struck her. "You two need a night out."

Mary stopped her rant on how much she spent filling up the tank this morning. "Oh, Mom, we can't do that. What about Emma?"

The vodka had done its job thankfully, and Virginia was more focused. "I can watch her for the evening. How about tomorrow? I have a friend who can get you reservations at the Space Needle. It'll be romantic." She'd have to call Jeremy, which was never pleasant, but the man adored her for some reason, so Virginia was positive she could get them in.

The way Mary and Derrick regarded each other, she knew she had them.

Emma, on the other hand, tensed her entire body. Her glare chilled Virginia. She wondered if she'd have felt any differently toward her granddaughter if she hadn't been her twin. It confused and muddled her mind. Grabbing her disguised cocktail, Virginia drank half the cup.

Turning to Mary, Emma pleaded, "I can stay at Abby's or Dana's. Grandma can have the whole house to herself."

Nice try, but watch the master. "It makes me very sad you don't want to spend time with me. That you'd think I'd do anything to my Roy..." Virginia made sure her voice choked up when saying his name. Then she went in for the classic. "I don't know how much time I have left in this world."

"You're not fooling me," Emma grumbled.

Little devil.

Virginia sniffed loudly, as if Emma's words cut her to the bone.

Dear Mary, with her forehead wrinkling, turned to her daughter lovingly. "Emma, I know the FBI agent showing up might have scared you, but this is your grandma."

Emma crossed her arms and practically snarled, "You mean showing up and basically saying everything in my dream was real? If you were susceptible to the Force, I'd make you believe me."

Mary closed her eyes, her daughter's attitude giving her obvious pain.

Enough for Derrick to join in. "Emma, come on."

Virginia wanted to laugh. The girl might be listened to if she stopped bringing in her fantasy nonsense. It was like religious people as soon as they'd bring up God, Virginia would tune the rest of what they'd have to say out. How could she take anyone seriously who believed in a higher being? Because if God existed, then he was a mean son of a bitch, letting her mother kill herself, giving her a father who beat her and gave her a wife's responsibilities in his bed. No. Virginia had to be her own god to survive this world. Anyone who claimed otherwise was a snake-oil salesman.

A sliver of pride sprung up at seeing Emma so determined to get through to her parents though. She really did remind Virginia of herself, not only in looks, but in sheer will, and bravery. Because the girl was absolutely right. Virginia had killed the people Agent Jackson showed Mary. She'd killed Roy, too. And yet, Mary and Derrick refused to entertain Emma's words.

Mary sighed heavily. "This is where your imagination makes things worse. The agent didn't accuse your grandmother of anything. He just wants to find Dad."

The capacity for delusion Mary had astounded Virginia, but she played into it whole-heartedly. "We all do. I've been on the phone all day, calling every neighbor. I even called...his mistress. Although she wasn't home."

Watching the shocked horror of Mary and Derrick's slacked jaws was delicious. She'd embed it in her memories forever. Because that part was true. Roy's mistress. He denied it, but Virginia knew the truth and she punished him accordingly.

"Oh Mom, I didn't know." Mary's hand went to her mouth.

"I didn't want to tell you. To make you think of your father any differently. But I called Agent Jackson to tell him. Roy may have left me for her." Virginia let out another choked sob. It was easier now that the booze fully flowed through her system. "He agreed with me and apologized for this afternoon. Anyway, Roy should be calling here as soon as the FBI contacts him."

Emma wasn't buying it for a second. Virginia could tell by the smirk on her granddaughter's face.

But Mary? She ate out of Virginia's palm simply because she *wanted* to. The idea her mother could be a monster was not a place she was willing to go. Better to write off Emma's warnings as a child who liked to lie. Reaching across the table, Mary clasped Virginia's hand. "I'm so sorry. I can't believe he'd do that to you."

Pushing her chair with her body dramatically, Emma stood. "She's changing the subject and lying!"

"Emma, sit down!" Mary ordered. "We are the adults, and you are the child."

Emma sat with a huff and another grumble aimed at Virginia.

With one more withering gaze at her daughter, Mary squeezed her mother's hand.

Virginia managed to produce a few more tears. "Let me prove myself to you all. I'll get Emma's favorite meal, whatever she wants to eat. And we'll rent her favorite movie." She tried her hardest to appear as sad as possible, but had no idea if she was pulling it off. "Come on, Emma. It'll be fun."

Before her granddaughter could answer, Mary nodded, beaming at her mother. "You know what? Yes. Thank you, Mom. Derrick and I will gladly take you up on your offer." Then her head swung to Emma. "No more talk about the Force or Winterbrook or any of it in regards to your grandmother. Your grandpa will be calling you soon, and then you can stop all this nonsense. You and your grandma will have a nice night together, and that's the end of it."

To her credit, Emma didn't argue. She simply took a bite of chicken and chewed. It was so dry, that bite alone may take another five minutes to swallow.

Taking another swig of her drink, Virginia let her mind go completely numb.

Mary would be devastated, of course.

But at least Virginia would be safe.

VIRGINIA

Walking toward her garden in Indiana, Virginia's feet crunched down on the frost covered grass, giving her a sense of satisfaction with each step. It wasn't quite winter yet, so the snows hadn't rolled in, but even then, the ground was so hard from the temperature that it made it impossible for her to bury any bodies.

Winter was her enemies' safe haven, she laughed.

Wait.

When did I get to Indiana?

A loud crunch echoed in the air.

Had her walking been that loud? But no, she stood still now. So where had the sound come from?

CRUNCH.

It came from her garden.

Hurrying the rest of the way there, Virginia skidded to a stop.

Arms busted through the frozen ground. The hands attached to them found purchase and began to pull the bodies they were attached to up to the surface.

All twenty of her wretches.

They were *escaping.*

The heads came next, rotted and gray like a zombie movie, eyes all staring at Virginia.

"No, you can't leave," she gasped.

She ran to the first body, Mr. Gastler. He'd cheated them out of a thousand dollars when Roy was stupid enough to fall for his pyramid scheme. Well, Virginia had gotten their money back and then some. Everyone assumed the man had fled town, but he'd never left.

Until now, apparently.

Virginia kicked his head, then jumped on it, trying to push him back down into the garden. "Get back down! You don't belong here!"

Mr. Gastler's head, now mangled further from her boots, laughed with what was left of the flesh on his face. "You can't keep us here forever!"

"Yes, I can!" she screamed.

The scenery around her dissolved into blackness, then rebuilt itself until she stood in her living room on Bentmer.

Roy danced a little jig as he reached the record player next to the television. Dropping the needle on the record, Elvis sang out of the speakers their song. *Can't Help Falling in Love.*

"Get me out of this memory!" Virginia yelled.

It was worse than her garden escaping.

She didn't want to feel anything for Roy.

And this memory tormented her.

Roy didn't hear, though. He leapt to her, pulling her into his arms, wearing a smile so big it always made her feet tingle. He led them into a slow dance, eyes sparkling the way they always did when he looked at her.

No. No. No. No.

Virginia didn't want to remember Roy this way.

Not now. Not ever.

She was stuck in his clutches though, no matter how hard she struggled to break free.

"I love you," Roy said as he dipped Virginia in a dramatic swing dance fashion.

"Get me out of here!" she yelled again.

Her insides churned.

She needed alcohol.

Roy still didn't hear her, pulling Virginia even closer until they were cheek to cheek. "Forever feels like heaven with you, my love."

"Stop!" Virginia desperately tried to push away from him.

Pain shot through her.

She didn't want to remember how he loved her.

He's gone.

He's *gone.*

And I killed him.

His hold on her grew stronger. Roy's eyes bore into hers, and his expression began to morph and distort.

"This isn't part of the memory," she panted.

Roy had made love to her that day, right in the middle of dancing to the song. They'd ordered in, drank wine, and laughed until their sides ached. It had been a perfect day.

Perfect until he ended up ruining any good memories when he cheated on her. He deserved to die.

"Did I?" he yelled, lips curving into an animalistic snarl. "Did I really deserve to be murdered by the love of my life?" Roy screamed.

Virginia struggled harder to be released now, but he wasn't letting her budge.

His face contorted with fury. "Maybe I should kill *you* now! It's only fair," he laughed maniacally.

"No, this isn't you." Virginia used all her force to finally free herself from his arms. The momentum caused her to fall to the floor.

Roy laughed as he towered over her. "Now it's your turn to be scared!" He stepped forward.

Virginia scrambled back, her veins pumping blood wildly.

A gun appeared in her husband's hand, and he howled triumphantly. "Oh, my dear, Virginia. See how you like it!"

BAM! BAM! BAM! BAM!

Each bullet pierced her chest. Sharp, then an explosion of agony.

She tried to scream, but only blood choked up from her throat.

He blew the smoke off the tip of the gun, like in an old western. "You really deserved that."

Virginia couldn't differentiate which hurt worse, the pain of the bullets, or the pain of Roy acting like...*her*.

Or worse.

Father.

At thinking his name, Roy's body transformed into Father's. He still held the gun, but seeing it in Father's hands washed away the sting of seeing it in her husband's.

Father tossed it on the ground, kneeling down to Virginia's level, his rope crawling up her leg. "My sweet girl. Did he scare you?"

Looking down at her body, Virginia saw she was a child again. She nodded at Father. "You made him stop."

"Of course I did. You're my little girl. My very special girl." Father reached out, touching her face. Then his hand moved down her arm, his eyes leered at her, and she knew where this was headed.

But Emma walked in, standing next to her. She knew it was her granddaughter and not her younger self because of the light in her eyes. The hope. Qualities Virginia never had. She only had emptiness and pain since she could form memories.

Father grinned. "Now, who's this beauty? Come here, little one."

Naïve and unaware, Emma jumped into Father's arms.

VIRGINIA WOKE WITH A START, HUGGING HER BODY, ROCKING HERSELF IN the bed.

She was awake.

It was just a nightmare.

Why?

Why was she being plagued by Roy? By Father? By Emma? What had she done to deserve this?

Virginia was only doing what was right.

It was her calling. Her mission.

Roy and Father got what they deserved.

And tomorrow night, so would Emma.

EMMA

Her feet planted on the pedals of her Schwinn Fair Lady, Emma rode as if she were being chased. She needed to be with Dana and Abby *stat.* They were the only ones who could help her. The only ones who *would* help her. Lewis made promises, and Freya vouched for him, but distance separated them. How soon could he really come to her rescue if she needed it? She'd have to call him first. He'd have to believe she was in danger. And then he would *maybe* send help.

No. Dana and Abby were close. They were family.

It didn't take long to arrive at Abby's with the speed Emma was going. Both her friends were in the front yard playing on the rope swing Dana had tied on a branch a year ago. It was only a couple feet long and fraying every which way, but it still held their weight, so they'd play on it until it died.

Dana ran up to the rope at full speed, grabbing onto the clump of fibers and swung high, jumping away when she reached peak height.

Landing on the grass yard like a comic book hero, fists down and in a perfect kneel, Dana exclaimed, "I have you now, Ares."

Emma laid her bike on the grass, approaching her friends.

"I'm next," Abby said defensively.

Emma couldn't blame her with a brother like Greg. She had to fight for any scrap of fun before he'd try and steal it away.

"Go ahead. I don't want to swing." Now that Emma was there, she didn't know how to tell them she was going to be stuck with her grandmother that night.

But when Dana walked over to her, her right eyebrow raised, Emma wasn't going to hide anything.

"What is it?" Dana asked.

Her tone brought Abby over, rope swing forgotten.

Emma plowed forward. "We have a code red. Grandma is babysitting me tonight, so we'll be completely alone."

"Spend the night at my house," Dana suggested.

"Already tried. She's got my parents fooled." *Maybe I should run away.*

"What about us coming over?" Dana said.

"I asked. Grandma wants bonding time." *She's got me trapped. I'm a fly, and she's the spider.*

But Abby stepped forward confidently, which surprised Emma. "Then you know what we have to do to your house?"

And like a telepathic bomb, Emma heard Abby's intentions loud and clear.

All three of them spoke in unison. "Booby traps."

The rest of the afternoon was spent in Emma's room creating the only type of booby trap that would go unnoticed by her parents and, more importantly, by Grandma Virginia. They had gathered anything with sharp ends or had some weight to it. Emma's favorite was her mom's old metal roller skates. She tied a string to each of them and secured the string to the hanging rail in her bedroom closet. One quick swing to the chest or face and hopefully it would be enough to buy her time to escape.

Heart beating fast, she gathered the rest of the objects they'd tied strings to. "Let's get these in the other closets."

Abby and Dana nodded, grabbing the strings holding the various "weapons." Wooden blocks, a Barbie Corvette, an Etch-a-Sketch, and even a Rubik's Cube. The last might be lighter than the rest, but the corners could do some damage if Emma swung it right.

Her parents weren't home as they were both at work, and luckily her grandmother was in the guest room resting, so they had free rein to hang all of their items. When all was said and done, Emma, Abby, and Dana ended up tying in three items in the hall closet, two in the basement closet, two in Emma's closet, and one in the laundry room closet. As they hung the last weapon, the sound of the garage door opening filled the silence.

"Parents are home," Emma announced as if the sound of the garage door had been the stroke of midnight in Cinderella.

"Let's go," Dana said

Standing in Emma's room, her worries lightened. She didn't feel as helpless as she had before. At least now she could do something if she was trapped.

A pang of panic hit her. "Hopefully, my parents don't see them and take them down."

"They won't," Dana assured her.

"We hid them well," Abby added.

Emma stared at her two best friends, and they stared back, an unsaid moment of understanding flashing between them.

"This is it," Dana said aloud.

"You got everything ready?" Abby bit her lower lip.

Emma waved Lewis's card. "I've got Agent Jackson's card. I got my booby traps. If she tries anything, I'll attack, then call." She tucked the card into her jean pocket.

"You sure we can't stay?" Dana shuffled nervously.

"Girls, it's time to go home," her mother's voice called from the living room.

"That answers your question." Emma hated they couldn't stay with her, but she'd begged and pleaded on her parents' deaf ears.

Dana and Abby leaned in and hugged her.

"Run if you have to," Dana whispered.

"Call us if you're scared," Abby added.

Pulling out of the hug, Dana said, "Good luck."

Emma could only nod, her voice evading her.

Dana and Abby gave her their last lingering worried looks until they'd left her room and she could no longer see them.

Walking to her bed, Emma pulled out Lewis's card from her pocket once more and stared at his name and number.

With one final deep breath, Emma found a kind of calm inside herself.

She was ready.

EMMA

Dressed up and ready for their date, Emma's parents walked down the stairs from their bedroom.

Their date where they abandon their daughter to a murderer.

Emma shook the thought from her mind. She was ready. She would fight if she had to, but more likely run to Abby's. She was willing to be grounded as long as it meant being away from grandma-dearest.

Kissing the top of her head, her mom smiled down at Emma. "Have a good night, sweetie."

Her father pointed at her while slightly lowering his eyes. "Be good."

Biting her tongue, Emma wanted to roll her eyes and yell to the rooftops how her parents were blind morons, but she forced a smile. "I will."

Lifting Emma's chin with her finger, her mother said, "You'll be nice?"

Are you kidding me? Say that to her*!*

But Emma grew the smile larger and threw in a salute.

Laughing, her parents waved as they walked through the door leading to the garage.

With the door snapping shut, Emma had the distinct feeling she was being sealed into her tomb.

"I'm going to bed." Plan A was to hide in her room all night. Can't murder her, if she can't reach her.

As she walked toward the hallway leading to her room, her grandmother grabbed her arm, yanking her to her side. "Your parents bought you a pizza. It's on the coffee table. Now let's watch that movie of yours." Pulling her to the living room, Grandma Virginia shoved her down on the couch, sitting so close their legs touched. "Put in the movie. Your mom said it was your favorite."

Her grandmother's voice was soft and kind, but Emma knew better.

No sign of creepy Great Grandfather or creepy twin, so that was good at least.

Emma walked over the television and placed the VHS tape of *Star Wars* into the VCR and pressed play.

With eyes like a predator, Grandma Virginia motioned for her to sit right next to her.

Emma hesitated.

She could run.

Run out the front door.

Run to Abby's or Dana's.

The 20th Century Fox logo music began to play. It was tempting to stay and watch. *Star Wars* was her favorite movie, but she didn't trust her grandmother for a minute. Eyeing the full glass of Pepsi on the coffee table, Emma readied herself to throw it in Grandma Virginia's face and lock herself in her room.

Her grandma obviously sensed Emma's hesitation because she began to stand up and reach her hand out.

Avoiding grabby-hands, Emma evaded her grasp and plopped

down on the recliner, giving herself a whole furniture-sized distance between them, the glass in easy reach.

Her grandmother didn't seem happy about it, but she didn't argue either. "Eat." She nodded toward the steaming hot cheese pizza.

Emma hadn't eaten all day, so her tummy grumbled at the sight.

Eat. Throw Pepsi in face. Run.

The blare of the *Star Wars* theme song filled the room, and it instantly gave Emma a sense of bravery. She could do this.

She'd probably watched it over a hundred times, and she knew she'd be a Jedi someday. That, or an X-wing fighter. Or, honestly, both. Sometimes late at night, she'd wait by her window, hoping the Rebels would come down and recruit her. She wished they'd recruit her now.

The smell of pizza became too tempting to refuse.

Emma picked up a slice and almost bit into it when she thought...

Almond Roca.

Grandma Virginia had accidentally poisoned Emma before. She could be doing it now *on purpose.*

With great pain, Emma tossed the pizza slice back into the box and inched her fingers toward the glass of Pepsi.

Chuckling, her grandmother asked, "You think your dear old Grams would poison you?"

Without hesitation she answered, "Yes."

"Suit yourself." She took the slice Emma discarded and ate a large bite.

Still not fully buying it, Emma waited until Grandma Virginia had eaten the entire piece.

Guess she wasn't trying to poison her. Didn't matter though. Emma was still on board with Plan Pepsi. But she needed fuel if she was to survive the night.

Deeming it safe, and the extra loud grumble from her stomach, Emma carefully took her own slice and sunk her teeth into it. Pizza was quite possibly the world's most perfect food. The buttery cheese mixed with the perfectly spiced tomato sauce, all placed on the soft salty dough, she was surprised her brain didn't explode every time she ate it. She gobbled down four slices before her brain finally told her stomach that she was stuffed.

Grandma Virginia shifted closer to her.

Nope.

Emma grabbed the glass of Pepsi and threw the bubbly contents directly in her grandmother's face.

"You little brat!" Grandma Virginia screamed as the brown substance dripped down her forehead and cheeks.

Emma ran.

Ran as fast as her legs could take her.

Turned out, it wasn't that fast. Every limb might as well have weighed about a thousand pounds and in five steps Emma fell to her knees. Even falling was in slow motion, as if she were underwater in the Johnson's indoor pool.

What was happening?

Emma blinked. She was suddenly on the Death Star, running toward the Millennium Falcon. At least she could move again. Glancing down, she wore the same disguise as Luke Skywalker had in the movie. The body armor of a Stormtrooper.

She knew this scene.

This was the scene where Obi-Wan Kenobi fought with Darth Vader.

Stopping in her tracks, Emma turned and watched in horror as Grandpa Roy, dressed in Obi-Wan's costume bravely fought Darth Vader. Their lightsabers clashed loudly with trails of blue and red light.

"Grandpa, hurry!" she yelled.

But the scene played out exactly as it had in the movie with her grandfather saying to Darth Vader, "If you strike me down, I will become more powerful than you can possibly imagine."

Vader swung the killing blow and Grandpa Roy's body disappeared, his robes dropping to the ground, empty.

"Grandpa!" Emma screamed.

Unlike the movie, no one else was in the room. Only her and Vader remained.

Vader turned to Emma, then took off his helmet.

It wasn't Vader.

It was *Grandma Virginia.*

"Emma, dear, wake up!" Jennifer Thatcher's voice called to her through the hangar deck of the Death Star.

Slowly coming to, Emma couldn't quite open her eyelids fully. It was as if they were made of lead. Her body jostled and jerked. She was moving, but not on her own.

"Open your eyes!" Jennifer screamed.

She pushed her eyes fully open.

Emma was in her grandmother's arms as she walked toward the door leading to the downstairs, hair still wet with Pepsi.

"Oh, you're awake." Grandma Virginia smiled. "I guess I didn't put enough of my sleeping pills on the pizza." She laughed. "I don't know how many times I have to tell you not to run down the stairs. You'll get yourself killed."

"Emma! You have to fight! Get out of her arms and run!" Jennifer yelled frantically.

It was as if sandbags were stacked on every part of her body, but the more Jennifer called out to her, the stronger Emma felt. Her mind slowly began to clear.

She drugged me with sleeping pills. Grandma is trying to kill me.

"Please, Emma. *Fight,*" Jennifer pleaded with her.

Grandma Virginia kicked the door open leading to the staircase and swung her body.

The momentum would surely make her fly.

Grandpa Roy materialized in front of her. He glowed blue and was still dressed in Obi-Wan Kenobi's robes. "If you can't use the Force, bite her!"

Seeing her grandfather again gave Emma the boost of strength she needed. She bit down hard on Grandma Virginia's arm.

Screaming, her grandmother's grip loosened and Emma squirmed free, dropping to the top platform of the staircase. Taking the stairs as fast as she could without puking or falling, she kept her hands on the railing just in case.

Grandpa Roy stayed by her side. "Hurry, Emma!"

His words sounded as if they were underwater, but she understood them. Grandpa Roy next to her, glowing the blue of Obi-Wan, Emma wanted to jump into his arms and never leave. She had her grandfather back. He may be in Jedi-ghost form, but she'd take it. "She struck you down, but you're more powerful now."

Jennifer Thatcher pushed slightly in front of her grandfather as Emma stumbled down the steps. "Hurry, child. She's right behind you."

It was difficult to focus. Moving fast didn't seem like it would be possible, but somehow her sloppy movements began to steady. The drug was wearing off, but not as fast as Emma would like.

Her grandmother thundered down the stairs after her.

The sight alone was enough for Emma to pick up her pace, and the more she moved, the more she gained her bearings. It helped having Grandpa Roy and Jennifer Thatcher by her side.

The downstairs closet.

Emma had enough wherewithal to remember there were booby traps waiting for her there. Stumbling toward the door, she tucked herself into the winter jackets, somehow thinking she might be able to hide, her brain still foggy.

Virginia swung the door open, hand reaching in to grab her granddaughter.

Clasping hard onto the metal skate, Emma swung it as forcefully as she could.

SMACK!

The skate hit with full violent impact directly into Grandma Virginia's nose and eye. Blood squirted out as if Emma had popped a water balloon. Her grandmother leapt backwards, swatting the skate away, holding her eye, grunting in pain.

"You've got to get out of this house!" her grandfather yelled in her ear. It echoed and shook her insides, enough to wake her up further.

Emma shoved the coats aside and stumbled toward Grandpa Roy and Jennifer Thatcher, who both stood in front of the sliding glass door leading to the downstairs deck. She charged toward them, unlocking the door and sliding it open.

A rush of awareness helped her steps become more assured.

But the more her mind began to wake up, the more Grandpa Roy and Jennifer Thatcher began to fade.

Grandma Virginia tore away from the closet, coming straight for Emma.

Almost on top of her, her grandmother reached the sliding glass door right as Emma slammed it shut. Unable to lock it from the outside, it bought her only seconds.

The blood oozed down her grandmother's face, revealing the monster she was.

Great Grandfather stood next to her now, his rope snaking out toward the glass, ready to catch its prey.

Racing across the deck, Emma's senses were still a bit fuzzy, but nothing as it had been. The fresh night air helped give her more strength as she skidded to the outside staircase leading to the main floor and garage.

Hearing the sliding glass door slide open behind her, pushed her to run up the stairs two at a time, but she had to use her hands to help keep her balance. Feeling more like a cat than a person, Emma kept her pace, as she saw she only had ten stairs left.

Grandpa Roy and Jennifer still ran next to her the entire way, but they were fading more rapidly now.

Grandma Virginia's feet hit the stairs creating loud thuds vibrating the steps as she scampered up. Her grandma may be in her seventies, but she was moving faster than Emma could ever dream. An animalistic scream from Grandma Virginia sent shivers to every part of her body.

She was coming.

And nothing could stop her.

EMMA

Reaching the top of the stairs felt as if she had won a marathon, the adrenaline almost completely freeing her of the sleeping pills' power.

Grandma Virginia's hand lunged toward her, fingers ready to grab an ankle, but Emma kicked out fast and hard, hitting her grandmother's nose, breaking it for sure now.

"Nice one," Jennifer Thatcher praised, but her body had almost completely disappeared at this point.

Emma opened the door in front of her and slammed it behind her, locking it from the inside. The smells of dust, gasoline, and must filled her nostrils.

She was in the garage. It was empty as her brilliant parents who she was a million percent ready to I-told-you-so them to death were on their date.

Jumping when the door handle rattled violently, Emma hurried away from it, thinking her grandmother would kick the door down. But the rattling stopped, followed by complete silence.

Jennifer and Grandpa Roy were almost entirely translucent at this point since Emma was more and more awake. As she glanced over at the second door leading inside the house, Jennifer said, "It locks from inside the house. She's going to double back."

"Hurry," Grandpa Roy said.

And with that, they both vanished.

"Don't leave me!" Emma screamed in panic.

Fully awake now, they'd both disappeared.

Slapping her hand on the garage door opener, the hinged sheet of wood slid up and into the ceiling. Grabbing her bike leaning against the wall, right next to her broken one, she hopped on the bike and bolted outside as soon as the door opened enough for her to leave.

The phrase "pedal to the metal" never felt more real for her as she flew past Virginia's empty car parked in front of the house and dashed toward Abby's.

In the distance, three shadows barreled toward her. Her heart leapt into her throat when she recognized Abby, Dana, and... *Greg?* They all rode their bikes and skidded to a halt when they reached her. She did the same. Emma couldn't fathom why Greg was there, but she had more pressing matters to consider. Like a serial killer grandmother out for her blood.

"We have to get out of here!" Thinking of her friends—even Greg—possibly being hurt because of her family created a hole of terror in her chest.

"We couldn't sleep. We were too worried! We had to come to see if you were okay." Dana's eyes were wide at seeing Emma. She could only imagine what she looked like to her friends.

"Greg caught us sneaking out, but when we told him you might be in trouble, he weirdly agreed to help." Abby side-eyed him.

"Hey!" Greg complained.

Abby ignored him. "Let's get to my house!"

The lights to her grandmother's car turned on, illuminating them in the darkness.

"Oh, *shit*," Dana exclaimed.

Screeching to a start, the car barreled toward them.

VIRGINIA

The roar of her car's engine sent a charge of anticipation through Virginia as her foot hit the gas. The chase was on. She was finally going to get rid of the holy terror. And if her friends ended up collateral damage, so be it. The time for games was over.

Her face ached from the dreaded skate and the kick to the nose. She was sure it was fully broken. Virginia was grateful it was nighttime so there wouldn't be any people around to see a bloody faced old woman with sticky Pepsi hair driving after a bunch of kids.

They were riding fast and erratic, obviously trying to evade her. But she only needed to hit *Emma.* She didn't care about the rest.

Young Virginia materialized next to her in the passenger seat. "You would have protected her once," she complained.

Pulling out her flask from her front shirt pocket, Virginia took a large drink. The tension in her neck loosened ever so slightly and her determination grew solid. She didn't glance at her younger self as she answered, "You see my mangled face? She's dead to me."

Even now, the rationalization hit wrong.

Her younger self whimpered in a corner, but Virginia couldn't be bothered with her.

She had a mission.

Focusing on Emma through the windshield, Virginia floored the gas pedal.

Father appeared in the back seat, his dark chuckle ringing in her ears.

She didn't like pleasing him, but right now they were the same.

EMMA

Grandma Virginia's car sped toward them, but Emma thanked her stars they were on bikes, as they all veered in different directions, avoiding the impact of the car. The screech of brakes as her grandmother obviously didn't know where to aim her giant metal weapon was music to her ears. But the car gradually sped up again, this time aimed directly at Emma.

Riding forward, the four of them all kept speed with each other now. In her peripheral view, Greg's eyes widened. "Holy shit! That's your *grandma*?" he panted incredulously.

Dana gave him a quick glance of disapproval. "Now you know what we've been fucking saying!"

"Go! Go! Go!" Abby screamed.

The car was almost on them once again.

"She's going to hit us before we get to your house!" Emma yelled. They were close, but not that close. "Turn around, then swerve!"

"But our houses!" Dana cried out.

They wouldn't make it. Her grandmother would plow into them

before they reached the door. “We can call Agent Jackson at a payphone!”

Right as her grandmother’s car sped up to hit Emma’s bike, they fanned out fast like the bike experts every ‘80s kid was. Then turned, riding in the opposite direction.

Emma remembered the payphone they’d used earlier to call the Bentmer Police Department. “Let’s get to the mall!”

Squeals from her grandmother’s car filled the night air, and Emma couldn’t believe no one had come out to investigate. They probably attributed it to a drunk driver and wanted it to go away. No one did much in the suburbs. It was a mind-your-business kind of life.

Greg pedaled next to Emma, their eyes meeting. An understanding passed between them. He was fully on her side. Rivalry or not, when it came to being in danger, his loyalty was instant.

“Forest way,” she said to the group.

Greg nodded and Emma led the way. Like a coordinated stunt team, they pedaled down the street and toward the towering pines ahead.

Bearings back, the car tore after them and was catching up fast.

Her legs ached from how hard she rode, but this was their only chance.

The car’s engine roared as it grew closer and closer.

Emma doubted if they would make it, but as her grandmother’s car almost caught them, the four riders, flew through the forest entrance.

They were momentarily safe from the car, but Emma knew it wasn’t over.

VIRGINIA

Backing up the car, Virginia stuck to the road but visually followed the trees where the kids biked through. They had to come out somewhere. The farther she drove, the farther she veered from the trees, which set a panic through her she'd never experienced before.

She'd never been caught.

She'd never been suspected, aside from Agent Jackson, who had absolutely nothing on her.

She hadn't even been that careful, which always amazed her, made her feel as if she were invincible.

But ever since Emma showed up in her dreams, Virginia had felt scared. Scared of losing everything. Of losing her life and everything she built.

The damn girl was just like her, and she wanted her *dead*.

"They got away," Young Virginia smiled.

Virginia sensed the hope in her younger self and wanted to squash it out of her.

Father leaned in from the back seat whispering in her ear. "You can't let her escape. She'll tell everyone what you are."

"I have to follow around this patch of woods. It has to lead somewhere." Virginia said her inner thoughts aloud, though she knew on some level she was talking to herself. Her dual sides had been with her so long they felt as real as any human at this point.

"Are you going to kill *all* of them?" her younger self asked shakily.

Virginia couldn't look at her. She focused on the road ahead of her and, out of the corner of her eye, the trees. In the distance, the street appeared to follow the forest once again.

Anticipation gripped her. "Children shouldn't be riding their bikes at night. It's dangerous, and poor old women like me can't see very well."

She couldn't fight the joy inside her when Father patted her shoulder proudly and laughed as if she'd told him the funniest of jokes.

Grabbing her flask, she took another drink, her vision blurring slightly.

She would need to stop if she wanted to catch them.

Being numb wouldn't help her do what she must.

Turning the corner, she drove directly toward the trees.

EMMA

Emma hit the bumps hard, her teeth smashing together every time she landed on a hole or patch of grass. She didn't remember it being this bad the last time she rode her bike down this path, but it had also been during the day and not in pitch darkness. She was amazed none of them had crashed as they charged through the forest heading for Four Tree Mall. The man-made path was narrow as well and soon they navigated single file, which slowed their speed.

"You think she'll find us at the mall?" Dana asked from behind.

Leading the group, Emma glanced behind her, quickly observing Dana was on her tail, followed by Abby, then Greg.

Fear and guilt threatened to drown her. "She seems to find me anywhere. You guys should turn around and go home. She's only after me." Emma had to say it again. She couldn't risk their safety.

Dana and Abby said in unison, "No way."

Greg was set with determination. "Yeah, not going to happen."

She swallowed the lump in her throat and blinked away tears.

She loved Dana and Abby more than words could express. Even Greg. She was still shocked that he came to help. She wouldn't forget it.

The four of them rode in silence until they finally exited the forest path. On solid asphalt now, they rode side by side, Four Tree Mall silhouetted in front of them. It looked different at night, giant shadows of buildings in the darkness, only a handful of lampposts in the parking lot gave any illumination.

As Emma pedaled to the phone booth, she scanned the area for her grandmother's car, but so far, there was no sign of her.

Within seconds they were in front of the phone booth once more. Emma lay her bike to the ground, while the others planted their feet on the cement but stayed seated. Better to be ready to book if they had to.

Pulling out Lewis's business card, Emma hurried to the phone, yanking off the receiver. She was about to punch his number onto the buttons when she stopped. "Oh, god. Anyone have a quarter?"

As a group, they frantically searched their pockets, but it was Greg coming in for the win handing her a shiny new quarter.

Emma dropped it in and punched in the number.

Ring after ring after ring, the phone almost slipped through Emma's fingers from nervous sweat. "What if he's not there?"

"Agent Jackson," Lewis answered, voice a bit groggy.

A weight lifted off Emma's chest at the sound of his voice. "Hi. This is Emma. You told me I could call." Now that she had him on the phone, the fact she was at a mall at night with her friends, her cheeks heated with embarrassment.

"Hi, Emma. Is everything okay?" Lewis sounded more alert now.

The people-pleaser in her weirdly wanted to play everything down, to not make him worry, but luckily her mouth said, "No."

"Tell me what's happening." Emma could tell by the way his voiced pitched, he was worried. Scared.

And so was she.

Beholding her friends, she swallowed any doubts she had. They were here for her, to help her, to save her. And she had to save them back. "Me and my friends. They came to rescue me." She needed Lewis to know. To know their bravery. Dana, Abby, and Greg ducked their heads at her words. But they were all still in danger. "But my grandma's searching for us with her car."

Through the phone, a rattling of what Emma could only assume was a cup full of pens, and the ripping of paper. "Let me write this down," Lewis said. "You said *her* car? You've left the house?"

"Yeah, she tried to throw me down the stairs," Emma admitted.

Dana's nostrils flared and if Grandma Virginia had been standing there, Emma had no doubt she would have had a bike thrown in her face.

"My god," Lewis's voice quieted as if he, too, would do something to her grandmother if he'd been there. "Emma, listen very carefully to me. I want you to go somewhere safe. Can you go to one of your friends' houses?"

Emma covered the receiver. "He wants us to go to one of your houses."

"Duh." Dana rolled her eyes.

"It's not like we had a choice." Abby backed up Dana's eye roll.

Uncovering the receiver, Emma said, "We can try, but she ran us off the road and this was the closet pay phone we could find."

At the far end of the parking lot, Emma spotted her grandmother's car slowly drive in.

"Oh god, she's here. I don't think she's seen us. She's driving really slow, but we gotta book." Emma's hands shook.

"Give me your friend's address and I'll get there immediately. And where are you now?" Lewis's voice was strong and steady, probably hoping it would rub off on Emma.

It didn't.

The car creeped along, her grandmother's head swinging left and right, searching. She still hadn't seen them yet.

"5555 North Crescent Road, and we're at the Four Tree Mall."

A roar from Grandma Virginia's car and a squeal of her tires.

"She sees us. Gotta go."

Slamming the receiver on the cradle, Emma picked up her bike and jumped on, and the four of them started to pedal.

VIRGINIA

"Don't let them get away this time," Father said, his voice stern.

His rope wrapped around Virginia's neck, but not enough to stop her breathing. He was simply giving her a warning.

She took another swig from her flask though she had decided not to earlier, but it helped loosen his grip.

Young Virginia clawed at the door, trying to get out.

"What are you doing?" Virginia asked her.

"You're a monster," she said dramatically.

Father moved to sit behind Young Virginia, eyes full of purpose and admonishment. He wouldn't let her act up. He never let her act up. There would always be consequences.

"You can never leave," Virginia said, then nodded to Father, an unspoken agreement between them.

If she was going to kill Emma, she couldn't have that whiny piece of her around.

BUMP!

"What the..." Virginia turned to see what she'd hit, Father did the same, forgetting his task at hand of ridding them both of the young one.

A cement parking block.

"Shit." Virginia concentrated on driving rather than her younger self throwing a full-on tantrum at this point, hands passing through the door handle as she desperately tried to get away from her.

Emma and her friends rode so damn fast. They maneuvered through the parking lot as if they were born on bicycles.

Swerving to avoid another cement block, Virginia couldn't pick up speed.

Emma was slipping through her fingers.

"Come on, you metal piece of shit!" she yelled at the car.

Virginia wouldn't let this heap of garbage deny her of her prize.

Hitting the gas, she raced after them.

EMMA

Almost through the parking lot, Emma glanced back at her grandma. Thank goodness for cement parking blocks, or she was certain they would have been a splatted Frogger by now.

Abby pulled alongside Emma, with Dana in the lead and Greg at the rear. "We have to get to my house!" Abby said.

Dana called from the front, "If we take the forest, she knows exactly where we come out!"

"We can go through Tuskee's vacant lot," Greg called from behind them.

"Let's do it," Emma agreed.

Mr. Tuskee was one of the coolest guys on their street. Always had the best Halloween candy, dressed as Santa Claus for the block at Christmas, and—most importantly—lived next to an empty lot with an incline perfect for bike stunts in the summer and sledding in the winter.

Emma spotted a small alleyway up ahead, and Dana veered toward it. "She can't follow us through there," she yelled to them.

As one, the group headed to the alley.

Grandma Virginia's car engine roared as if it knew its prey was getting away. The loud thumps and crashes as her grandmother apparently decided avoiding the parking blocks was overrated. Luckily, it didn't speed her up, only slowed her down.

Flying through the alley, Emma judged the size of the entrance with a small sigh of relief.

No car could make it through here.

Maybe they really could make it to Abby's before her grandma caught up.

VIRGINIA

Screeching to a halt, Virginia almost rammed into the alleyway. Her depth perception wasn't working particularly well. Drinking did that sometimes. She slammed her hands on the wheel in frustration, then whirled to her younger self, who still clawed at the door to get out.

"This is your fault!" Virginia yelled.

It was always *her* fault.

She shouldn't have avoided the parking blocks. She should have driven over them like she did for the last leg. She would have caught up to the kids before they biked through this damn alley.

"No, it's your fault. It's always been *your* fault." Young Virginia clamped her hands shut in defiance.

Virginia nodded to Father.

Father smiled as he controlled his hanging rope to wrap around Young Virginia's throat. Yanking her small body clear over the front seat, he used his hand to pull the rope tighter as her younger self screamed in-between choking. With barely a puff of dust, her younger self disappeared.

Good riddance.

Climbing over from the back of the car, Father joined her in the passenger seat. He said nothing, watching Emma and her friends slowly disappear in the distance.

Virginia reversed the car, then sped out of the mall parking lot.

EMMA

Only one lamppost lit Tuskee's lot, and at this time of night, it created stark shadows from the surrounding trees. A small incline, the ground itself was mostly dirt with a few patches of grass. Much easier to ride bikes on than the forest trail, but still difficult in the darkness.

Emma, Dana, Abby, and Greg rode across it.

"Almost there. We just have to go down Suicide Hill," Abby called.

So far, no sign of her grandmother, but they hadn't lost her. With a certainty twisting her stomach, Emma knew Grandma Virginia would find her anywhere, in waking or in her dreams. She'd never escape her.

Ever.

But she couldn't give up.

And she certainly couldn't let her friends get hurt because of her.

Riding through the lot, they reached the flat street leading to Suicide Hill. With lampposts set every two hundred feet, the patches of darkness in-between didn't faze them from the countless times they'd ridden this way. Emma led her group, but they were close behind her.

Almost there.

The roar of Grandma Virginia's car filled the air. It peeled around the corner, coming toward them fast.

Pedaling faster, Emma spied the car behind them, then turned to her friends, who now rode parallel to her. "Go ahead down Suicide Hill. I got this."

Dana shook her head. "No. We're not leaving you."

The car sped toward them.

"You won't be. I have an idea," Emma lied.

"No!" Dana yelled.

The car was at the most ten seconds away.

"I swear, I got this! GO!" Emma screamed.

It spurred the three of them forward, and Dana, Abby, and Greg were mere seconds from Suicide Hill.

When her friends crested the vertical hill, Emma rode sideways to force her grandmother to follow her and not them.

It worked.

Grandma Virginia's car swerved toward *her* bike, picking up speed.

One Mississippi.

Two Mississippi.

Three Mississippi.

Her friends would be halfway down by now.

It was time.

Steering a hard left into a full turn, Emma sped back the way she'd come, zooming past the front of her grandma's car and toward the hill. She spun her legs as fast as she could.

Grandma Virginia's car squealed loudly as she steered it into a full 180-turn, racing toward Emma once more, now having to gain momentum once more.

Emma prayed it was enough of a stall for her to make it to Abby's.

Suddenly Emma was there.

At the top of Suicide Hill.

Without hesitation, Emma plummeted forward.

Catching air as she flew down the infamous hill, she slammed onto the asphalt with a jarring impact.

Queen Madelis appeared in the sky above her like she had before and threw a bolt of blue lightning at the road.

The asphalt rose, teeth chomping to eat Emma alive.

Her grandmother's car almost took off into the air as well, but it pounded down onto the steep hill's surface, almost hitting the bike as it did.

So much for a lead.

Glancing back, Emma saw the car's grill grow teeth, snapping at her, trying to swallow her as well. Great Grandfather sat in the front passenger seat next to her grandmother. He was in charge now.

Her friends were almost to the bottom of the hill. Almost clear.

The car edged forward, but was still about seven feet from Emma's bike.

This was it.

Emma had to stop Grandma Virginia and her car, or she and her friends were dead.

She pulled one hand free from the handlebars and threw a white beam of magic at Queen Madelis. The queen screamed and disintegrated mid-air, instantly destroyed. The road returned to normal.

Both hands back on the handlebars, Emma was free now. She set her teeth, bowed her head. She knew what she had to do. The stunt.

The elusive stunt.

Halfway down the hill, wind racing through her hair, Emma jumped her feet onto the banana seat.

Her grandma's car was two feet away.

Legs bent, Emma readied herself to stand.

One foot away.

She took one hand off the handlebar.

The car almost touched her back wheel.

One more hand.

Swallowing down her fear, she took the other hand away.

Wait.

Was this real?

Was she actually balancing on her bike with no hands?

A rush of adrenaline.

Yes.

Emma had done it.

No hands, standing on the seat.

She'd really *done* it.

Abby, Dana, and Greg, now at the bottom of the hill, watched with wide eyes.

Emma leapt to the left, kicking her bike directly into the car's front grill.

SMASH!

Bike collided with car, spinning her grandmother out of control. The vehicle veered a hard right, smashing into a rockery.

Her friends and Greg pedaled up to Emma.

She slowly got up off the ground.

Abby's frantic expression said it all. Still, she asked, "You okay?"

Nodding with only minor scrapes, Emma climbed onto her friend's bike.

They all stared at the crashed car in shock.

Turning to her brother, Abby said, "Better go get Mom and Dad."

Greg paused and turned to Emma, eyes open in amazement. "That was incredible. You saved us."

The awe on his face almost made Emma speak, but before she could, he hopped on his bike and pedaled toward home.

Abby turned to Emma. "I think that's the nicest thing he's ever said...to *anyone*."

Emma didn't know what to think about Greg, so she stared at the wrecked car.

There was movement inside.

VIRGINIA

Peeling her face off the steering wheel, Virginia couldn't remember a time when her head had throbbed this much.

Where was she?

Did she get into an accident?

"You're useless. Old. *Dying.* The little girl is stronger than you ever were," Father shouted angrily.

She hated it when he was mad. It meant the belt if she was lucky, the brick if she wasn't. And Virginia couldn't figure out what he was talking about. "Little girl? Rachel? She's your daughter, Daddy."

"You can't let him hurt Emma. Think of what he did to Rachel."

Through blurred eyes, she stared at...herself? Was she seeing things? How could she be sitting next to her own body?

"Where's Rachel?" Virginia asked, suddenly panicked. If her father was angry, he might take it out on her sister instead, and she couldn't let it happen. Not ever.

Blinking away blood, Virginia reached up and held her forehead to keep it from throbbing, but it didn't do much.

Where was she again?

Surveying her surroundings, she realized she was in a car.

I can drive?

Obviously not. She apparently got into an accident.

Searching out the window to see where she ended up, she saw herself again, but this time she was standing next to two other girls, each holding a bike.

"Who is that?" she asked Father.

"Your granddaughter. Your replacement," he said and grabbed the passenger door handle.

All Virginia's memories flooded back into her mind at once, and she immediately vomited on the dashboard.

She wasn't a little girl.

She was an old woman.

A *killer*.

Father left the car.

Her younger self clenched her hands into fists. "You didn't save Rachel in time, but you could save Emma."

Rubbing her chest, to wake herself up more, Virginia yelled, "I saved Rachel. I killed the son of bitch!"

"He'd already put his hooks into her. You *couldn't* save her."

Virginia flashed to the memory of her sister hanging from a rafter, exactly as they had staged their father.

Father turned to her from outside. "Rachel would rather be with me than live with a killer like you."

Virginia opened the car door and clumsily put one foot out, then the other. "It's your fault I'm like this, why Rachel killed herself."

Father pointed at her. "At what point will you stop blaming me for all your sins? *I* never killed anyone. What's your body count?" He eyed Emma with optimism. "She has the spark. Like you had."

Observing her granddaughter and her friends, a wave of alarm surged through Virginia as she struggled to her feet. "*No*. You can't have her."

"What do you care?" He seemed done with her, annoyed. "You've wanted her dead since she saw who you really are."

His words hit her like blows. Is this why she wanted to kill her granddaughter? Shame? *No.* She brushed away the thought. "She was going to turn me in. She sided with Roy."

Father laughed. "Lies you tell yourself." He started to walk toward Emma.

"No!" Virginia cried out. She stumbled toward him, her younger self by her side.

"Save her. Don't let him hurt her," Young Virginia begged.

"Leave me alone. You're weak. Like Emma. Like Rachel. I don't need you!" Virginia lashed out.

"And *he* makes you strong?" Young Virginia asked incredulously.

"I *am* strong. He has nothing to do with it," she spat.

"Then why have you held onto him so tightly?" her younger self asked.

A question Virginia didn't have an answer to, and didn't want to think about.

Ignoring the little menace, she limped toward her retreating father, his noose dragging behind him.

EMMA

Virginia stumbled toward them.

"This is seriously like a horror movie," Dana said in shock.

"But with a little old lady," Abby's voice quavered.

Emma saw Great Grandfather walking in front of her grandmother. Confident. Determined.

Her heart pounded wildly. "Um, guys?"

"Oh god, what is it? Is it Mr. Waller?" Abby's brows furrowed.

"*Abby!*" Dana scolded.

"Sorry." Abby cringed.

"It's Great Grandfather." Emma's voice cracked. "He's coming towards us."

Sirens sounded in the far distance.

"Oh, thank goodness," Abby said.

Great Grandfather was only ten feet away, his rope longer than she'd ever seen it, whipping in the air.

Emma's knees shook. "They're not going to get here in time."

Dana and Abby pulled at Emma protectively.

"We gotta run, then," Abby whimpered.

"Don't you see? If I run now, it won't matter if she goes to prison. She's like me. If she dies, her ghost would haunt me. If she lives, she'll haunt me in my dreams. Either way, if we leave her like this, with her dad always telling her to be evil, I'm stuck with her *forever.*"

"What do you want us to do?" Dana's teeth slightly chattered, but her legs stood strong in fighter stance.

Emma raised her shoulders questioningly. "United front?"

Abby and Dana nodded, one of them standing on each side of her. A line of defense against something her friends couldn't see.

Glimpsing her grandmother in the distance, Emma noted Grandma Virginia's facial expressions kept shifting from fury to confusion to total innocence as she stumbled toward them.

Emma eyed her great-grandfather and his rope inching its way toward them. "The accident mottled her brain, so I don't know what this figment of hers is capable of."

Stepping forward, Emma spoke to him when he was only a few feet away. "You can't have us."

He laughed, his voice echoing with Grandma Virginia's. "I only want *you.*"

"I'm protected," Emma said as bravely as she could muster.

Dana and Abby took the declaration as their cue to step forward next to her once again.

Her grandmother limped to a stop. "Leave her alone. She's *mine.*"

Emma knew Grandma Virginia was talking to Great Grandfather, but Dana assumed it was directed at her and Abby. "Go ahead and try. You'll have to go through us first." She grabbed Emma's right hand, and Abby grabbed Emma's left.

A human chain. Now linked, a gold glow formed around them.

Great Grandfather laughed, his rope growing and growing, racing its way toward them.

Abby and Dana's heads swiveled from Emma, to each other...to Great Grandfather.

"Oh my *god*," Dana whispered.

They could see everything.

VIRGINIA

Watching Father stare down at Emma, towering over her like the giant she remembered him to be, gave her momentary pause.

He's not real.

He's part of you.

The rope from his noose started wrapping around all three of the girls' feet.

Father reached down, touching Emma's cheek. "You're like my Virginia. Which means you have it in you, girl. The rage. The righteousness. The cruelty. I only need to unlock it," he cooed to Emma, like he had to Virginia the night she'd killed him.

His spirit, or whatever this was in front of her, had come to her that night. Told her how powerful she could be.

And she'd listened.

Where had it gotten her?

Where would it get Emma?

"*No.*" Virginia stepped in front of Father. "She needs to *die.*"

Her younger self stood to face her. "You'd rather kill her than corrupt her?"

Hands shaking, she nodded. "Yes. She'll be better off. Trust me."

Young Virginia huffed. "But we don't have to do *either*."

Father's rope was still working its way up Emma and her friends. They struggled to free themselves with their legs, not wanting to use their hands and let go of each other.

Loyalty.

Love.

Emma had it.

Virginia never did.

Her younger self's eyes bore into her. "Lies! You had *all* those things! You were too stupid to believe it!"

She leapt into Virginia's body.

Like fire in her blood, Virginia screamed as her younger self melted inside of her.

Father's face contorted, his rope suddenly loosening its grip on Emma and her friends.

Flashes of every person Virginia hurt or killed rotated in her brain like a wicked carnival wheel, one after the other until it landed on Roy.

Her husband.

Her *love*.

Virginia screamed from the pain of it.

She'd killed him.

Killed the man who loved her with all of his being.

He didn't know who she really was, though.

The golden glow from Emma, Dana, and Abby traveled toward her, touching Father and then herself.

Both of them screamed as it burned them.

If Roy had known who she was, he never would have loved her.

She had to kill him before he saw her.

Before he saw her the way Emma had.

The gold grew larger and stronger, pulling Father toward her until his body absorbed into hers, joining her younger self until both sides burned so hot she thought she would die right there. Now, there was only darkness and light battling *inside* her. No longer in an external form.

The pain seared like nothing she'd ever experienced before.

She wanted it to end.

Virginia could physically see the dark and light hissing and snapping and breaking each other, spilling outside her body from the war they fought.

The golden glow from her granddaughter weaved the dark and light within her body. She screamed so loudly she thought she'd wake up the entire city.

It dropped her to her knees.

Emma stepped closer, no longer holding her friends' hands.

It was like a thousand snakes battled inside of her, body shaking, writhing. Only grunts left her lips as the pain had reached a point where it was too difficult to bear.

Her granddaughter's eyes were full of fear, but she reached down and touched Virginia's face. "Grandpa said I have to love you extra hard." Her words barely had meaning, but somehow a part of her held onto them like a lifeline.

Before she could respond, the girl wrapped her arms around her, folding her into a tight hug. The battle between light and dark intensified, and the tighter Emma held her, the more the pain lashed out like whips.

Virginia lost the ability to breathe, the pain and deafening noise of fighting battled on.

The golden glow blazed stronger, brighter than the darkness and light itself. Dana and Abby joined the embrace.

The golden glow surrounded everything Virginia saw.

And right when she thought her body would explode, she saw a figure behind the girls.

Roy.

Watching her.

He's going to judge me. Condemn, me. Hate *me.*

But staring into his eyes, there was only light.

"You really loved me, didn't you?" Virginia choked.

Roy's eyes filled with tears, and he nodded.

BOOM!

They were gone.

Father and her younger self.

Darkness and light.

Two sides melting into their creator.

One now, as it should be.

All that remained was Virginia.

On her knees.

Crying into her granddaughter's arms.

And Roy right behind.

It was all too much for her mind to handle.

Everything went black.

EMMA

Shaking Grandma Virginia gently, Emma said, "Grandma?"

Abby checked her pulse. "Still alive."

"She might have a concussion from the accident, and whatever it was we just saw." Dana's knees buckled slightly. "Which was *insane*, by the way."

"Hello, Emma."

Her breath caught in her throat.

She recognized that voice.

Grandpa Roy.

All three girls whirled around.

There he was.

Smiling down at them.

"You guys can see him?" Emma asked, her voice breaking.

The sirens grew closer.

Abby and Dana nodded, unable to speak.

"I don't have much time." Grandpa Roy reached down to touch Emma's cheek. "But you need to know, none of this was your fault.

I should have listened to you."

Tears streamed down Emma's face unbidden. "But I should have *saved* you!" she cried.

He kneeled to be at her eye level. "Emma, you did save me. All three of you did."

"What do you mean?" she was in disbelief, continuously wiping fresh tears.

"Yeah, what do you mean?" Abby apparently had gotten over her shock and needed answers, too.

"I found the door to Winterbrook." Grandpa Roy's smile radiated peace and awe.

All three girls exchanged shocked expressions.

Two police cars screeched to a halt, followed by a sedan with flashing lights.

"Speaking of which, I need to go back." Grandpa Roy nodded toward the sedan. "Tell Lewis that Freya loved him and she's at peace now. She made it to Winterbrook, too." Hc winked.

And through her tears, Emma smiled. "I love you, Grandpa."

"Yeah, we love you," Dana agreed, backed up with an emphatic nod from Abby.

"I love you, too. Now, go tell Lewis what I said."

Emma turned away and headed toward the FBI agent, who ran toward them.

When she glanced over her shoulder, Grandpa Roy was gone.

EMMA

Emma walked toward the kitchen door leading to the garage. It had been a week since her grandmother had been arrested.

Her grandma had won her battle with her demons.

She had seen it. Seen all of Grandma Virginia's bile and hate dissipate as if it had been made of smoke. Emma had nothing to worry about when it came to her anymore. No hauntings. No dreams. Only a jail cell for her grandmother.

Lewis had been so worried as he hovered over Emma, making sure she, Abby, and Dana were okay.

She had told him exactly what Grandpa Roy said about Freya and where to find her.

Lewis had looked sad, but at peace as well.

Her parents had even let her go to the island with him, now fully believing her and in her ability to see ghosts.

There had been seven bodies in total, including Grandpa Roy and Freya. It was enough to lock her away for a long time. And her grandma didn't argue.

She confessed to it all of it, didn't want a trial. Even told them about her "garden" in Indiana.

Emma had felt the change in her that night.

Her grandpa had been right.

Loving her had set her free.

Opening the door to the garage, Emma nearly lost her breath at the beautiful sight in front of her.

Her dad had taken both her broken bikes and created a new one. Roses burst out of the metal, with green vines wrapping around every surface.

"What do you think, kiddo?" he asked.

Emma's entire being lit up at the sight of every stunning rose blooming all around the bike, just like Grandpa Roy's rose garden. "It's the best bike I've ever seen."

Her father laughed as he rolled the masterpiece over to her. "How you holding up?"

Not being able to peel her eyes away from the bicycle she answered, "I'm okay."

Pulling her face away from the bike by touching her hand with his finger, her dad said, "She's in jail, and she's never coming out. You're safe now."

Her parents had been devastated when they arrived to police cars in front of the house. And when they heard what happened from Lewis, Emma didn't think her mother would ever forgive herself.

She had thought she would have had satisfaction in being right when her parents had refused to listen to her, but she didn't feel that at all. Emma only felt sad her mom now had to accept that her own mother was a killer and had murdered her father. And had almost killed her daughter.

Since then, both her parents had been showering her with gifts. Her favorite foods, having Abby and Dana over almost every night. Emma suspected they wanted her forgiveness, but they had it. She'd told them a million times.

Dana told her to enjoy it, but she couldn't quite do it. Not yet.

Part of her was still scared.

But mostly, she was just sad.

She missed her grandfather.

Her father studied her a moment longer, then hit the button to the garage door. It slowly opened. "I know you've been looking for the door to Winterbrook. I think I found it in our front yard. You might want to check it out. Dana and Abby are coming over now."

"What?" Emma didn't think she could open her eyes wider.

When the garage door was fully open, she gasped.

In the center of the front yard was a metal door frame and a door inside it, bolted to the ground.

Elation surged through her.

"*What?!*" she exclaimed.

Before she took her bike, she hugged her dad fiercely.

He might have built that door, but she knew it could still lead to Winterbrook.

"Thanks, Dad."

Her father kissed the top of her head. "I don't know why you're thanking me. The door just appeared ten minutes ago."

Emma smiled so large, she felt it radiate through her entire body. It grew even larger when she heard Abby outside.

"Holy crap! It's the door to Winterbrook!"

Emma laughed. She jumped on her bike with twisting and turning roses and vines, joined her friends, and they all raced toward the door to Winterbrook.

TRUE OR FALSE

I thought some of you might be interested in what was true in the book and what was made up. Though this is a work of fiction, the broad strokes are not. Because, truth be told, if I had written this as an entirely fictional piece, I would have saved Grandpa Roy and he would have helped Emma take down Grandma Virginia.

It was very difficult for me to write Roy's death scene. First off, because it was triggering and emotional to re-create what happened to him in real life. But also, professionally as a writer, I didn't want him to die. I wanted him to fight back, to escape, to foil her plans. That's the type of stories I normally tell, wreaking havoc on the main characters, but it always ends up happy in the end. And they always get the bad guy.

But this book, though fiction, is based in reality, and I wanted to tell Rolf's story through Roy. The way I remembered him. A grandpa figure to me, when both my paternal and maternal grandfathers were gone before I was even born. He had a smile for everyone, had gifts that "Santa" forgot to give us at Christmas (I still have the teddy bear he gave me, and I keep it by my bedside), and he always had time to help me find the door to Narnia.

Rolf Neslund was a good man who didn't deserve what happened to him.

The names Virginia and Roy: Not True. The character of Virginia is based on Ruth Neslund, and Roy is based on Rolf Neslund.

My age when Rolf was murdered: I was actually seven years old when Rolf was murdered, not eleven, like Emma is in the book.

Ruth and Rolf were my grandparents: Not True. They were my great-aunt and great-uncle. But my grandmother (Ruth's sister) lived in Ohio with the rest of my mom's side of the family, and we only saw them once every couple of years, so Ruth and Rolf felt like my grandparents. (Also, fun fact about Rolf: He's actually famous for destroying the West Seattle Bridge in 1978 with his freighter ship, the MV Chavez. There's actually an Easter-egg in the book about it).

Ruth and Rolf lived on a remote island: True. They lived on Lopez, a small island in the San Juans.

The FBI Agent: Almost true. He wasn't an FBI agent, but Deputy Raymond Clever never gave up after his interview with Ruth. And because he kept the investigation open, it eventually led to her arrest.

Timeline of the murder and eventual arrest: Not True. No, this didn't all take place in a week like in the book. It actually spanned over 6 years, from the murder in 1980, to Ruth being charged with first-degree murder in 1983, to her being convicted in 1985, and finally being sentenced in 1986. She was allowed to pay bail and be under house arrest until she could appeal, but in 1987 she got drunk and hit two bicyclists with her car and sent them to the hospital, and was sent to prison for that.

Witnessing Ruth's first attempt to kill Rolf: True. Aside from spirits, ghosts, and best friends, it happened just like in the book. I heard them arguing and went to check it out and saw her punching herself while leveling a gun at Rolf. He had his hands up and was pleading with her, but she only stopped because she saw me in the doorway watching. From then on, I became a "witness" in her eyes.

Abby and Dana on the island when witnessing Ruth's first attempt to kill Rolf: Not True. That was my sister. Yes, I have a sister. I had to give her the news that her character wouldn't be in the book, but she laughed and completely understood the vibe I was going for with Abby and Dana.

Me being asleep the morning everyone went to the grocery store: True. And it was, in fact, Fish Lady (more on her later) who woke me and told me to hide in the doghouse. Whether she was my subconscious warning me, or guardian spirit, is something I leave up to the reader to decide for themselves.

ovember 20, 1985

s Neslund adm

confrontation with Rolf hurt her left breast and se," Stroup said.
en Stroup — fighting ith her voice broken — y Attorney General a what she remembers ing next:
Bob held him and I nd he's now outside barrel.'"
d she called her aunt the day, and "she rue." Ruth Neslund ed" her original sto- Stroup said she slund home a num- the following days, would answer the wasn't true."
he also phoned her nith, who lives in

'... she said she was going to send me 30 pieces of silver ... indicating I was a Judas, a traitor.'

Donna Smith

Seattle, and the two of them testified in the 11th day of New- lund's trial that they made efforts after Aug. 8 to talk to Rolf Neslund, or to see him; for exam- ple, Smith invited Ruth and Rolf to

Dream of Rolf's murder: True. My great-aunt had called my aunt right after she'd killed him. My aunt and my mom had to testify to that in court. But I'd also had a dream that same night about Rolf. Like in the book, my mother comforted me all night as I was shaking uncontrollably, telling her what I saw. For the story's sake, I made the mom a nonbeliever because Emma confused imagination with reality. In real life, my mom may have been scared of my dreams, but she was always there for me.

Murdering her husband: True. Ruth was convicted and sentenced for life for the murder of Rolf where she shot him, chopped up his body, and burned him in a barrel.

Murdering Rolf alone: Not True. She had the help of her brother, Robert. He was never charged and was even offered immunity to testify, but he was living in an Illinois nursing home with dementia, so they didn't extradite him. Some family members believe his involvement broke him and that it wasn't dementia that made him lose his mind. There are theories that Ruth had planned yet again to make it look like self-defense while her brother was visiting, but then he ended up helping his sister get away with it. We'll never know what the true story is.

Hiding in the doghouse while being stalked with a butcher knife by my great aunt: True. But instead of a chase scene like in the book, what stopped Ruth is: simultaneously, the phone rang and everyone arrived in the RV from grocery shopping. Talk about the

Universe looking out for me. It was my mother who was calling, and she was in a panic, knowing I was in trouble. For the book, I didn't make the mother character have any psychic abilities, but my mom is a highly sensitive person, and she knew her baby was in trouble.

Ruth staying with us after the murder: Not True. In real life, so much time passed between the murder and when she was finally arrested. For the story, I brought her to Emma's house right after.

Ruth trying to throw me down the stairs: Not True. It's worse. She actually tried to throw me off a three-story deck. I had been hiding from her in the closet, wrapped in a purple blanket, when the family reunion moved to our house. She found me, scooped up the blanket trapping me inside, then announced to the room that she'd found the One-eyed, one-horned, flyin' purple people eater, and that she needed to throw it off the deck. She began the countdown: "one, two..." and I screamed as loud as I could, causing Rolf and my dad to yank the blanket from her hands. She claimed she was just having fun, but I know she was going to "accidentally" throw me over the side as this was only a day after the doghouse-butcher-knife incident.

End confrontation with Ruth: Not True. I hate to be the bearer of bad news, but I did not have an epic spirit battle with my great-aunt in my old neighborhood. In fact, I never really got to confront her at all. And there was no car chase. But, like I said earlier, she had gotten drunk, and ran into bicyclists, which finally landed her in jail.

Now that we've covered the true crime elements, let's talk about what else is real in this book.

Ruth was a serial killer: Not True. Not that we know of, anyway. Would any of us be surprised if we found out she'd killed others? Absolutely not. But as far as anyone knows, Rolf was the only person she ever murdered.

Ruth was abused: Allegedly true. There is no way to know with absolute certainty since all the parties are deceased, but according to family, the physical abuse was true.

Man that stalked my mother: True. Though Ruth didn't kill him (that we know of). When my mother told Ruth about her ex-boyfriend stalking her, Ruth told my mother she had a talk with him and that he moved back to Ohio. Did anyone ever check this out? No. But even if she didn't hurt him, now in hindsight, I can't help but wonder what she said to him.

Abby and Dana: True. Heck yeah. I'll refrain from doxing the real Abby and Dana, but they were the bestest best friends a girl could have growing up. And like in the book, they always had my back (still do).

My obsession with dares: True. You could pretty much get me to do anything by just putting the word "dare" in front of it from the ages of five through eighteen. There are many things I will never admit to that I did on a dare. And the beauty of being a child/teen of the '70s and '80s is there is absolutely no visual proof I did anything. I'm actually shocked so many of us made it out alive.

The bike dare: True. And I did in fact ride down Suicide Hill, standing on the seat with no hands (and no helmet because this was the '80s).

Lying to my parents (a lot): True. I went through a lying phase, and grounding me didn't work because my room was my happy place. But finally, they came up with a punishment that made me stop lying for life. They grounded me from watching the season finale of

The Misadventures of Sheriff Lobo. I'm sure this show would be extremely problematic now, but my god did I love it as a seven-year-old child. The show was canceled after the finale, and because it wasn't popular enough, they never played it in re-runs. To this day, I have never seen the series finale of *Sheriff Lobo*. Longest grounding ever!

***Star Wars* obsessed:** True. Um, duh. Always was, always will be.

Using the Force on parents: True. I tried baking something in the kitchen one day and made a mess. And when my mom came home, she wanted to know who did it. I proceeded to use the Force and tell her "I did not make this mess." She looked at me with crossed arms and said, "I'm not weak-minded." I cleaned that mess up so fast!

The Schwinn Fair Lady: Not True. It was the knock-off: The Pink Lady. But I loved her just the same.

The ghost Freya: True. Kind of. I had an imaginary friend I named Fish Lady. I named her that because I could see her very clearly, and she had seaweed wrapped around her body.

Being chased by dogs: True. But not me. It was my sister. Ruth thought it would be funny to sic her dogs on her when she was just three years old. No one else thought it was funny, obviously. For a good chunk of my sister's life, she had a massive fear of any dog. But I'm happy to say that when she met her wonderful boyfriend, he had the most loving, sweetest dog, Sally, and she helped my sister heal from that traumatic event. (Also, the names of Ruth's dogs were not Caesar and Taco. Those were actually the names of dogs on our street growing up that were extra territorial and barked and chased all the kids that dared walk past their houses. Definitely not helpful in getting rid of my sister's fear of dogs).

Bike bribe: True. Yes, my aunt bribed me with a bike to say that I wasn't homesick. Because she had no idea what had just happened. None. I never told anyone. She honestly thought I was just homesick (which was very common for me back then–the throwaway line from Mary of Emma faking food poisoning to go home from sleep-away camp was a hundred percent true. Two other kids genuinely got sick and I jumped on that bandwagon so fast that I was on the next ferry home an hour later). Now, if my aunt or my mom knew what had actually happened, they would have taken us away from there instantly. As an '80s kid, we just didn't share. We didn't tell. We kept everything a secret from our parents. It was just "normal" back then. Maybe it was because we came from the generation where we'd leave the house in the morning and come back when it was dark, no questions asked. That's just how we played back then.

Never losing at Monopoly: True. I have strangely never lost a game. Except for the time I flipped the board, because that was also true. But I flipped it on my sister and not "Greg." She did buy Boardwalk just to spite me, like all older sisters do.

Rope swing: True. We did in fact tie a rope that was only a few feet long onto a branch in front of "Abby's" house. And we did play on it until it died. It just so happens to be that I was the last person to swing from it. I can still hear the rope cracking when it snapped in half right before my head hit the rock and I lost consciousness. "Abby" and "Dana" tried to wake me up and couldn't, so "Abby" ran down to my house and told my mom I fell out of a tree and died. By the time my mom arrived, frantic, I'd woken up in "Abby's" mom's arms as she carried me to their kitchen. One concussion later, I was back to playing on rope swings. It really is a wonder any of us survived the '80s.

Searching for the door to Winterbrook: True. Though it was Narnia and not Winterbrook. Winterbrook is a story I wrote when I was twelve and reference it in both my books: *Jeraline's Alley* and this one.

A DAY WITH GREAT-AUNT RACHEL

PRINT EXCLUSIVE SCENE

EMMA
JUNE 1982

Kicking random tufts of grass in her grandparents' side yard, Emma wished Abby and Dana were there with her. Not that she didn't have fun playing alone, but when she was stuck with a bunch of adults, it made her miss her best friends. The side yard led to a forest that surrounded her grandparents' house on Bentmer Island. She'd never truly explored these woods before, but all the adults were inside watching a football game, so Emma figured she'd go exploring.

As she passed by a few straggling pines, within seconds she was fully immersed inside the forest, and wait...

...whirling around, Emma discovered she'd found the world of Winterbrook. She could tell because the bark on the trees was a deep red that only grew in the Dunlop Forest.

A thrill of adventure tingled her toes as she reached down and picked up a fallen branch. As soon as it touched her hand, the gnarled piece of wood transformed into a wizard's staff, a bright blue magic crystal caged in its top.

“Emma, lunch is in an hour!” her mother’s distant voice broke her out of her fantasy. The wizard staff now just a stick.

“Kay!” Emma yelled back. She waited for an answer, but it seemed that was all her mom needed to hear and must have gone back inside.

Sighing, she walked farther into the forest trying to imagine being in Winterbrook once again. *The Chronicles of Winterbrook* was her favorite book series. Grandpa Roy read them to her before she’d go to sleep every time they came to stay. It was always her favorite part of coming to visit.

“I wouldn’t go down that way,” a female’s voice sounded from behind Emma.

She turned around and a woman stood amongst the trees, pointing to an area of the forest ahead of Emma. “I’m your great aunt Rachel,” she said with a friendly smile. She wore blue high-waisted pants with six silver buttons in two vertical rows of three, and tucked inside, a white short-sleeved fitted sweater with a tight collar around the neck. Her dark hair was shoulder-length, parted to the side with large loose waves. Red lipstick framed her bow-shaped lips, and her eyes were large and blue, with a small straight nose. She was quite possibly the most beautiful woman Emma had ever seen.

“Great? Like a queen?”

Rachel laughed, eyes twinkling. “I wish, but no, it just means I’m your grandma’s sister.”

Emma reared her head back, a bit surprised. Her great-aunt looked like she couldn’t be more than twenty. Not anywhere close to her grandmother’s age. Then another thought hit her, “I thought Grandma was an only child.”

Rachel shrugged. “I died young, so she doesn’t like to talk about me much.”

Oh.

Emma understood now.

Great-Aunt Rachel was a ghost.

This was still new for Emma and difficult for her to tell the difference between the living and the dead. She'd met her first ghost a couple years ago on the playground.

His name was Joel and they'd played for the entire recess, but when she walked back to class, Abby and Dana had said she'd been playing alone. Joel disappeared after that.

When she told her parents, they just smiled and said he was an "imaginary friend." She had a lot of those, apparently.

"Why don't you want me to go over there?" Emma looked in the direction Rachel had pointed but could only see dark shadows. Was that tree black?

Rachel crossed the small distance between them and nodded in the opposite direction. "Let's go over there. It's safer."

"Are there dragons? Because some of them can be really nice. Daltorine is the bravest soul in all of Winterbrook."

"No. No dragons. Just bad things. Things I don't want you to see." Rachel led Emma toward a different part of the forest. "What's Winterbrook?"

Deciding to ignore whatever "bad things" might mean to a ghost, Emma welcomed the subject change. "It's another world filled with magic and adventure. It's a book series Grandpa Roy reads to me. Some people from our world have found doors that lead there, but I've never been that lucky. I keep looking though," Emma confessed. "But playing make-believe is just as fun. You wanna play with me?"

There was just something about her great-aunt that warmed her, and she found that she didn't want her to leave, spirit or not.

"I didn't do much playing as a child." Rachel ducked her head. "I'm not really sure how to do it."

"Oh, it's easy." Emma beamed. "I'll be Olivia—she's the main character in the *Winterbrook* series—and you can be Daltorine in her human form." A growing excitement charged through her.

Rachel's eyebrows crinkled in confusion. "Didn't you say Daltorine was a dragon?"

"Yes, but, like I said, you'd be her in human form. She can turn into a human when she wants. It's how she infiltrated Queen Madelis's guards and broke into the castle to save Olivia in book four."

"Are there some kind of noises I should make?" Rachel asked, shifting her feet.

Emma had never seen someone so embarrassed or scared to *play*. Playing was the simplest thing on the planet. But maybe it truly had been a long time for her great-aunt. Viewing her clothing, it could have been centuries. Or at least a couple decades. It was all the same to her.

Great-Aunt Rachel may not have played much as a child, but she was about to get a crash course from her niece.

"Follow my lead." Emma asserted herself.

As they walked farther into the trees, the bark on the giant boles turned red once more as they entered Dunlop Forest. "Queen Madelis's castle is just up here. The wizard Tovias is being held captive in a prison tower. We have to save him."

Straightening her sweater, Rachel grabbed a stick off the ground. "I brought my magic wand to help." The piece of wood morphed into an elegant wand of white oak, its tip glowing a bright yellow in anticipation of a fight.

Eyes wide at the transformation, Rachel analyzed the wand more carefully. "It's really a wand now."

"Of course it is," Emma laughed. "Oh, and be careful, you're turning back into your dragon form."

Bright red scales formed on Rachel's forearms and as she turned to examine them in awe, they shimmered gold with her movement. "Beautiful."

"I wish you could see yourself when you're flying, but there aren't a lot of floating mirrors in Winterbrook. You'll just have to take my word for it. But you better hide your scales. We're approaching the castle." Emma nodded toward the looming dark monstrosity in front of them.

Like a jagged saw with broken teeth, Queen Madelis's castle was frightening to behold. Spires of black and charcoal reached the swirling storm clouds above, making it feel as if her home was endless.

An endless nightmare.

And Tovias was stuck in one of those towers.

"You know what? I think we can get the wizard much easier if we go in my true form. Here, you take the wand." Rachel handed her the magic stick.

Emma took the wand into her hand, then stepped back in awe as Great Aunt Rachel metamorphosized into the creature of her dreams. Within seconds, the magnificent dragon Daltorine perched before her. Even with the waning illumination through the storm clouds her scales glimmered red and gold, and with each new crack of lightning, she glowed like a treasure chest full of rubies and coins.

"Daltorine," Emma said with her mouth agape.

"Climb on, and let's get Tovias!" Rachel/Daltorine roared with elation.

Emma didn't need to be told twice. Tucking the wand into the back pocket of her jeans, she hopped onto the scaled back. She held onto the golden ridges that lined the top of Daltorine's head and down her neck with ease. Emma was made to ride dragons.

"Hold on tight!" Rachel/Daltorine called back to her.

A rush of wind blew through her hair as the great dragon flapped her sparkling red wings.

And they were airborne.

Flying in the darkened sky directly toward their target.

Queen Madelis's castle.

They'd been spotted by the guards and volleys of arrows flew toward them, but none hit their target. Even as they flew closer to the topmost spires, the arrows that found their mark, bounced harmlessly off the dragon's hardened scales.

"Which tower is he in?" Rachel/Daltorine yelled over the wind.

"Let me use the wand!" Emma yelled back.

Pulling the wand from her back pocket, Emma swirled it into the air as she said, "Show us where Tovias is!" A gold beam of light burst out of the tip of the wand and shot up higher than Emma even thought possible, to the very top of the highest tower. She laughed. "Queen Madelis must have forgotten you could fly to put him here."

"Her mistake!" Rachel/Daltorine laughed with Emma.

Flying to the end of the golden light, the dragon hovered next to the arched dark stone opening that served as a window. Black wrought iron bars kept anyone from climbing out, but being this high up, Emma didn't think anyone would ever try.

Suddenly, hands clasped the iron bars and the Wizard Tovias's face appeared behind them. "Olivia, Daltorine. You've come to save me!" His eyes brightened with surprise and relief.

"Of course, you silly wizard. What did you think we would do? Leave you to Queen Madelis?" Emma waved her wand and the bars dissolved into dust. "Hop on!"

"Not so fast," Queen Madelis materialized on the roof of the tower. "You fell right into my trap. Now I have you all!" She cackled maniacally.

Daltorine's wings froze mid-air, but she stayed afloat. They were caught in some sort of magic spell from Queen Madelis.

"Not this time, witch!" Rachel/Daltorine roared, and fire poured out of her mouth, encircling the queen until she was forced to teleport away.

She could never die, she was immortal, but she could be defeated.

And as far as Emma was concerned that's just what they'd done.

Daltorine's wings were back in motion and they were free.

With a cheer, Tovias climbed on her back just behind Emma and the dragon flew them far away from the castle.

They spent the rest of the day celebrating and feasting and telling each other war stories of other battles with the queen.

"Emma! Where the hell are you?" her mother broke her and Great-Aunt Rachel out of their play.

They were back in the forest and it was dark.

Uh, oh.

"I'm over here!" Emma called out. She turned to her great-aunt. "I'm in trouble."

Rachel smiled gently. "Thank you for today." She paused, then tears stained her cheeks though she still smiled. "It was the best day I've ever had."

"Me, too," Emma smiled back. "You want to come see Grandma? I'm not sure if she could see you, but you could at least see her?"

Rachel shook her head. "No. I don't want to see her. You go. I think I'm going to go back to Winterbrook. I like it there."

"Lucky," Emma grinned.

"Emma!" her mother sounded out of patience.

When Emma turned to say goodbye to Rachel, she was gone. Sighing, not sure if she'd ever see her again, she figured the next best thing would be telling Grandma about her day.

Racing toward the house, Emma couldn't wait to tell her.

ACKNOWLEDGMENTS

Thank you to all my friends growing up: Erin, Megan, Diedra, and Tara. You made my childhood and young adulthood full of love, imagination, and adventure. Even though you knew about my great aunt, you still treated me the same, and for that, I will be forever grateful.

Thank you to my family, for giving me their blessing to write this. It helps that it's fictional, but the key events are not, and that's not something everyone is always comfortable sharing. I thank every single one of them for always being supportive and loving me unconditionally. Love you all! But most especially, my parents, Donna and Mike, and my sister, Julie.

And the found family, of course:

Marni, what would I do without you? My sister. The Crazy Eight to my Weird-'O'. You've been there since I was a wee eighteen-year-old moving to Los Angeles to become a writer. We've been to hell and back, and we can still laugh about it. I think out of all my friends, you've seen some form of version of this story the most, and your feedback has helped make it the story it is today!

Faith, we've shared so much over the years! From our instant bond when we met, to writing books together, to sewing little Supernatural dolls for our Etsy shop, to our reaction channel on YouTube. We'll forever be 2NerdGirls.

KaShay, my twin! I feel so lucky to have found you and have you in my life. I don't know what I'd do without our daily texts, lol! Your encouragement, feedback, and love have helped me grow as a person and a writer!

Natasha, your friendship over the years has brought me so much joy. We've come a long way! And my stories would not be the same without your amazing feedback. You always tell me like it is, and even if I squirm because I don't want to make the changes, I've come to the conclusion that you're always right lol!

Kate, finding your YouTube channel back when I started mine, and experiencing the ups and downs of writing a book in a month, is something I'll always cherish. Look how far we've come! We've had so many wonderful adventures from the west coast to the east! And I hope we have many more! I'm so thrilled to be on this journey with you! And I can't wait for your book to come out in two months! *Gah!*

Hudson Mcarthy, the woman who asked the question: "Why *can't* Virginia be a serial killer?" I'd been sticking to everything that had really happened, that I'd been so hesitant to fully dive into the fiction of it. And you were the one who helped me push past that final barrier to write something that could be fully both fictional and non-fictional. Thank you for your friendship and for letting me vent whenever I'm about to explode lol!

My Chillicothe Coven: Jess, Kate (same Kate as above lol), Wallis, Davaisha, Katie Ann, and Lindsay. Our writing retreats have been everything! So much of this story was written and conceived during our adventures together. You all have made me a better writer. I can't wait for the next retreat!

Stig, who knew that *Agatha All Along* would be the thing that brought us together lol! Your support and friendship has meant the world to me. I can't wait for our Hobbiton meet up for your 40th! I'm already planning!

And all the amazing people I've met and written with from our tiny little community on YouTube. Phoebe, Malin, Nia, Jules, J.C., Laura N., Esther, Mars, Natalia, Tiffany, Morgan Lee, Michael, Liselle, Laura, Kevin, Holly, Marta, Anne, Anna, and Brooke.

Thank you, Christian Storm, for my awesome cover.

And of course, Zara, for taking a chance on me and this book. Our nerd-bond brought us together, and I'm just so grateful that you're in my life!

ABOUT THE AUTHOR

Becca fell in love with storytelling at an early age. The first book she ever read was *The Lion, The Witch and The Wardrobe*, and she's been looking for the door to Narnia ever since! She's a passionate reader, consuming any mix of paranormal, mystery, thriller, sci-fi, or fantasy. So it's no surprise that she writes in these genres as well. When Becca is not writing, she loves to sew, from cosplay to elaborate magical creature bags, she just loves to create!

ALSO BY BECCA

The Dream Guy
Jeraline's Alley

Riser Saga
Riser
Reaper
Ripper

***Atlas* Series**
Atlas
Grigori Returned
The Underworld

***Riser Saga/Atlas* Series Finale**
Atlas Rising

***Alexis Tappendorf* Series**
Alexis Tappendorf and the Search for Beale's Treasure
Alexis Tappendorf and the Search for Atlantis

***Dream Diaries* Series**
Dream Diaries
Blood Ties

The Hexsphere Chronicles
The Severed and the Hunted